Consumed

BOOKS BY EMILY SNOW

Standalone:

Tidal

Wrecked

Uncovered

The Devoured Series:

All Over You (Book 0.5)

Devoured (Book 1.0)

Absorbed (Book 1.5)

Consumed (Book 2.0)

The *Savor Us* Series:

Savor You (Volume 1)

Consumed

A NOVEL BY EMILY SNOW

Consumed

ISBN-10: 1494920697

ISBN-13: 978-1494920692

DEDICATION

To my family …
Thank you for supporting all my dreams.

PROLOGUE

Lucas Wolfe

Easing my Audi A8 off the main road and down the private driveway leading to

Sienna's house, I drop my gaze to the dash.

It's 8:57 PM.

I've got about three minutes before the video starts, and four minutes and thirty-nine seconds after that until I know whether or not there's a future for the two of us. The digital clock moves forward, the neon lights flashing 8:58, and I feel the same way I did the first time I stepped on stage. A complete fucking mess.

It's just about dark outside, but someone—I'm betting it was Sienna's grandmother—has installed two neat rows of solar lights on either side of the walkway, all the way up to the wooden front steps. I start to drive forward, and let the slight glow from the garden lights draw me to Sienna, but then I think better of it.

This needs to be a surprise.

Parking the car, I kill the ignition. When I get out, closing the door as silently as possible, I notice that I'm closer to the road than to the cabin. It's a little ironic. At one time, this place belonged to me. Five months ago, I wagered it away to get Sienna close to me. I offered her the chance to work for me for ten days in exchange for her grandmother's foreclosed home, which I had purchased.

But in the end, I'd lost both the woman and the house because of fear.

"Fucking idiot," I mutter aloud.

During my three-hour drive from Gatlinburg—where I just bought another vacation home—I had plenty of time to think about all the times I've messed up with Sienna to bring me to this point. After I let it all roll through my brain like the worst type of poison, I thought about stopping for flowers or a gift, but I immediately axed that idea. She's not that type of woman, never has been. She'll take my apology, or she'll tell me to piss off, but she doesn't want what my money can buy.

She's not like Samantha.

Clenching my fists at the thought of my bitch of an ex-wife and her outstretched hand, I go up the front steps and lean my shoulder up against the door. Out here, I can hear the sound of my own music—my first solo project, my first *real* attempt to fix something I've screwed up to pieces since what I dub "The Sam Days". As I wait for the song to stop, my chest feels like I've swallowed a shot glass or two filled with acid. I'm not a stranger to pain—it's all I feel whenever I see my ex, whenever I let her pull my strings, whenever I think of what *I* did—but I never expected the last five months to be this goddamn bad.

Then again, I never expected to fall so hard I don't want to get back up again.

The music gradually fades to silence. I hear her take in a huge breath. She's waiting for more—it's what I want her to do—and I know that I've got to be the one to give her that ending. Face to face.

I've played shows in front of thousands of people, but I'm nervous as hell knocking on the door.

She takes a while to answer, so long I almost feel like she may just refuse. She's smart. There's a good chance she already knows that I'm the one out here waiting for her. She knows that, from the way I see it, her not opening the door will be a bigger middle finger than if she said the words outright to my face.

But at last, the door creaks open a couple inches, then a few more, until I can see her face. Adrenaline compels me to finish the song I wrote for her. I've purposely left it unfinished just so this one last piece can belong to us alone.

"Say that what happened isn't it for us," I breathe, my voice cracking on the last note as I run my hand along the curve of Sienna's face.

She shivers, looking just as beautiful as when I left her in Atlanta. Instead of a slinky black dress that I want to rip apart just to get to the center of her, she's wearing tiny faded denim shorts that make her legs look impossibly longer and a tight white tank top. Her long red hair is yanked into a ponytail on the top of her head and not loose, the way I like it. The way that's always driven me crazy with the desire to possess her.

The only thing that's exactly the same as the last time she was this close to me is her expression. Wide blue eyes, damp cheeks, and clenched teeth—she's afraid, and I feel like a bastard for doing this to her a second time.

Angrily, she shrugs away from my touch. "What are you doing here, Lucas?"

I'm here to tell you that I'm so sorry, to say I love you.

"You've got two days left." My voice is once again that of a cocky rock star, and it must piss her off. Her mouth drops open, and she looks at me like there's a dick growing out of the center of my forehead.

"You *dismissed* me."

Does she think I've forgotten? If she only understood that the moment I sent her away from me is one that won't ever leave my mind, no matter how many years pass or how many people come and go in my life.

I've got a short list of regrets, but that moment made its way close to the top spot well before the hotel room door slammed behind me. There's only one thing I regret more, and it's been fucking me over for the last several years.

Drawing her eyebrows together until they meet in a furious line, Sienna steps into the house. She's going the wrong way, and I know that I'm losing this. Losing her. And that's something I can't afford to do because I need her.

"You signed a contract," I remind her. It's a low, *low* move on my part, and she shakes her head in disbelief as she grips the door, ready to slam it in my face. Softening my tone, I add, "And, I'm a fucking idiot."

Admitting I'm wrong helps because not only do her bewildered blue eyes dart up to mine, but a choked noise come from the back of her throat. She releases the door and makes a hesitant move in my direction. Then one more.

One step backward and two steps forward.

I can live with that as long as it means I'm getting somewhere.

"I'm not going to give this up." I yank her to me. She smells good, so goddamn good, like that apple bodywash she used when we first met. "I'm not going to give *you* up," I repeat.

Because I'll always want her, and I was fucking crazy to think I could make myself forget.

Several emotions pass over her face. Lust and anger. Love. Fear and *pain*. I'm fully aware that I'm responsible for all of those feelings, and I hate myself for all the bad.

She releases a long exhale and then hisses, "What you did hurt, Lucas." She drops her chin to her chest, and I watch the top of her ponytail as it moves slightly. She's counting. Once she reaches five, she rips her gaze up. "You wanted me to give myself to you just so you could tell me to screw off."

That's not the case. I wanted to keep her—I was just too selfish and wrapped up in being with her to remember that Samantha refused to let me enjoy even an ounce of happiness. That my ex-wife's threat of taking me down, and Sienna along with me, was dangerously real.

Sienna clears her throat, tearing my thoughts away from my Sam and back to the present, back to her. "And now you want me again?"

I tighten my hold on her, because her body is trembling. "I've *always* wanted you. It just took me awhile to tell the shit holding me back to fuck off."

"Sam?"

I nod. And when I told Sam that she was holding me back from living, she'd cried. She'd begged. And finally, after months of going back and forth with her, she'd calmly agreed to back off—as long as I agreed to her terms.

The agreement had been worth it.

I dip my face until my nose touches the tip of Sienna's, which is still damp from her tears. "If you were with me, she'd try to ruin me. She'd try to ruin you because she knows I love you. You've got to know that. You've got to know what she has on me—" But when she cuts me off by putting her fingers over my lips, I'm relieved. What the hell was I even going to say next?

You've got to know what she has on me might take me away from you, from everything. And I don't think there would be any going back.

"Damn you, Lucas," Sienna says, but she's wearing a soft smile. She lets her hand slip from my mouth down to my neck, and I turn my head slightly to kiss the inside of her delicate wrist. She trembles, but even still, she doesn't let go of me.

"I know you're angry," I begin. She'll probably be that way for a long time— months, maybe even years. "And I know that it'll take work, but I just want you to try. To give getting through my fuck-ups together a chance. I need to know that you can give a shit about me again."

For the longest fucking minute of my entire life, her face is an emotionless mask. A hundred thoughts—each a little shittier than the one before it—roll through my brain before she moves her head to each side incredulously and mumbles something that sounds like "dumbass." She lays her head on my shoulder, and her tears seep through my tee shirt.

"A lot can happen in the two days I owe you," she whispers. "But you're right.

You *are* an idiot if you thought I ever stopped loving you."

"I love you too, Sienna," I growl. I frame her face with my hands. "I won't ever stop." Then my hands are all over her as I bring her close to me. Her lips part willingly, and her tongue darts into my mouth. She tastes sweet, and I make myself a promise that I'll never lose the taste of her again.

I'll fight to keep this woman beside me.

Her eyes are still squeezed together when she pulls away, but when I press her hand up against my cock, they open and she glances between our bodies before clearing her throat. "I need to fuck you," I say, and she leans back, rubbing her hand across her chest. "If we were anywhere but here, Red, I'd be inside you right now."

"Gram's not here—" But then she shakes her head. "There are hotels just a couple of miles away from—"

"Come with me."

"What?"

I gesture to my parked car. "Two days. I want those two days now." It's a bold ass move, but she doesn't immediately shoot it down.

She chews on her bottom lip. "Right *now*?"

"Yeah." I stroke my thumb across her lips to stop her from nibbling them. Keeping her eyes focused on mine, she bites the tip of my finger instead, and I groan in frustration. Why does she have to do shit like that? "I'm sorry, Si, and I need a chance to prove it."

She backs into her house, motioning for me to follow behind her, but I remain in the doorway. "I'll have to go pack my things," she says, jabbing her thumb over her shoulder to point at the staircase. "And I've got to call Gram—she's not here." Her face is flushed, and I can tell she's mentally making a list of what all needs to be done before she can allow herself to come with me. But suddenly, her expression clouds over, and her lips pinch into a frown. "Lucas, you're not going to—"

And there goes that burst of hot pain exploding in my chest again. She doesn't trust me, and it about destroys me. But what can I expect?

"Nothing will happen to you while you're with me," I promise. Then I lift my eyebrows and add, "Nothing bad. I'm going to do what I should have done before. I need you with me because there's no music without you."

It is that promise that completely wins her over.

She tugs me to her by the collar of my tee shirt and grabs me by the back of my neck. Her lips are rough and demanding, making me reconsider what she'd begun to say earlier about the hotels. I drag myself away from her, putting a good amount of space between us.

"No more of that or I'll change my mind about fucking you right here in this doorway," I warn.

Control is your motherfucking friend, I remind myself, taking a deep breath.

"Give me an hour to get ready." She walks backward into the house. "I won't be long."

It only takes her half that time. After I load her luggage into the trunk of my car, which I drove closer to the house while waiting for

14

her, she slips into the passenger seat next to me. Dragging in a shaky breath, she lays her head back against the smooth leather headrest and then turns to look at me as I put the car into drive. "I love you, Lucas."

Goddamn, I'll never get tired of hearing those words come from her lips.

"I love you too."

As I near the top of the driveway, a thought enters my head, and I slam on the brakes. She frowns in confusion, but then I produce a wide red strip of fabric from the center console. The corners of her mouth slide into a knowing smile. "Another one of your attention exercises, Lucas?" she questions, as I cover her eyes with the blindfold.

"No, but surprises are your new best friend."

For once, she doesn't protest.

CHAPTER ONE

Sienna Jensen

Lucas' car comes to a slow stop, and he cuts the engine, stopping Cavo mid-song. At the sound of his door opening and closing, the air suddenly flies out of my lungs. I embrace this moment of breathlessness, the sudden burst of uncertain excitement that hums through me.

Where are we, and what have I gotten myself into?

Grasping the hem of my shorts, I let my imagination run wild as I go through a list of places he might have brought me. I rule out a hotel or airport. We've been on the road for what seems like hours, and Gram's house is only a stone's throw from

Nashville's airport.

So where does that leave?

Exasperation kicks in, and I bring my hands up to my blindfolded eyes, but then the passenger door swings open. Lucas clears his throat. Even though I can't see him, I swear I can feel his hazel eyes blazing a hot path down the side of my face as he looks at me.

"We're here," he announces, answering absolutely zero of my questions.

"I figured as much. Where exactly is here?"

His hand closes around my wrist, the rough pads of his fingertips kneading into my skin, and he tugs me out of the car toward him. I stumble a little, the front of one of my flip-flops bending enough that the warm pavement brushes the tips of my toes.

Lucas quickly stops me from falling, steadying me by placing his other hand on the curve of my hip.

"Careful," he teases, "I want you in one piece."

Now, we're chest to chest. The late night breeze whispers against our skin, but I'm not cold. Not when he's so close. I can practically taste the spearmint on his tongue as I breathe him in.

And no matter how many times I've attempted to convince myself otherwise, I have missed breathing in everything about this man.

"Lucas." My voice is thin and strained. "Where are we?"

Releasing my wrist, he glides both of his hands up my body, his touch setting my skin on fire. He doesn't stop until he's holding either side of my face, and when he chuckles lightly, I can almost bet it's because my cheeks are so flushed.

"You ask too many fucking questions. You always have." He works his fingers beneath the silky blindfold and dips his mouth next to my ear. "Enjoy the moment."

"Hard to when I can't see a damn—" I begin, but he lowers the fabric from my eyes, and I lose the ability to breathe for a split second.

Blessed with exotically good looks—olive skin, full, sexy lips, and a perfectly straight nose—Lucas' long, muscular body towers

18

over me by a good five or six inches. I drift my gaze over him, starting at his shoes, working my way up to his tattooed arms, and stopping when I reach the top of his head, which is covered in dark brown hair that's so long it brushes over his neck. This man is all male, all gorgeous, and from what

I understood tonight, all mine.

I swallow hard. Yeah ... it's a lot to process.

"You look stunned," he points out.

How does he expect me to look after everything that's happened between us just in the last several hours? "I doubt that'll go away any time soon."

A new emotion passes over his features—one that makes me uncomfortable— and I use this moment to glance away to get a good look at our surroundings. Beneath the pale glow of moonlight, there's nothing but mountains and lush trees as far as I can see. The only house around is the one we're parked in front of, a luxurious three-story cabin—twice as large as my grandmother's place in Nashville—with floor-to-ceiling windows on the second level.

"Where are we?" I repeat.

"Gatlinburg," he confirms, and I lift my eyebrow. "I needed you all to myself. These two days without interruption, to win you back and make-up for those fuck-ups the right way."

Two days to make up for being an epic dick? Leave it to Lucas to be completely convinced of his power of persuasion. Twisting my lips to the side, I almost tell him what

I'm thinking, but then I bite my tongue. "All to yourself, huh?"

A few locks of his hair fall over his eyes when he nods. "The way I should have done months ago. A new start." Spinning me around so that I'm by his side, he runs his palm down the inside of my arm, lacing our fingertips together.

I hold on to him tightly, not wanting him to release my hand, to release me.

While Lucas removes our luggage from his car, I explore the cabin's main floor.

Other than the ceiling-height gray stone fireplace located in the center of the entertainment room, the house has none of the usual rustic charm I've come to expect from cabin living. From the black sectional leather couch that wraps around the fireplace in a U-shape, to the equally dark cherry wood furnishings, and even to the gleaming black granite countertops found in the kitchen next door, something moody and sexy pulsates through the atmosphere.

It's definitely familiar.

I rest my back against the stainless steel refrigerator, scanning my eyes across the open, state-of-the-art kitchen. It has everything— double ovens, every appliance I can think of sitting on the granite counters, and a horseshoe-shaped center island complete with an overhead wine rack that's filled with dozens of bottles.

Then it hits me: the interior of this house reminds me of Lucas' place in Los Angeles. I've only been there once, more than two years ago, when he took me there for what had been a catastrophe of a date, but it's impossible to forget.

Pushing away from the fridge, I head through the double doors at the left side of the kitchen and back into the living room and stop short at the sound of the front door slamming. Lucas is standing in the foyer with his back turned to me. Even with the dim, recessed lighting, I'm able to admire his hard muscles and the intricate ink etched over them.

My mouth goes dry. There are so many, *many* more tattoos hidden beneath his clothes, and I'm anxious to uncover each and every one.

The sound of me shoving my hands into the pockets of my shorts, causing a few coins to jangle, demands his attention. He turns slightly, giving me a clear view of the profile of his face. "You should eat something since we didn't stop."

"I had dinner an hour before you showed up." I step in his direction. "This place is absolutely amazing." Two more steps closer, each one wider, each one making the pit of my belly clench a little more. "This isn't just some weekly rental, is it?"

As I step foot into the foyer, he turns all the way around. I'm struck by the look in his hazel eyes. Lucas Wolfe has never been the type to do emotions—well, none except for anger, disinterest, and lust. But tonight?

Tonight he's mind-fucked me. Coming from him, it's something I could get used to.

"It's yours," he says.

"Wait, *what?*"

He inches closer to me. "You heard me, Red, I bought this house for you." Clearing his throat, he rubs his large palm over the gorgeous angles of his face. "I'm a shit gambler and lost my last vacation house in a bet. So this one is for us, Sienna. You and me."

For us. You and me.

21

Those words catch me off guard—wrap around my heart and give it a firm squeeze. Giving me one of those smiles that leave panties dropping in its wake, he turns to set the alarm system on the wall by the front door.

Wow. Just … wow.

If someone had asked yesterday whether or not I'd ever see Lucas-*Fucking*-Wolfe again, I would've laughed off the question. Lucas and I were through; he hadn't wanted me—at least not enough to make us work—and besides, I had no place whatsoever in a rock star's world.

Just when I realized that I'd fallen in love with him, he had sent me away.

Now, standing inside of a house that he said is meant for *us*, I decide it's a good thing nobody has ever asked me about the probability of a future between Lucas Wolfe and myself. My answer would've been dead wrong, and I would have looked like an ass. The alarm beeps twice, startling me. I look up to see his thick eyebrows knit together.

"You okay, Sienna?" I nod, but he doesn't look convinced. "Because, you've got that fucking look."

Now it's my turn to frown. "What are you talking about?"

The soles of his classic black Converse squeak on the hardwood as he takes two long strides to reach me. I'm incredibly tall for a woman—five-foot-ten to be specific— but he's several inches taller than me. I have to I tilt my head far back to stare up at his face.

"It's that look like you've got something you want to say. Trust me, I want to hear it."

I start to cross my arms over my chest, but he grabs both my wrists and pulls me hard against his body. This is the first time he's put his hands on me since he removed the blindfold, and I crave more of his touch. Less than five hours with him, and already he's like a drug to me.

God, I hate my body for acting so stupid when I should be asking him a hundred and one questions.

"Answer me, Si."

I lift my shoulders into a tense shrug. "I'm shocked you didn't try to screw me on the way here."

"Would it make you feel better if I told you that every time I looked at you I thought about saying fuck the steering wheel and pulling you on my cock right then and there?" He pauses to take in the flush that blooms across my cheeks, the corner of his mouth jerking into a teasing grin. "But this time, I wanted to do things the right way."

Without warning, he pulls the band out of my high ponytail, breaking the rubber with his fingertips. He growls something under his breath when my red hair tumbles in tangled waves around my shoulders. He's always had a thing for my hair. "Anything else you got to say?"

"No." My voice is tragically unconvincing.

He places his fingertips over my lips, working the tender flesh between his rough thumb and forefinger for a few seconds before giving me a serious look. "We won't leave this spot 'til you get it out, Red, so might as well make it easy."

Closing my eyes, I swallow and count to five to collect my thoughts. The last thing I need to do is ramble and come off sounding like a blubbering idiot. "You sing a song about me," I start tentatively. His thick hair sweeps back and forth across my forehead as he nods. "Don't get me wrong, "Ten Days" has got to be the most *ridiculously* romantic thing anyone's ever done for me. But then you show up at my grandma's house. You tell me that I owe you two days and that you've got somewhere to take me. You bring me here, to the mountains."

"Yes."

"And you told me you *love* me." The last two words come out in a fierce whisper. "That's a big word, Lucas." One of those words that has always terrified me, because of all the weight it carries.

"Open your eyes." When I don't immediately give in to his request, his fingertips thread into my hair. Electricity hums through every part of my body, making it hard for me to keep from shivering. "Open your eyes."

I comply and take a deep breath. "Happy?"

He responds with a broken smile. "I brought you here because I didn't have the patience for Los Angeles, where I should've taken you months ago. You're here because I plan to enjoy every inch of your body and fuck you senseless without interruption." His mouth is just a mere centimeter away from mine. I can smell the spearmint from the gum he chewed while he was driving intermingling with the scent of the cologne he uses. It's intoxicating, a beautiful interference from the issue at hand.

"I love you," he continues, "and I plan to love you on my terms—at least for the next few days. And you came with me. Don't ever forget that."

What in the hell? What exactly does he mean by on *his* terms?

24

I jerk away from him and put enough distance between our bodies to give myself a chance to think clearly. Once my ass hits the bannister behind me, I stop moving. Lucas cocks his head to the side.

"What about *my* terms?" I squeeze the wood behind me for support like it will help boost my confidence. "You're not going to pull a bunch of shit on me again, Lucas. You're not going to use me for two days, or two weeks, or however long, and screw me over. I won't let you."

"No, I'm not."

"Because, if you tell me to leave again, I …" But my voice gives. I don't actually know what I'll do if Lucas pulls a repeat of what had happened in February. Or what happened in Los Angeles two years ago.

What I *do* know is I'd rather not have him at all if the bitter reality of our relationship will be a repetitive loop of crushing break-ups and over-the-top make-ups.

He stalks over to me and traps my legs easily between his so it's impossible for me to walk away again. With nowhere to go, I challenge his gaze.

"I'm with you now." He hooks his index fingers under the tight waistband of my cutoff shorts and presses his thumbs against the strip of pale skin exposed right above them. "I'm with you." Each word is a harsh, staccato whisper.

Ninety percent of my body molds against his as if we were *made* to do this with each other and nobody else, but I firmly lay my palm flat against his chest to prevent him from claiming my lips. "For how long?"

"I'm keeping you this time. You're mine, Sienna."

Letting my hand go limp between us, I let him close the remaining space between our bodies. His tongue parts my lips roughly, without hesitation, and I moan at how delicious he tastes as I grasp the soft cotton of his tee shirt.

"I can't get enough of you, Sienna, and I sure as fuck don't want to try to stop," he groans as soon as he breaks away from me. He tugs my bottom lip with his straight white teeth before releasing it and making a low noise in the back of his throat. The sound I manage is just as guttural and pleading. "You taste like sin—the best kind imaginable."

This isn't the first time Lucas has told me this, but it doesn't make it any less sexy. Now, there's a raw desperation in his voice. It just makes me want him even more. "I need you." I point my gaze to the top of the staircase behind us, and then back to him. "*Now.*"

"We should eat," he whispers against the column of my throat, as his hand squeezes between my legs. "There's food in the fridge." His fingers glide under the hem of my shorts. "I should take you in there to eat because if I don't—" He sucks in a sharp breath between his teeth. "Fuck, you're wet."

Shaking my head, I respond in a breathless voice that doesn't sound at all like me, "No food—not now, okay? Just you. Just me."

This does the trick. His eyes sweep over me a few times, and then he nods.

"Upstairs."

Our mouths are still connected, tasting and exploring, reluctant to break apart as we fumble up the stairs. When we reach the top, I shove him against the log-paneled wall. He leans his head back, gazing at me incredulously as I push the bottom of his shirt up.

"Patience is a good thing," he drawls, amusement evident on his face.

But he's already finishing the job for me, dragging the dark cotton over his head, revealing a chest and abs that only come from years of gym dedication. I touch him— draw my fingertip around the outline of the dagger-filled heart tattoo in the center of his chest.

"This coming from the guy who couldn't wait until he got back to Los Angeles? Hypocrite." I scrape my fingernail along the last dagger. Before I reach the hilt, he grabs my hand, sliding my finger into his mouth and skimming his straight teeth along my skin.

"Never claimed *I* had shit for patience, Red." He motions me down the hallway and into the master bedroom. Like the rest of the house, this room is incredibly similar to his bedroom back in Los Angeles—decorated in a startling erotic contrast of red and black. There's a king-size, four-poster bed in the center of the room covered in a black duvet, partially pulled back, revealing deep red sheets. On either side of it are matching black wood nightstands that are bare except for an alarm clock on the edge of one. Directly across from the bed is a long dresser with a cylindrical glass vase of flowers sitting in the center of it—a splash of scarlet and cream calla lilies.

Lucas supports his shoulder against the doorway and trains his hooded gaze on me. "Get naked," he commands and then says, "You're doing it again. That thing with your teeth that drives me fucking insane."

Slipping my tongue between my teeth, I quickly unbutton my shorts and shimmy them down around my hips. When they fall to the floor around my feet, his chest visibly constricts. "Do you know how many times I've thought about you?" he asks, and when I pause to answer him, he motions me to continue undressing.

As I drag my white tank top over my head, I hear his footsteps drawing closer. "Do you know how often I've woken up needing you?" He kneels down in front of me and presses his mouth to the cotton "V" of my panties.

My knees buckle. "No," I admit, letting my top fall to the floor.

His warm breath fans my skin when he continues. "Every single day since you left." He skims his hand beneath the pink fabric of my underwear and lets out a low, animalistic growl when I tremble at his touch. "So no, I'm not letting you go this time,

Sienna. There's not even a chance."

And I believe him. By the way his hands are holding onto me as if I'd disappear if he so much as let me go, I know there's nothing in hell that will keep Lucas Wolfe away from me.

Not even Samantha.

My hands clench by my sides as he drags my panties down my hips. No, I refuse to think about his crazy ex, at least for now. There will be plenty of time for him to give me answers about her later.

Right now is meant for him and me.

Running my tongue across my dry lips, I find my voice. "What? You going to tie me to your bed to keep me with you?"

He finishes pulling the pink lace down my legs before lifting his eyes to mine. They're full of lust and need. He gestures for me to step out of my panties. "Maybe later."

Though I didn't believe it possible, even more heat pools in the pit of my stomach. "God, Lucas—" I start, but he drags me down onto the floor with him, causing my breath to rush out in a gasp. "What are you doing?" I struggle to get up, but he places one of his hands firmly over my belly button to hold me still.

"Don't ask obvious questions." He eases my knees apart with his strong body. "I'm going to taste you, Sienna." Even though I'm expecting it, I still jerk against him and grasp at his thick brown hair the moment his tongue darts out and circles around my clit.

"That feels so …" My words of pleasure are muffled when I yank his hair harder. He retaliates by sucking greedily on me until my teeth clench together and my hands shake too much for me to grip anything.

Satisfied, he replaces his mouth with his fingers, spreading my slick folds, his strokes fast and insistent—seconds away from sending me over the edge. "Do that hair pulling thing again, and I'll tie you to that bed." He jerks his head in the direction of the black four-poster bed several feet away from us.

My thoughts instantly go back to several months ago, to the infamous red guitar pick he'd flicked across my breasts whenever I gritted my teeth, and I lay back, curling my fists into tight balls.

Lucas dips his head and kisses a hot trail from my stomach to my inner thigh and then back up again, stopping only once to touch his mouth to my center. "I'll never get enough of the way you taste," he breathes against my flesh.

Any response I might have come up with is cut off by the hoarse gasp that slips through my lips when he circles his tongue around my center roughly. He draws back.

"Make that noise again." When I do, he splays one hand on the inside of my thigh, digging his fingertips into my soft skin before he uses his other hand to slowly glides two fingers deep inside my body. "I want everything from you."

Everything.

There's a part of me that wants to give him everything he wants without asking a single question, but there's also an alarm blaring in the back of my head.

"What'll you give me back?" I dig my fingernails into my palms a little deeper.

"Everything?"

"Always," he confirms, and I feel my heart beat even more erratically. "Whatever you want." Then he lowers his mouth back to my pussy, tasting and touching me until I cry out and my back arches up. Whenever I grind my teeth, he stops, pulling completely away for several seconds, denying me until I manage to control myself.

This is torture—both pleasure and pain.

"I want you," I finally manage to say in a coherent voice.

"You're going to have to do better than that."

I buck my hips against his mouth. "Fuck me, Lucas."

Hazel eyes stare up my body wickedly, and he shakes his head. "Not yet."

"Why?"

"Come first," he orders, and when I try to protest, he reaches up my body and covers my lips with one hand and my breast with the other as his tongue picks up speed. I taste myself on his fingers, and my hands wander down to his broad, tattooed shoulders. I scratch into his flesh, digging my nails into his skin.

I'm hardly aware I've tangled my fingertips into his hair again until his hands leave my mouth and breast to clamp around my wrists. He doesn't release me until I come, until I'm writhing and moaning beneath his lips. Even then, I'm still saying his name over and over again.

Slowly, he crawls his body up mine. He doesn't stop until we're heart-to-heart and eye-to-eye, and he's grinning. "Why are you looking at me like that?" I pant. I run my fingers along his jawline, and he grabs my hand, bringing my palm to his lips. "Because, I want to be inside of you. Right now."

About damn time.

"Yes," I half-shout in eagerness.

Coming to his knees, he pulls the blindfold away from my neck. Dangling it on the tip of his long finger for a moment, he glances between it and me, trying to decide what he wants to do next. Ultimately, he takes my hand in his and begins wrapping the fabric carefully around my wrist.

"But first, I'm going to tie you to that bed," he says at last.

"What happened to later?"

He kisses my fingers slowly before tying the first knot. "It was moved up when I felt your hands in my hair again."

CHAPTER TWO

"Why did you make me leave?" I ask Lucas a little over an hour later. He's several inches away from me on the California King bed, the sheets pooled around his strong hips, the back of his finger stroking my right palm in wide, circular motions. It feels good, *right*. "I've wanted to know why since it happened."

He traces my center life line, his short fingernail softly scraping my skin.

"Because even I mess up." I wait for him to continue. Then, I wait a little more.

And nothing.

Tugging the Egyptian cotton red sheets over my naked breasts, I turn my head toward him. It's dark in here, but I can easily make out his frown thanks to the sliver of light coming from beneath the bathroom door several feet across the room. "Okay, I get that, but what exactly happened?"

"Does it matter now?"

I sink my teeth into my lip to suppress my snippy response. How can he even ask if it matters? One moment we're making plans that would turn our temporary arrangement into something permanent once we returned to Los Angeles together, and the next hc's telling me I need to leave. His change of heart had come out of left field.

"Oh yeah, it matters," I say.

"It was all new to me, and I froze. I was—"

When he stops, I ask, "Afraid?" He doesn't confirm or deny, so I continue, "Of your first wife?"

He immediately corrects me, his eyes gleaming cold and hard at the mere mention of Samantha. "Of what she might do to *you*." As if to drive his point home, he loops a thick red strand of my hair between his fingers before pressing it to his lips.

"There was no fucking way I was going to let her screw with you to get to me."

I attempt to get up, but the crimson-colored blindfold is still binding my left wrist to the bed. Maybe he predicted we would have this conversation and had tied me up just so I wouldn't throat punch him when he started with the evasive maneuvers. Lucas uses this opportunity to slide closer to me, yanking the sheet back down to my waist. Sitting up, he lowers his lips to my waist and glides his tongue around my belly button.

I will *not* let what he's doing take my mind off what happened between us in Atlanta.

"You should have given me an option. You should have given me a—" I shiver and dig my toes into the sheets as he presses his fingertips against the sensitive part of my hip. "God, don't do *that* right now."

This time he uses his mouth, making a sensual path from my navel to my hip, keeping his eyes on mine the entire time. "The point is, I'm a big girl, Lucas," I gasp.

"Sam is a crazy one, though," he reminds me.

That much was obvious from the night I met Sam, but the question is, why? Why is she like this, and why is she obsessed with ruining Lucas' life? "What does she have on you?"

Lucas smiles, probably to make me feel better about the situation, but the reassurance isn't reflected in his eyes. "Nothing."

Nothing, my ass. When he came to me last night right after I finished watching the "Ten Days" premiere, I was sure he was ready to tell me what Sam was dangling over his head.

And now this?

"Don't you dare treat me like an idiot."

"I'm not. You need to understand—"

"Will you understand if I decide to go my own way?" I clear my throat. "If, after I finish the two days that I *owe* you here, I go back home to Nashville?"

Sitting up abruptly, he looks down at me, narrowing his hazel eyes into dangerous slits. For a lengthy, awkward moment, he doesn't say anything else, and all there is between us is the sound of angry breathing.

At last he snaps, "Don't do that shit. It's what she would do. I love you, and I'll do whatever the fuck is necessary to keep you by my side, but I don't need you doing what she's done to me already."

I suck in a breath of air through my nose. Squeezing my eyes closed to stop the burning at the corners, I exhale through parted lips. I will absolutely not cry, because that won't get anything accomplished.

"I'm sorry," I say. I don't want to make demands or be anything like his ex, and I feel wretched that he even made the comparison.

35

I've only met Samantha once, at a birthday party for Cilla, the lead singer of Wicked Lambs, but I learned all I ever wanted to know about Lucas' ex-wife during that brief encounter. But at the same time, I want to know the truth about why she has so much control over him. I need honesty just as much as I need Lucas.

He traces the oval-shaped outline of my face, studying every freckle and laugh line, every long black eyelash, and every twitch of my lips. Finally, he reaches across my body to unravel the fabric from my wrist. Once my hand is free, he lowers his lips to mine, running his tongue over the center of my lips until I part them and give him complete control of my mouth.

My body reacts to his almost immediately, and I drape my arms around his neck, desperate for some part of him to hold on to.

Screw him for making me feel this way.

When he draws away, his expression is pained. "Let me deal with Sam, with my past. I promise I'm going to keep her away from you. All you need to do is just let me love you."

God, if only it were that easy.

"I don't want you to get hurt." I clench his shoulders harder, pushing my fingers against the center of a black and gray five-point star tattoo on the right side. It matches the stars on his wrists. "You said it yourself that she'll try to ruin us if we're together."

The cocky look that dominates Lucas' face is achingly familiar, but I can't help wondering if it's not all an act now. If he's not just as worried about Sam. "I said she'd try. I won't let a goddamn thing or person touch you."

Why does he have to sound so confident all the time?

I'm still worried, but I murmur, "Okay."

"Good."

He plops back down on his side of bed, grasping my hips to pull me on top of him. I dig my knees into his side, which only prompts him to smack my ass. I gasp at the sharp sting, and of course, he grins.

"Sienna?"

"Mmmhmm?" I trace along the intricate tattoos on his forearms, following the pathway my fingers make with my blue eyes. "What is it?"

"I want everything from you."

"You told me that already," I tease as his hand tangles into the hair at the nape of my neck. Warmth spreads through my body, from my scalp to between my legs, and I move my hips.

He lets out a low growl and sits up enough for his mouth to touch the delicate bones of my throat. "No, I mean, I want you to work for me."

When I realize he's said these exact words to me before, the day he offered me the opportunity to save my grandmother's house by working as his personal assistant for ten days, I frown and push him away from me, leaving us eye-to-eye. "We're not role playing, are we?"

The fact that I'm shoving him away doesn't deter him from touching me—his fingers are still in my hair, and he drops his other hand to the curve of my hip. "As hot as that would be, no, we're not. YTS is going on tour in a week and a half."

YTS, Your Toxic Sequel, is the band Lucas fronts. They're best known for their raunchy lyrics, kickass live performances, and, well

... Lucas-*Fucking*-Wolfe himself. I'd forgotten that they were going on tour this summer, even though I frequently talk to

Lucas' sister, Kylie. Aside from last night when she told me to watch the music video that he had dedicated to me as an apology, she hasn't exactly mentioned her brother, his music, or the band.

"On tour?" I repeat, and he nods.

"Different city every night or two, big-ass bus full of shitheads with too many vices." He lifts his shoulders. "You'd like it."

I'm certain I know where this conversation is going, and immediately, I'm desperate to jump to another subject. I manage a shaky laugh. "You're not asking me to be a backup singer are you? Because I seriously blow at music."

Releasing my hair and my hip, he moves both his hands down so that he can grip my ass. "Oh, I don't know about all that. Never met anyone who plays piano like you." He looks so ridiculously sexy right now that I can't resist moving my face closer to his until our lips brush. "Besides, if I wanted you to sing, you'd do it," he taunts in a low voice between kisses.

"Abso-fucking-lutely not," I counter as he moves his erection up against me.

He shifts his hips, rolling me onto my stomach in a couple of well-executed motions. "Put your hands against the headboard." I am utterly vulnerable to him— completely his—and I feel the wood against my fingertips just as he nudges one finger inside of me. I cry out.

"Come on tour with me, Sienna."

And there it is. Five words not spoken in a question, but an order, and each word scares the hell out of me. Not even twenty-four hours have passed since Lucas literally forced his way back into my life. Since he ran out on me earlier this year, I have an entirely new list of commitments.

"I want you with me," he insists.

I peek back over my shoulder at him. "What about—" I start to mention my job, but another one of his fingers finds my body, and I splay my hands out on the headboard and squeeze my eyes shut. "Fuck," I groan, burying my face into pillows.

"I'm getting there," he promises, and I open my eyes to see the grin he's wearing widen. "But after you say yes. And before you ask, you'll have a job. I need your wardrobe expertise, but I'm not going to lie and tell you my reasons for wanting you with me aren't mostly fueled by greed."

The part of my brain that's not a blurry hot mess from what he's doing to my body realizes just how much sense his proposal makes. I've been working as a personal wardrobe consultant ever since I moved back to Nashville—and I've worked freelance for a few musicians. Plus, Lucas' music and my job are the reason why we initially met two and a half years ago. I'd worked wardrobe on the set of the "All Over You" music video, and Lucas and I had hit it off. Clearly, it hadn't worked out, but my time on set with his band had a lasting impression on me.

"I'm not much for cramped spaces," I blurt out.

"I am." He gives me a wicked smile as his fingers thrust faster inside me. I dig my fingernails into the pillows, the headboard— whatever my hands come in contact with— and he rubs the pad of his thumb around my clit. "Besides, we'll probably be in hotels more than on the tour bus."

But we'd still be on a bus. And despite what Lucas has said about wanting to keep me around, anything could happen. I'm not aware that I've started to clench my teeth until Lucas stops touching me. It's always been a nervous habit of mine, and it drives him insane. "Please don't stop," I beg.

"Come on tour with me."

He's asking a lot, he has to know that. I can't give him a direct answer right now because it's not possible—how can it be when I'm shivering beneath him, and I can feel every inch of him pressed up against my hip as he touches me?

I run my tongue over my lips and nod. "I promise I'll think about it."

His shoulders relax a bit, and I let out a satisfied moan when he slides his erection deep inside of me. He takes his time, going agonizingly slow, until he's balls-deep, and I'm biting my lip to keep from clenching my teeth. And then he sighs. Lucas-Effing-Wolfe actually sighs. For me.

"I'll just have to fucking convince you to come," he growls. I assume he's talking about the tour, because right here in bed, I don't need any convincing.

CHAPTER THREE

Over the next couple of days, Lucas doesn't come right out and directly ask me to go with him on the band's tour again. Instead, he uses his mouth and hands and body, and his music, to persuade me to join him on the road. By the time he drives me to the airport in Knoxville on Friday morning, I'm half-tempted to tell him I need another couple days of convincing, despite the fact that I've had a very limited amount of sleep in the last several hours, and my body feels like I've spent days doing nothing but hardcore Pilates.

Then I remind myself that I have been contracted to do a job this weekend— wardrobe for a singer's debut album photo shoot in downtown Nashville. I have to go back home, even if it's just to take care of one obligation.

My flight is scheduled to leave at 10:45 AM, but Lucas gets me to the airport with an hour to spare. As I check my bag in, I can feel his eyes on me. I know he's expecting me to give him an answer about the tour before I leave, but I'm not sure if I'm ready to do that just yet.

And, frankly, he deserves to be the one left hanging for a change. As much as I hate to admit it, deep down I'm still pissed off about his refusal to answer any of my questions about Sam.

I need time to let my brain process everything, because it's nearly impossible for me to think clearly when I'm with Lucas.

"When are you driving back to L.A.?" I ask as he walks me to security. His hand is on the small of my back, and we're close enough that the sides of our bodies brush with each step.

"Flying," he tells me. "I'm leaving this evening, and Kylie's driving my car back after she uses my place over the weekend." He gives me a distant smile. "I want you coming home with me, Sienna."

I'm sure that if I could see his eyes, I'd tell him anything he wanted to hear. Luckily, he's wearing sunglasses—the same aviators he put on the few times we left his house over the last forty-eight hours. It's kind of a useless disguise—any diehard Your Toxic Sequel fan would be able to spot him from a mile away. He's that memorable, plus the tattoos on his arms are unique and don't exactly help him blend in.

A few feet from the security checkpoint, he stops moving and drags me to him, burying his face in my hair. "What have you done to me?" He takes a deep breath. "I've never cared about goodbyes and then you come along and make me need you."

I swallow, trying to push down the tightness building up in my throat. I don't want to be a big baby and cry, especially since I know that, for once, this isn't it between us. Still, goodbyes are painful—they rip into you and slowly tear you apart no matter how long they actually last. "I love you."

He looks me in the eye. "Come on tour with me, even if it's just for a few cities."

And I think it's because I hate goodbyes so much that I nod and say, "I'll think about it, okay?"

We kiss then, like it's for the last time, though there's a good chance I'll be with him for nearly a month and a half on the road. By the time I board my flight forty-five minutes later though, I already have a sick feeling in the pit of my stomach.

We couldn't even last ten days with each other before, so what do I expect to happen when it comes to forty-five days of nonstop togetherness? He can't even be honest with me about whatever it was that ripped us apart five months ago. I want him—God, do I want him—but right now there's a tiny piece of me that wants to tell him to fuck off.

But then … I think of the music video he made, and how it made me feel.

As I shuffle down the aisle to take my seat near the center of the plane, I try my best to shove the negative thoughts from my mind. I refuse to let them screw up my emotional high after my time with Lucas, at least for the time being.

To my surprise, my brother is actually at the airport on time to pick me up when my flight touches down in Nashville. Dressed in his usual attire of cargo shorts, bright boat shoes, and Polo shirt, with his short blondish brown hair still damp from a shower, Seth greets me at the baggage claim.

"You look surprised to see me," he says. He seems more cheerful than usual, and I regard him carefully.

"And you look incredibly Chuck Bass." When he gives me a look of confusion at the *Gossip Girl* reference, I shake my head and continue, "Didn't think you got my text." I sent him a message early this morning asking him to pick me up, but he never replied, and I figured I would be stuck catching a cab home since Gram has a doctor's appointment today.

"I got it," Seth assures me. Four and a half years younger than me, my nineteen-year-old brother is notorious for not picking up his phone. "And besides, do I ever let you down?"

I snort and lean over to grab my oversized bag off the conveyor belt, but he immediately steps up and plucks my luggage out of my hands, slinging it over his shoulders. "I was busy when you texted, but next time I'll make sure to stop just to let you know I'm on my way, deal?" He wiggles his light brown eyebrows at me.

My nose wrinkles at the thought. "God, Seth, seriously? You have to tell me that?" He grins as I move my head from side to side. "Thanks for making this conversation totally awkward."

"Anytime I can make shit weird for you, Si."

Seth's old Dodge Ram pickup truck is surprisingly void of its usual collection of Burger King bags and old mail when I climb inside of it ten minutes later in the short-term parking lot. I sniff a few times. The only thing I smell is wintergreen air freshener and after a quick onceover, I locate two—one dangling around the rearview mirror and the green string of another poking out the dashboard.

"So ... is she nice?" I ask as he starts the engine. She must be if he took the initiative to clean his filthy truck.

"Nice enough. Maybe I'll, you know, bring her to meet you and Gram if things work out." He merges onto I-40. "I think you'll like her."

I turn on the radio, which is tuned to a station I know he hates because all they play is pop music. The sound of The Pussycat Dolls blasts through the truck for about ten seconds before I jab another button, switching to a rock station that's in the middle of airing an ad for the end of a local car dealership's Christmas in July sale.

"This *is* serious," I say, shocked. "You've given her control of your radio."

"Don't be such a nosy ass." After he switches lanes, he looks over at me, his eyes searching my face. "You went on a work trip to Knoxville? Why didn't you just drive?"

"Now who's being nosy?" I counter. Seth isn't exactly Lucas' biggest supporter, mainly because of the dilemma with Gram's house earlier this year. I take a deep breath before saying in a sugary voice, "But, yes, something like that. The front-man of Your Toxic Sequel has asked me to be his personal wardrobe consultant during their national tour." My words sound so professional and rehearsed, I'm sure my face looks just as surprised as Seth's.

"Damn, that's awesome, their new music is—" He pauses and scowls. "Wait, that's Wolfe's band, isn't it?"

"Yeah, it is. And?"

Seth's top lip curls. "And that son of a bitch is the front-man. You told him to fuck off, right?"

"No." My voice exudes confidence that's impossible for me to feel at the moment.

"I didn't. I haven't given him an answer, actually."

"Jesus, Sienna, don't you think—" he starts, but I hold up a hand to cut him off.

"If you start with your preaching, I will kick your ass. Let me take care of myself, okay?" When he starts to protest again, I continue, "And besides, working for this band would be killer for my resume."

I don't add that it's already on my resume from when I worked with them two and a half years ago.

"So you definitely haven't said yes yet or signed any contract?"

I shiver, thinking of the last contract I signed for Lucas, and then I shake my head.

His brown eyes dart up in relief. "Good. I don't want him screwing you over."

My cheeks flush when my mind automatically goes to all the ways Lucas did screw me this weekend – over, under, sideways, on the floor, the shower, the deck railing, hell, even the rocking chair on the front porch.

"Neither do I," I manage in a small voice. Because even after the amazing two days of bliss I spent with Lucas, I won't ever be able to forget all the crap that's happened between us. Not completely, at least. To my brother, though, I smile brightly.

"But if I say I'll go, I'll be fine. I swear."

"Are you going to tell Gram?"

I bite the inside of my lip. "Do I have a choice? If I leave home for two months I'm probably going to have to say *something*." Besides, I've made it a point not to lie to her.

My mother has done enough of that to last Gram, and the rest of us, a lifetime.

Seth's lips twitch. "What about Tori?"

This makes me flinch. Tori, my former roommate from the years I spent living in

Los Angeles, is one of my closest friends. If Seth's the vice-president of the "Castrate Lucas-Fucking-Wolfe" Fan Club, then Tori's the president, thanks to how many times shit has hit the fan between us.

"Yeah." I wring my hands together in my lap, causing Seth to give me the most sympathetic look he can probably muster. "I mean, it's business, right? She'll be alright."

But that night, as I lay on the porch swing outside of my grandmother's Nashville cabin—the same house that had brought Lucas back into my life when he bought it in a foreclosure sale—I glance at my phone. Tori's number is pulled up and ready to dial, but I haven't been able to hit send. When I'd told Gram about the tour this afternoon, she'd been cautiously optimistic. As much as I love Tori, I'm still too high from the last couple days to deal with listening to any "what-ifs."

I have enough of those running through my own brain without any of my friends' help.

Before I know it, I find myself calling Kylie, Lucas' younger sister.

She picks up her phone almost immediately, and I swear I can hear the smile on her face. "So, what did you think?"

"I'm guessing you knew about what he was going to do for a while, huh?"

"Not *that* much longer than you," she assures me. "And it was very unlike Lucas, which is why I agreed to ask you to watch it."

47

"Thank you. Thank you for asking me to watch." My voice is shaky, and there's a moment of silence between us. I grip the swing's chain to steady myself, even though there's no threat of falling. "Looks like we might be seeing each other soon."

"What are you talking about?"

"The YTS tour."

"Ah," she hedges, the single word drawn out.

"Lucas didn't tell you he invited me?"

She lets out a low whistle. "No, it's not that. I knew he was planning to try and convince you to go. The thing is, I'm not going to be going on tour with the guys this go around."

I sit up on the swing so fast it makes me dizzy. "Seriously?" Kylie has been Lucas' personal assistant for years, so I expected her to be with the band every step of the way during their tour.

To hear otherwise worries me.

"I can't be around Wyatt—not in that type of environment at least. Not if we're going to keep making things work."

Wyatt McCrae, Your Toxic Sequel's bass guitarist.

Make things work.

Okay, this is definitely new.

"Did you dump the new guy?" For the past couple of months, every time I asked her about her love life she's vaguely mentioned some guy she met at a music awards show.

"Sienna, I—" Kylie starts, and then she groans. "Screw it, I guess I might as well tell you. Wyatt's the guy I've been living with in New Orleans."

And then she tells me everything. How Wyatt showed up in New Orleans while she was on vacation there several months ago.

How he demanded a second chance with her. How he ultimately screwed up.

What was with the guys in Your Toxic Sequel and their massive screw-ups and their penchant for showing up at women's doorsteps unannounced?

Kylie continues her story, but while she tells me about the road trip she and Wyatt took back to Los Angles, my front door opens. "Hold on," I say, as Gram pokes her head outside. She mouths that dinner is ready, and I give her a thumbs up. "Just a second, Gram."

"Tell her I said hello," Kylie trills, and I comply. Once my grandmother goes back into the house though, I reiterate to Kylie that I'm still not following her. She takes a long pause before she answers. "We got back together a few weeks after I left New Orleans, back in February."

"And the guy at the awards show?"

"Well hell, I guess you and Lucas *didn't* talk very much while you were in the mountains." She releases a sound. "Sienna, that's just the bullshit I've been telling almost everyone so Wyatt and I can have a chance to … adjust."

Adjust? My breath hitches. "Oh my God. Kylie, are you pregnant?"

CHAPTER FOUR

Kylie makes a noise in the back of her throat that sounds suspiciously like a sob.

I chew on the tip of my nail. "Are you okay?"

"No," she says, and this is when I realize that the sound she's making isn't her sobbing but rather laughter. "I mean, yes. I'm fine. The no was for the pregnancy question. I'm not knocked up. I swear, that's the first thing people say whenever I tell them. I need to buy a shirt that says there's zilch in my oven."

"That you're—?"

"*Married*. After an award show back in late April," she explains. "Well, the morning after the award show. We've been pretty quiet about it because we want to make it work. I *need* for this to work."

I don't know all that much about Wyatt McCrae—I haven't spent enough time around the band to form a solid opinion—but I do know that his history with Kylie is rocky, and that's wording it lightly. The last time I saw him, back in February and right before he went after my friend, he was cozying up with an assistant at the studio where the band was recording tracks for their upcoming album.

And now—now he's married to a woman I care about just as much as my own family.

I massage the bridge of my nose between my fingers. "Congratulations."

Kylie releases a weak sigh. "Thanks, it means a lot to me that you're not pissed that I kept it from—" I hear something buzzing loudly on her end, and she groans. She mumbles something about fire extinguisher and dinner and tells me she'll be right back.

When she returns to the phone nearly two minutes later, she's out of breath.

"I blow at cooking," she explains. "We're just *now* getting around to telling most people that we're married, so please don't think I kept you in the dark for too long."

I can only imagine the way she broke the news to her brother.

"Today you need to call the head of your record company. Go to a photo shoot at two thirty. Buy a wedding gift for Wyatt and me—oh, by the way, Lucas, I married him back in April."

I bite the inside of my lip to keep from laughing. "How's everyone taking it?"

The silence that immediately encompasses the conversation is a good indicator that her answer is going to be no. I don't nudge her to speak this time, but after thirty seconds of a quiet hum on her end, she laughs. "Just about. Lucas shocked the hell out of me because he's been the most supportive. My parents—well, you met them. They're all smiles and glad I'm settling down. Sinjin, on the other hand…"

Just hearing the drummer's name makes me a little uneasy. High on prescription pills and who knows what else, he had confronted me back in February. It ended badly, with Lucas furious and Sinjin going back to rehab.

"It's not his life," I say, my voice tight. "He'll be fine."

"He's getting there. He's just worried Wyatt is going to screw up and hurt me. I worry too—don't get me wrong—but I want it to work. I don't need the people closest to me making it worse."

This I completely understand. The last thing I want is to decide to go on the road with Lucas and then have my family and friends tell me what an idiot I am. It wouldn't sway my decision, but the divide it might cause is something I don't want to deal with.

Kylie shouldn't have to either.

"What matters is you're happy." I dig my heel between two of the porch's wooden floorboards and rock the swing back until it creaks. "Sinjin will get over it."

"He will," she agrees. "Thanks for listening. And I know it still doesn't make sense why I won't go on tour with you guys, but I just can't. It'll cause too many problems and jealousy issues on my end. It's just best if I sit this one out so I won't end up going all

Kylie smash on some groupie."

"You're making it sound like I've already decided to go." And after this phone call,

I wonder if I should step a foot on that tour bus.

When I say as much to her, she pulls in a breath. "Shit, babe. Do me a favor and ignore *everything* I just said."

"I'm still shocked he showed up. I don't even know what we are yet, but I know I don't want to backtrack just because I have to see him around a bunch of horny groupies."

"Lucas isn't like that at all, I swear it. Not when he's in a relationship, and that's what you are to him now. You don't have a damn thing to worry about."

There's another uncomfortable pause in our conversation, and once again, she's the one who breaks it by saying she has to go. For the first time since I began talking to Kylie on a regular basis, I'm actually eager to get off the phone. She's given me a lot to think about in the last fifteen minutes, and there's no doubt I'll be up late tonight, gazing up at my ceiling with a hundred and one thoughts hurtling through my head.

"I'll talk to you soon, okay?"

"You know it. Look, Sienna, think about the tour long and hard, okay?" She pauses. "Ugh, I just heard you snort, you dirty bitch."

"I did no such thing."

This time, she snorts. "Whatever. But, back to what I was saying—I swear the bus isn't just about tits and ass." Before I have a chance to call her on that bullshit, she amends her statement. "I swear my brother's part of the bus won't be about tits and ass. Better?"

"You have no filter, do you?"

She laughs. "Filters are for pussies."

"Good night, Kylie. And seriously, take care of yourself."

She promises to call me sometime next week, after she drives back to Los Angeles from her weekend getaway, and then hangs up. I remain on the swing for a few more minutes before I wander into the house. The mouthwatering aroma of chicken teriyaki immediately assaults me. My grandmother is already in the dining room that's on the other side of the kitchen, so I slide down into one of the seat across from her at the massive formal table.

"His sister called to talk you into going on tour with that band?" she questions.

I blow a few errant strands of red hair out of my eyes. "She's not even going." Gram's brow knits together over her bright blue eyes in confusion, and I add, "She married the bass guitarist a few months ago and doesn't want to be on the road anymore."

She chews an oversized bite of chicken and broccoli slowly, carefully considering what to say next. "So, now that you know she won't be going, what do you think you'll do?"

"I'm going." Even if it does scare the hell out of me. If Kylie is willing to give Wyatt McCrae a chance for the umpteenth time, I can deal with being on tour with Lucas. "At least I'll go for a couple of weeks."

I pay no attention to that nagging little voice in the back of my head warning me that a couple weeks may be all it takes for Lucas to tell me to fuck off again. I ignore it because if I listen, I'll never be happy. Besides, I'm almost certain that if I spend some time with him, I'll finally be able to get some real answers.

Gram wipes the corners of her mouth with her napkin. "I think it will be a good thing for your career. Good for you, too."

I give her a little smile before I pop a forkful of stir-fry into my mouth. "Let's hope so."

A few hours later, after Gram has gone to bed for the night, and I'm lying in my own bed stressing over the wardrobe job I'm scheduled to work in less than ten hours, I call Lucas to tell him that I've made up my mind about the tour. His phone goes to voicemail after a few rings, so I end the call and lay my phone face down on the bed next to me. It's 1:19 in the morning here, which means it's 11:19 PM in Los Angeles. There's a chance, and it's a really small one, that he's already sleeping or that his flight back to L.A. hasn't landed yet. I consider sending a text but then I decide against it— this is something I need to say directly to him, even if it is through a message.

I redial his number to leave a voicemail.

He picks up on the second ring. At first, all I hear is the deafening sound of a rock song in the background, but then his voice comes on the line, a sexy growl over the loud music.

"Couldn't stay away?" he asks, and I laugh past the lump forming in my throat.

God, how am I going to survive being on tour with him when I turn into an emotional mess from just talking to him for a couple minutes?

"Is this a bad time?"

There's a shuffling sound on the other end, but after a few seconds it's gone, and the sound of the music has just about disappeared. "Sorry, couldn't hear for shit in there. You make up your mind?"

"Yes, I—" I start, but then I hear a husky female voice say something to him. The scratching noise comes back—which I easily recognize as him covering the phone. "Do you need me to call you back?"

"Why the fuck would I want that? I need as much of you as I can get."

"Sounds like you might be busy," I say, each word clipped.

"Ah, Red, don't tell me you're already letting your imagination run all over the damn place. Promise there's no woman tied to my bed right now." I make a noise—one that I'm not entirely certain is relief or surprise—and he lowers his voice. "I'm at Wicked

Lambs' release party."

Sitting upright, I bring my knees to my chest. If there's one woman out there who loathes me as much as Lucas' ex, it's Cilla Craig, the lead singer of Wicked Lambs.

She's known Lucas for years and made it clear to me last winter that she's in love with him. Lucas has made it just as clear that Cilla's just the woman he grew up with—that she would never be me.

Still, I'm only human, and hearing that she's around bothers me big time.

"You still there?" he asks.

"Yeah, I am." Even though the late July heat makes my upstairs bedroom an inferno, I drag my old pink and orange hibiscus-print comforter up and over my knees, tucking it under my chin. It's comforting—the same sort of thing I would do as a child after my mother freaked out on me. I squeeze my eyes shut. "I called to tell you yes. I want to go with you on the tour."

It sounds like he drags a breath in through his teeth. "And you're fucking sure you want to come with me?"

Of course I'm not. I'm scared to death of things not working out. "Very."

"I—" he starts, but then the shuffling sound returns once again. "Wyatt wants you to know he's happy you came to your senses." He covers the phone once more, and I purse my lips. "Fuck, Wyatt and Cilla are killing me here. They said they'll see you in a week."

My lips part to answer him, but then I pause and let what he just said sink in.

"What do you mean *they'll* see me?"

"Have you—you don't know much about the tour, do you?" There's the faintest tinge of surprise, not to mention hurt, in his voice. It catches me off guard. When I don't answer—or make any noise for that matter—he repeats his question, this time sounding like the ridiculously confident man I fell in love with. "Google is your friend, Sienna. You should use it before you agree to stuff."

After the incident in Atlanta, I did my best to put Lucas Wolfe out of my mind. Ignored the magazines with him on the cover in the supermarket. Changed the channel when anything Your Toxic Sequel came up. And I sure as hell didn't look him up online.

"No, apparently Google is my worst enemy," I mutter. "Lucas … Wicked Lambs is touring with YTS, aren't they?"

I know the answer before he confirms it, but it doesn't stop the tension from spreading across my chest when I hear his words. "I thought you already knew."

CHAPTER FIVE

Lucas

Call me a goddamn idiot, but up until twenty seconds ago, I truly believed she was already aware of Cilla being on our tour. Sienna's surprise and irritation tells a different story, though. She's hesitant now, giving me short, clipped answers. *Yes. No. Fine. Okay.* It drives me fucking insane, and there's nothing I want more than to bend her over my knee and spank that perfect ass of hers.

There'll be enough time for that later.

We talk for another few minutes before she fakes a sorry ass yawn and tells me she has a wardrobe assignment in the morning. "I'll call you later this weekend, okay?" she says. Does she think I'm too oblivious to notice the break in that sexy country accent of hers?

Cilla and Wyatt are smoking only a few feet away from me, but I don't hesitate to stop her before she hangs up on me. "Wait!" I urge, and I hear her breathing pick up. The muscles in my neck tauten as I sit down on a nearby bench. "You really think I'm letting you go that easy?"

"I really am tired."

"Sienna," I begin, but a cough coming from Cilla's direction makes me pause. Out the corner of my eye, I see her glaring at the ground and tightening the vice on her cigarette until it comes close to snapping in two. She's listening to every goddamn word I'm saying. It's no secret that I don't want Cilla on the same tour as me, but because I don't want to hurt her, I drop my voice to a whisper. "Sienna, I love you. And I'm so happy you'll be with me."

She laughs nervously, and she's probably nodding her head briskly and skimming her teeth over her bottom lip. "I'm your wardrobe consultant, remember?"

The way she says *wardrobe consultant*—in a whispery, professional voice— makes my cock go hard. Damn I need her. I start to tell her that I'll be on the earliest flight to Nashville in the morning, but then I remember I've already made plans to fly to

Atlanta.

Fuck.

It's a trip that can't be avoided if I don't want to lose my mind anytime soon.

"I know exactly what you are," I say. I catch Wyatt's shit-eating grin, and I turn away so he won't attempt to read my lips when I add, "And I'm going to have one hell of a time with you in and out of that wardrobe. Bending you over—"

Her voice is strained when she interrupts me, and I know she's forgotten all about Cilla and Wicked Lambs. For the time being, at least. "You shouldn't talk like that."

No shit, I shouldn't. All I'll be able to think about for the rest of the night, and tomorrow morning on the way to Atlanta, is the warmth of Sienna's skin beneath mine, the tiny beads of sweat on the small of her back, and the sweet scent of her apple body wash lingering between her shoulder blades. When I go to bed—alone and with my dick throbbing—all I'll be able to imagine is her bound hands and her hips grinding against me.

I blow out a harsh breath. "Sienna?"

"Yes?"

"Later, when you touch your pussy—because I know you will, and there's not anything I can say to make you wait for me—I want you blindfolded. I want you thinking of me inside of you, tasting you. And after you're done, after you've called my name into your pillow and you're shaking, I want you to tell me."

"You don't know that—" she argues, but I cut her off with a rough noise that leaps from the back of my throat.

"Don't play games."

Cilla flags me down by tossing her black hair around so dramatically I've got no other choice but to notice. When I make direct contact with her blue-green eyes, she juts her head toward the entrance of the club, where her band's party is happening, and gives me a pissed off look. "I'm going inside," she mouths before hobbling up the brick steps on her spiky red heels. Her shoulders tremble as the doorman murmurs a few words to her before letting her inside. I stare at the club's black metal door long after it closes.

"Did I lose you?" Sienna interrupts my thoughts. "I said good night and that I love you."

There it is again. That strange feeling of warmth crawling through my body because of a few words mumbled by a woman who was supposed to be nothing more than a one-night stand.

"Don't forget what I said, Sienna." I remind her.

"And what if I don't do what you're asking?"

"I know you. You will."

After she's gone, I'm silent and oblivious to all the shit going on around me despite the Friday night traffic less than fifty feet in front of the club and the sound of

Wicked Lambs' new music blaring behind me. When I finally decide to give a fuck again, I realize that Wyatt is on the bench beside me. Tossing his cigarette butt in the nearby receptacle, he cocks his head to the side and gives me a nosy look.

"I hate the smell of those things," I bark. The scent of cigarettes has always brought up memories of Sam and all our arguments just before our marriage tumbled apart. It never failed—mid-argument, she would always light a cigarette while telling me to leave if I didn't want to deal with her. The scent is a reminder that when I left, I should've stayed the fuck away. "And stop looking at me like that."

He leans forward, supporting his forearms on his knees. "How did she take the

Cilla thing? I'm going to go out on a limb here and say not well."

"Did Kylie take any of the shit you did to her well?"

He winces, but quickly shakes the jibe off. Stretching back, he starts to light up another, but thinks better of it when I look at him like I'm about to throw him into traffic. "Here's how I think shit's going to go down." He shoves the unused cigarette back into the green and white box and closes the cardboard lid. "Cilla's going to run her drunken mouth and call Sienna 'Pepper' or tell her how many times you've fucked her in the past and then she'll get her ass kicked."

"Just so we're clear here—which one's getting her ass kicked?"

"Cilla. Least that's what I hope will happen."

Wyatt, Sin, Cal—they're all just as adamant about not wanting Wicked Lambs on the road with us, but the combined tour was what our label wanted. And all of those details were worked out long before Sienna came back into the picture.

"They won't fight," I say, hoping I'm right.

Later, after Cilla has had several more drinks, she stumbles up to my table and offers to come home with me in front of everyone we know professionally—Cal, Wyatt, our tour manager, and her own drummer. I take this as my cue to leave, but when she follows me, I pull her into an empty alcove close to the club's entrance to let her down as easily as I can.

That shit doesn't happen.

"I won't tell Pepper," she argues. Her ruby red lips stretch up into that slow grin she does when she thinks things are about to go her way. "Not that I care what she thinks—"

"Cilla." I grab her wrists, one hand closing around the Tiffany bracelet Sinjin had given her a couple years ago, when she tries to rub her hands down my chest. "We're not doing this—we won't ever do it. Her name is Sienna, and believe me, I give a whole lot of fucks about what she thinks, how she feels. If I'm with her, there's no me with anyone else."

She jerks out of my grasp like I've burnt her and stumbles backwards. "God, who are you? Not my Lucas." She shakes her head belligerently. "Not anyone I know."

This shit is getting really old.

"You're right," I sneer. "But I've never been your Lucas." I turn abruptly to leave, and this time, she doesn't come after me when I leave the club.

My driver gets me home in record time, and after I get into bed—the same one I'm going to share with Sienna once the tour is over in a couple of months—I check my phone. I'm not surprised to find a message from her that was sent just over an hour ago, at 3:22 her time, but it's the self-portrait she sent along with it that knocks me on my ass.

The makeshift blindfold covering her blue eyes, combined with how her flushed face is turned to the side, is the sexiest thing I've ever seen. She's got me rock hard just staring at it. The text below the photo is simple:

1:22 AM: *I needed YOU more.*

Because of my history with Sam, I avoid going home as much as possible, usually making the trip when my mom becomes too insistent for me to deny. But the next morning, after I've signed some autographs at LAX and smirked for a few photos with a group of college girls from New Zealand claiming to be Your Toxic Sequels' biggest fans, I board a flight bound for Atlanta. Unlike the last time I came to town, there's no limo to pick me up when I arrive. I rent a pearl white Suburban from one of the airport kiosks and head straight to my ex's place.

She's still living in the same overpriced, luxury apartment on Peachtree Street, still driving the same Mercedes that she's had for a year and a half now. When I walk past it, I want to kick the grill in—I paid for the goddamn thing—but I keep my shoes firmly planted on the pavement and go inside of her building. A woman dressed in Under Armor workout clothes walking out with her dog twists around to rake her eyes over me, the look on her face inviting and curious, but I give her a cold smile.

No, not much has changed, but does it ever?

The only thing that's remotely different about this visit is that Sam's not expecting me. And the way she looks when she opens the door for me.

The last time I saw my ex was this spring, and even then she was skinny as hell. Now, with a pair of cutoffs hanging from her pointy hips, her tits nearly non-existent beneath a baggy tank top, and her short hair surrounding her face in limp, greasy strands, she looks like she's aged five years instead of five months.

Does she know what she's doing to herself? Or has she reached the point where she just doesn't give a shit anymore?

Sagging her tiny body back against the wall, she takes in the sight of me, starting at my Converse and ending at my black baseball cap.

"Are you hiding from someone, baby?" she sneers. This is how I always look when I travel, but she already knows that. Not that it did me much good this time; it was too hot to cover my arms, and the stars on my wrists, which were the result of a bet I lost to Sinjin seven years ago, are now my trademark. "Well, are you?" Sam probes.

"No, not hiding." Not anymore.

Her eyebrows pull down together. "I told you I'd come to you next week, so why the fuck are you here?" she yells.

I shove the door completely open and let myself into the apartment. There's an unmistakable stench of gin and vomit that she's tried to get rid of by dousing the place, and herself, with expensive perfume. Sam doesn't bother to stop me, but I don't expect her to. She looks too weak to walk across the room, much less start an argument with me. And besides, she probably needs the money too much to try anything stupid or play games.

That's the only time she ever cooperates with me. When she's broke.

"Not happy to see me?" I ask at the sound of her creeping up behind me.

"As a matter of fact, I'm not. I'm—" And this is where I tune her out and focus instead on all the U-Haul boxes scattered around her living room. Most of the boxes are open, with their contents spilling out. It gives me the idea she's in a hurry to go somewhere.

"Moving?" I turn to face her, and her large gray eyes go even wider in surprise.

They're the biggest damn things on her entire body.

"Why do you care?" She stares at a cigarette burn on the oak floor, but I know she's seething. I already knew before coming here that there was a ninety-nine percent chance she's run through the money I gave her this spring, so I don't even flinch at what she tells me next. "Yes, I am moving. Downgrading to a smaller place—not that it's any of your business. That's why I told you I'd come to you, asshole. You know that—"

"Save me the 'you're inconveniencing me' bullshit. I wanted to get this over with." Leaning over her abstract, designer coffee table, which is covered with stacks of mail and a couple of overflowing

66

ashtrays, I drop the envelope holding the last cashier's check she'll ever receive from me. It lands on a letter from her electric company marked *URGENT*.

She's not just downgrading to a smaller apartment, she's been evicted from this one. Chances are this money will let her keep this place. "Saved you a trip."

Sam shuffles around the coffee table, not once looking at the envelope, until she's on the opposite side of me. Calmly, she sits down on the edge of her white leather couch and places her forearms on her bony thighs. She remains eerily still for over a minute before she speaks. When she does, her voice is off. Dazed.

Fuck, I bet she's high right now.

"Then we're done," Sam lisps. "I told you this would be it for me and you, and I meant it."

I take a couple steps back but keep my face blank. "We're not doing this anymore."

"I told you we wouldn't. I have no plans to contact you again, Lucas."

I expect her to scream. Or tell me that she's changed her mind about leaving me alone and that she'll be around to fuck me over until the day I die. She doesn't. She just sits there, her gray eyes empty, running her hands over her bruised kneecaps.

"I'm leaving. Take care of yourself, okay?"

Her gaze snaps up, and the hatred in her eyes makes me wonder if all that love she once swore she felt was nothing more than another game. "Then go. Make sure you tell Shannon and Dan I said hi," she barks. "I'm sure you're going to see them as soon as you leave here, and I know how much your parents adore me."

I give her a cold smile. "Get some help, Samantha, but don't bother me again." I make it halfway to the door before I hear her call my name out in a weak voice. When I look back at her, I'm already prepared for the deluge—for her to physically come at me, but she hasn't moved from her spot on the sofa.

"And I'm the bad one." Her pale lips curve into a grim smile. "I'm the fucked-up, heartless bitch."

"You haven't made it any easier."

"*I* didn't hurt anyone, Lucas," she scoffs. "*I* only reminded you of what a goddamn coward you are." Her words pierce right through me like a knife to the gut, but I keep myself together. I've got no other choice if I'm going to get out of this apartment without losing all of my shit.

When I don't speak, she continues, "You're the fucked up one, Lucas. You are … for what *you* did."

I force the corner of my lip up. "Fair enough."

She slides back until her shoulder blades hit the white cushions. She doesn't look at me, but she doesn't have a reason to. Sam knows exactly what she needs to say— what she needs to do—to cut me to pieces and remind me of what I am. "Good luck on your fucking tour, Lucas." Her hands shake as she reaches over to the end table to swipe up her pack of cigarettes. "You'll need it."

"Yeah, fuck you too, Samantha."

She doesn't say goodbye, but I don't expect that from her either.

CHAPTER SIX

Sienna

For the next few days, after agreeing to go on tour with Lucas, I completely throw myself into my job. Since I moved from Los Angeles back to Nashville at the end of April, I've been able to start a name for myself. Keeping that reputation is important to me. I don't want to go back to being a wardrobe assistant—I'm not saying that my time working for Tomas, my former boss, on the set of *Echo Falls* wasn't invaluable, but it was a living hell, too.

By Tuesday night, not only have Lucas and I verbally agreed on two dates when I'll return home from the tour based on my current work assignments, I've also personally spoken with all my clients to let them know about my plans.

I spend the majority of Wednesday with my friend Ashley, who helps me get ready for my flight to Los Angeles the next morning. Ash is a diehard Your Toxic Sequel fan—her off-and-on boyfriend (they're currently on) plays in a YTS cover group, and she's seen the actual band in concert a few times. The entire time we pack my bags, she gushes over the album-like quality of their live shows and even takes a fifteen minute break to make a playlist for me on Spotify.

"Their best songs. Ever," she tells me, her eyebrows nearly touching as she kneels in front of my laptop at my tidy corner desk, concentrating on her list.

I fold a plain black tank and place it on a pair of gray jeans inside of the new

Samsonite bag that I bought yesterday especially for the band's tour. I figured I needed something a little more heavy-duty than my old luggage that's, literally, coming apart at the seams. "Why do I feel like this list will have *all* their songs?"

Ashley rolls her eyes before shrugging. "Not quite all of them."

When it's time for her to leave an hour later, I'm surprised when she reaches into her purse and hands me a typed list titled *Ashley's YTS Bucket List*. Her name has been marked through with a series of X's and above it, she's written my name— correction, *Sienna-Fucking-Jensen*—in her loopy handwriting with a metallic pink Sharpie.

As I scan over the list, I slide down on the front porch swing. "Body shots with Cal backstage. Get Sinjin's sticks signed. Stroke Wyatt's Kramer." Cocking an eyebrow, I glance up at her. What the hell is a Kramer?

While I am reading, Ashley walks down the wooden steps, and now she's standing in the yard with her back turned to me, digging around in her purple Coach bag for her car keys. Since we reconnected several months ago, I've learned enough about Ashley to know she's waiting for more of a reaction from me before she responds.

"I'm assuming that's a guitar and not a nickname for Wyatt McCrae's boy bits," I say dryly.

Sure enough, she spins to look at me with a wicked gleam in her eyes. "Right."

She puts her hands on her hips, covering Jared Leto's face on her Thirty Seconds to

Mars t-shirt. "But I wouldn't mind stroking his—"

"So, I'm guessing you didn't give this to me just for shits and giggles?"

She shakes her head, her turquoise and pink-dyed hair swinging around her pierced heart-shaped face. "Um, no." Sighing, she jogs back up the steps, crosses the porch, and sits down on the swing beside me, crossing her legs at the ankles. "Oh come on, Sienna, I want you to do this for me. Take pics and everything so I can live vicariously through you."

"Why don't you be vicarious and come to the show *here* in September?"

Ashley shoots me a determined look. "Trust me, I'll be there, I've had my tickets for months. But think of how much fun you'll have getting to know the band by doing *that*." She gestures dramatically to the piece of paper I'm clutching, reminding me of a cheesy talk show host. "This is one hell of an icebreaker."

I've spent, at the most, maybe a total of twenty-four hours with the other members of Your Toxic Sequel. That entailed a music video shoot that I was eventually fired from, and then last February when I filled in as Lucas' temporary assistant. Both situations were awkward, and the only member of the band who didn't seem to automatically dislike me was Cal.

"You like putting me on the spot, huh?" But it's not like Ashley's begging me to sneak her backstage or onto the bus. And

71

besides, what she's suggesting really would be a good icebreaker—well, everything except for the body shots off Cal Romero. I fold the list in half and use it to swat away a mosquito. "I doubt I'll get signed sticks from

Sinjin, but I'll try my best. He's not my biggest fan."

I'm not exactly a fan of his either. Sinjin is a certified dick.

Ashley seems to think otherwise. "He'll do it. And thank *you* for doing this for me." She gives me a quick peck on the cheek, no doubt smearing her dark red lipstick across my pale skin. She stands and starts toward her car again. "Just so you know, I'm incredibly jealous of you."

I can hear the grin in her voice, so I smile at her back as I get up from the swing. Folding the list one more time, I slide it into the back pocket of my high-waist shorts. "I'll make sure I tag you in each of the photos."

She throws her head back and laughs. "See you in a few weeks and don't get into too much trouble, okay?"

"I won't," I promise.

Several hours later, over dinner at Gram's favorite restaurant in Franklin, my younger brother echoes Ashley's warning to stay out of trouble. Except Seth's advice isn't teasing, and he even goes a little further by giving me advice on how to have safe sex.

Gag.

At first, I'm not sure if he's joking, because as he tells me to make "the asshole wear a rubber," my brother is slathering butter on a dinner roll with the most relaxed look imaginable on his face. Plus, my grandmother is sitting right next to him, and I feel like even Seth is smart enough not to talk about my sex life in front of her. When I don't respond, his brown eyes move between Gram and me.

"You're both looking at me like *I'm* the douche right now."

Gram's bright blue eyes tighten into thin slits, a look that always made us quickly correct bad behavior when we were kids. "Since you put it that way, I guess you've gone ahead and called it right." Her usually soft voice is full of steel. "The shoe fits you well, son."

Seth's forehead creases. "Oh, come on, I just don't want to see her hurt, Gram.

That asshole she dated a few years back—he has nothing on Wolfe." He gives me a pleading look to help him out, but I press my lips together into a tight line. There's no way I'm helping him get out of this one. "Here, I'll filter myself: Don't let him screw you over. Better?"

No, not really.

Still, despite how calloused and rude Seth is sometimes, I know in my heart he means well. My grandmother and I are the most important people in his life. We rarely see our dad, who lives in Maine with his second wife, and Mom has been in prison for the last several years.

Ugh. I bite the inside of my cheek. Thinking about our mother makes me sort of thankful for Seth's lack of a filter. At least he doesn't beat around the bush, using manipulation and bullshit to get his point across like she always did.

Bending forward, I reach past the bottles of steak sauce and ketchup in the center of the table and cover his hand with mine. "Look, Seth, I love you—" I start, and he groans. Gram smacks him hard in the back of his head, ruffling his fair hair. Scowling, Seth gestures for me to continue. "It means a lot to me that you're worried— trust me, it really does—but I'll be alright."

"Sienna deserves to do this for herself," Gram adds with a smile that's so encouraging, so warm, I fall in love with her all over again.

Jerking out of my grip, Seth lifts his hands up defensively, palms facing me. "Damn, I never said she doesn't deserve to be happy. She does. I'll drop it, okay?" He doesn't speak again until Gram excuses herself to the bathroom. The moment she's out of earshot, he says, "I just want you to be careful."

I spear a piece of steak, roll it in sauce, and pop it into my mouth, ignoring the fact that it's cold and too rare as my brother and I stare each other down. I start a mental countdown from ten so I won't say something to him that I'll regret later even if he does deserve to have his ass handed to him.

Once I reach one, I take a sip of my Coke and clear my throat. "I promise I'll be careful, but this is the last time I want to talk about this with you. You're making things weird."

"Aw, Si, don't—"

Ugh, this is going nowhere. "Seth, I *am* going to be *exactly* like that. You let me worry about me, and you worry about yourself."

"You worry about everyone but yourself. You can swear your ass off that you don't, but I'll call you out on your shit every time."

I place my palms flat against the laminated surface of the dining table so I won't reach across and snatch him to me by the neck of his American Eagle t-shirt. I'm *that* frustrated with him. "Of course I worry about you and Gram. She turns eighty in November. And you—you're barely twenty. It's my job to make sure you're not screwing up your life."

"Don't start with that shit—" he begins, but out of the corner of my eye, I spot our grandmother coming back, and the muscles in my shoulders and neck tense up.

"Can we not completely ruin the rest of tonight?" I plead in a harsh whisper. "At least for Gram's sake? Let's drop it for good this time."

His expression is conflicted—like he absolutely wants to spend the rest of dinner telling me just how dumb he thinks I am for going with Lucas—but finally, the moment before Gram slips back into her seat, he scratches his fingers through his hair and lifts his shoulders dejectedly.

"For what it's worth, Sienna, I love you too," Seth says, and I feel myself begin to relax. That's the thing about my brother, always has been. Even when I should be angry with him, he has a way of melting through my defenses by saying things like that.

But then, maybe that's the thing about me. I've always been a sucker for white flags and kind words.

As Gram settles back into her seat, I clench my teeth for a moment and then work my mouth into a smile for my brother's benefit. "Everything is going to be alright. *I'm* going to be alright. It's a music tour, not a wedding."

But once again, I'm listing all the reasons going on this tour is a bad idea in my head.

Too anxious to fall asleep until the wee hours of the morning, I nearly miss my flight first thing in the morning. My brain is still fuzzy from the two hours of sleep that I managed as I go through the security checkpoint. Tossing my shoes and purse inside of a rectangular gray tub, I try to remember whether I parked my old Mercury sedan in short or long term parking, and it's not until I've boarded my first flight that I realize I left the bag containing the majority of my shoes sitting by the front door in Gram's foyer.

Dammit.

Closing my eyes, I attempt to get comfortable in my seat. "Get your shit together,

Jensen," I admonish myself through my teeth.

During my layover in Phoenix, I text Seth and ask him to check on my car (since he has the only spare key) and to send my shoes as soon I get a good address to receive overnight mail.

While I wait for him to respond, I receive a Facebook alert on my screen. It's a new message from Tori, my former roommate whom still lives in Los Angeles.

Victoria Abrams: *Wait, did I just wake up to read that your ass will be* here *tonight and tomorrow night? I'm squealing in anticipation, but I've got to admit, I'm kind of worried. What's going on? You're not taking your job back on* Echo Falls, *are you?*

During my sleeplessness last night, I contacted Tori to let her know I'd be in town for the next forty-eight hours since Your Toxic Sequel's tour will kick off in Pomona tomorrow night. I didn't mention Lucas or my agreement to go with the band, but it would be an ass move to go to L.A. without seeing her.

Taking a sip of my lukewarm caramel macchiato, I message her back.

Everything is good, I promise. I'm coming to town to see Lucas.

76

Just like Kylie always does when we're messaging back and forth, Tori takes forever to respond. When the IM finally does come through, it's just one sentence that I know she wrote and rewrote several times because she didn't quite know what to say. I swear Tori was born stressed out—hell, she even has a stress ball for every occasion.

Victoria Abrams: *Is this about that "Ten Days" song that's all over the radio?*

I scrunch my nose. Of course, she would have already heard the song—her daily commute is a bastard, so she blasts music to keep the level of road rage to a minimum.

Before I can respond to her question, my phone rings.

"Morning, Victoria," I answer.

She's out of breath when she speaks up. "One, don't call me that. My mother calls me that, and I hate it. Two, the song … it *was* about you, wasn't it?"

"And just last week you said your boss told you how much you sucked at inference," I joke. Silence follows, and I bite the inside of my cheek before adding, "But to answer your question, yeah, the song is about me."

The woman sitting next to me grunts and shuffles around in her seat noisily before covering her face with a purple and gold LSU throw blanket. I give her a hard look, even though she probably can't see it.

"Hold on for a second." Grabbing my purse, carry-on bag, and my cold coffee, I shuffle to a gate with fewer people. Once I find a secluded spot to finish my conversation, I drop my stuff by an uncomfortable-looking chair and put the phone to my ear. "Are you still there?"

"Oh, you're so not getting rid of me right now." She's still winded. I start to ask her why, but then I catch a glimpse of the time at the top of my phone's screen. It's 8:05 in Los Angeles, meaning she's more than likely getting ready for work. She has less than an hour to be inside of her cubicle, and chances are she's not even finished getting dressed.

Some things never change.

"Okay … are you *with* Lucas Wolfe again?" Tori's question is blunt and completely to the point. In my head, I can even hear the words left unsaid: Are you actually back with Lucas after he treated you like shit last winter?

Bending at the waist, I rest my forearms on my knees and glare down at the rounded toes of my yellow ballet flats. "We're going to give it a try," I say cautiously, and Tori goes quiet again. I can picture what she's doing right now: She's half-dressed, sitting on the edge of the micro suede loveseat in the tiny apartment we once shared and nodding her head—hair still probably wet from her shower.

"You're going to be late if you don't get your ass up and get dressed," I warn, and she begins to laugh.

"I'm not mad if that's what you're thinking," she says. I hear her shuffling around as she heeds my advice to get ready for work. "And as much as I don't understand it, I can't blame you for wanting *him*. I'd fall all over myself if Micah wrote me a song like that. But I swear to God, if you get hurt, I'm going to torch his house."

I work my lips into a smile. "Don't worry, we'll light it up together, and I'm pretty sure his sister would even join in."

78

"His sister's a smart girl."

Considering the deep-rooted disdain she's shown for Lucas during the last several months, Tori is taking the news of our reunion really well. This is the same woman who'd freaked out at her boyfriend for playing Your Toxic Sequel's music at a party we hosted several months back. I feel relief, though. I know it's unnecessary to get anyone else's approval to be happy—really, I do—but not having to hear bullshit from my best friend makes everything so much easier.

"You're being scary quiet," Tori points out, and I sit upright.

"I love you, you know that right?" I ask. "There you go, silence broken."

She laughs and then mutters something about mascara and raccoon eyes. "I support everything you do, woman. I'd be a petty bitch if I got angry about you dating someone."

"Then thanks for not being a petty bitch," I mock, and she snorts.

The mood of the conversation suddenly more relaxed, the rest of our call goes smoothly. For the next forty-five minutes, I talk to Tori as she drives to work about everything but Lucas. When it's time for her to go, I take my belongings back to gate 19, and an hour later, I board my flight to Los Angeles.

Back to Lucas, the expected, and the completely unexpected.

CHAPTER SEVEN

When I arrive at LAX and power on my phone, a message from my brother immediately pops up. Seth promises to stop by the Nashville airport to check on my car—and move it if necessary—and to send me my shoes as soon as I give him the word.

There's also a single text from Lucas.

11:48 AM: *Your driver will be there when you get off at one. Then you're all mine.*

I can practically hear his sexy voice growling the last part of the message directly into my ear, and my body immediately reacts. The tiny hairs on my arms and the nape of my neck stand on end, and the flutters in my stomach skim the line of pain and pleasure. Exhaling, I begin to type my response, focusing on what's important at the moment as I make my way toward the baggage claim.

12:15 PM: *I think you gave the driver the wrong time. I'm here already.*

He messages me back quickly, and I find myself grinding my teeth as I read the text.

12:16 PM: *Shit, are you serious? Sit tight.*

Sit tight?

"Nice move, Mr. Wolfe," I mutter under my breath. Tapping my foot rapidly against the floor, I wait for my suitcase to come around on the carousel. Once I locate it, I lug everything to a row of chairs nearby. It's too hot for me to wait outside for some driver to arrive, so I have no other choice but to take Lucas' advice and literally sit tight inside the airport.

No sooner than when my butt makes contact with the hard seat do I hear snippets of a conversation between two women who are walking in the direction of the taxi exit.

" … I have all of their CDs. I could spot him from a mile away. It was definitely him, and you—*you* are stifling me!"

What the hell?

I twist around in time to witness the shorter woman with the black, asymmetrical bob narrow her chocolate brown eyes at the tall, leggy blonde. "And just last night you said they're on tour. So which is it, Kate? He's on tour, or he's bullshitting around this place?"

"Or maybe," Kate snaps, "Lucas is catching a flight because of his tour. Did you even consider that before you dragged me away?"

Lucas is already here?

I clamber to my feet, allowing the argument between Kate and her friend to fade into the background as I scan the area around the baggage claim for Lucas as far as my eyes can see. There are couples reuniting all around me, and what appears to be an entire busload of people holding up signs that announce "Welcome Home, Gloria," but no sign of him. I'm about to grab my stuff and go look, but then I see him. Heading directly toward me. His stride a little faster than it normally is, his soft grin entirely too confident, his hazel eyes cocky and yet so full of need.

God, that man and those eyes.

He's wearing destroyed jeans and an olive green t-shirt that brings out the green flecks in his eyes. His muscular arms hang relaxed by his side, but when he comes close enough for me to breathe in the clean, airy scent of his cologne, I notice that he's worrying something between the thumb and forefinger of his right hand. I squint down at it as the toes of his Converse brush up against my ballet flats.

"Damn, Red," he drawls, "looks like you're more interested in my hands than my face." But then he opens his palm, holding it six inches from my face. My throat constricts as I take in what he's holding.

It's a guitar pick.

Holy hell.

"Don't grind your teeth." The volume of his voice is barely above a whisper and yet so powerful. I hadn't realized I was doing it, but as soon as he calls me out on my worst habit, I stop, running my tongue from side to side between my teeth instead.

"There are so many things I think of doing to you when you grind your teeth."

Dragging my stare up to meet his amused expression, I cross my arms over my breasts and rock back on my heels. "I almost feel you're carrying it just so I'll do it." He gives me a noncommittal shrug, but I know he's thinking of the night we spent in Atlanta five months ago when he'd punished me for grinding my teeth using a guitar pick. Possibly the very same one he has now. A flush spreads through my body at the thought.

"I thought you said a driver was—" I begin, but he interrupts me mid-sentence by jerking me to him. I gasp. And he smirks.

"Did you really think I'd send a driver to get you? Or that I'd forget the exact moment you were due to arrive?" He moves the tip of his guitar pick along my back, tracing the outline of my lacy bra through my shirt. "I'll deal with any airport bullshit just to get to you first."

I cast a mock glare up at him. "Suck up." He slides the guitar pick across my shoulder blades, a look of sheer satisfaction taking over his face when my body curves against the contours of his. "But, I'm glad you did, I wanted to strangle you when I read that text."

"You're sexy when you're aggressive." He dips the pick dangerously low, tracing it along the plunging V neckline of my white and yellow peplum blouse, and I let out a tiny squeal. "And when you're nervous."

He would try to screw with my head, with my body, right in the middle of freaking LAX. "If you're going to kiss me, you should probably do it now before you draw a crowd," I respond hotly.

"But I'm not going to kiss you, Red." When he notices the look of disappointment, and surprise, on my face, he brushes his thumb over my slightly parted lips. "Because when I do, I'm going to be the only thing on your mind. Not what's running through the heads of everyone walking past us, you understand?"

The commanding lilt of his voice sends a thrill through my veins. *God, I'm putty in his hands and he knows it.* "Yes, Mr. Wolfe."

"Smart ass." With a grin playing at the corners of his mouth, he stuffs the guitar pick into the back pocket of my jeans, letting his fingers linger there for a moment.

Breathing heavily, I'm unable to stop myself from moving my hand over the spot his fingers just touched. I can feel the rounded, triangular shape of the pick through my pocket.

"Gives me more to look forward to," he promises against my ear before stepping away to examine my luggage. "You packed light." He grabs the handles of my bag and carry-on in either of his large hands. He jiggles the larger bag. "I expected there to be at least one more of these things."

"There was, but I had a crappy memory this morning." At the confused look on his face, I twist my lips to the side before I explain, "I left a bag of shoes at Gram's. Don't worry, it's carry-on size, too." Though judging from what he just told me, he doesn't really care how many bags I bring along for the ride.

He gestures his head to the left of us, and I fall in step beside him toward short-term parking. I resist the urge to brush away the hair that's just fallen into his face. "I'll get you new ones."

There's no doubt in my mind he will, if I ask him to. Which I won't. "No need for that, Mr. Wolfe. My brother's going to send them as soon as I know where we'll be stopping for our first ... off-night."

Instead of arguing with me and commenting with something utterly Lucas-esque—like "I can buy the whole fucking shoe store"—he gives me a sideways glance.

"Off-night?"

"Not a rocker. Don't know the exact terminology."

I hold one of the double glass doors open for him. Unexpectedly, he stops for a moment to bend his head to mine. He keeps his word by not kissing me, but murmurs against my lips, "Go

85

ahead and give him my address. If he gets it out today, you'll have them before we take off in a couple days. Or I'll just buy you new ones." When I press my lips together and shake my head, he laughs and adds, "And I'm glad you're not a rocker. Trust me, I like you better doing clothes."

No, you like me better without clothes, I think, as I follow him out to the parking lot to a black Jeep. It's one of the enormous Wranglers Rubicons with all the bells and whistles, including incredibly high lifted suspension. Even though I'm freakishly tall (Tori has always called my height Amazonian) it takes some effort getting in. As soon as I'm in my seat, Lucas comes around before I close the passenger door. He stands close to me, his hazel eyes searching my face, until finally I give in and move his hair away from his forehead.

"So, about that kiss?" For once, I could care less where my voice has gone. As I trail my fingertips down the side of his face, he shakes his head.

"Patience is a beautiful thing." Says the man with absolutely none to speak of. He pulls my fingers to his mouth, pressing them flat against his full lips, kissing the pads of my fingers. Each tiny movement of his mouth is delicate, sensual, and need flares through me.

"Let's go home," I say, and he reacts immediately to me calling his house 'home.' His eyes flare with heat, and he kisses my palm once more before slamming the passenger door and walking around to take the driver's seat.

Lucas keeps his eyes glued to the road as he speeds down streets that I've driven many times myself, and others—the wealthier parts of the city—that I've rarely been to. When we pass a luxury condo community that I vividly remember seeing the only other time he brought me to his place, I release a shaky sigh.

This gets his attention. He turns his head slightly toward me, his dark eyebrow raised.

"What ever happened to the Maserati?" I ask.

"What?"

"I'm thinking about the night you first took me to your place. The blue car you picked me up in that time. That's what it was, right?"

He refocuses his gaze on the road, and I slide closer to him to see that he's wearing the tiniest smile. "I remember it, just surprised that you do. Sold it a year and a half ago. Wasn't right for me." He turns left onto a street that's about a half a mile from his gated community. "Anything else?"

"Tori," I say hesitantly. "My friend Tori still lives here, and I want to go see her tonight or tomorrow since we'll be on the road so early the next morning."

He slows the Jeep down at the security gate but doesn't rush to roll down his window. He jerks off his sunglasses, tosses them on the dash, and turns to me, his hazel eyes direct. "I don't want you to misunderstand what this is."

"Then please, fill me in." Although I want to sound badass, absolute uncertainty laces my voice.

"You're mine, Sienna. You're with me now, but you don't need to get confirmation to see your friends. Invite her to the damn show and the after party if that's what you want." A self-assured grin tilts the corners of his lips, sending a sharp pang through my chest. Dear

God, why does he have to look at me like that? "I want to possess you, not treat you like a child."

We're both hushed as he lets down his window to punch in the gate code and drives through the neighborhood to the big Mediterranean-style house he lives in by himself. The only thing he says to me after parking in his winding paver stone driveway is that we'll come out and get my luggage later. As soon as we're inside and the door is locked, he turns to me.

"Do you remember where my bedroom is?"

I glance at the top of the stairs before returning my gaze to him. "Is it possible to forget?"

"You're blushing," he points out. "Which is why I'm not going to take you up there.

Not yet."

Without warning, he reaches between our bodies and cups my sex through my skinny jeans. I release a hoarse gasp and grab hold of his upper arms. As he shimmies my tight pants down my hips, he drags his fingertips down my skin, the sensation causing my legs to tingle.

"Lucas, I'm going to—" But he stops my words with his mouth, pressing his lips against mine roughly, offering me that kiss he promised in the airport, commanding the breath from my body. He tastes sweet—like spearmint—as his tongue darts in and out of my mouth teasingly. This is a dangerous game. I know that it's impossible for me to win, but honestly, when it comes to Lucas, I don't want to.

When he pulls me away from him, leaving my world spinning violently, he nods his head down to the floor. "Right here. Right now. That's how I want you, Sienna."

On the stair landing, I add silently. With the mid-afternoon light streaming through the shutters in the foyer, and my luggage still waiting out in the back of his Jeep—this is the night we reconnected all over again. Aloud, I say in a shaky voice, "What happened to that 'patience is good' mantra?"

"Fuck patience—I'll just have to try that shit again later. I need you." Driven by that need to get to my center, he continues to nudge my jeans down my legs. "I've thought about nothing but you and *this* since you sent me that picture. You've worked your way into my goddamn head, into my soul, and most definitely into my skin." He draws away from me for a moment to finish pushing my pants down around my ankles.

"Into your head, huh?"

Confirming my question with a slow nod, he kisses my left kneecap, and then the other before standing back up. "I've pictured every way I can enjoy your body, and believe me, there will be many. Don't think that being on that tour bus will stop any of those." The way he says this—in that growl he uses whenever he sings—sends electricity prickling through every vein of my body.

"Your poor band mates," I breathe.

"I'm going to take you right here. On top of me, bent over, beneath me. I want you in my bed and in my kitchen and in the fucking shower, but first, I want you here."

I step out of my jeans, kicking off my shoes in the process. "You're right." I'm not ashamed to admit that I want this too. "Screw the bedroom."

Keeping our bodies pressed together, he spins us around until his back is facing the steps. I follow him as he undresses quickly—each step slow, each breath I take heavier with anticipation—until he stops right in front of the stairs. His expression is something that's soft—that hurts my chest—as he eases down on the second hardwood step from the bottom.

"Get over here." He tugs me to him using the first thing his hand makes contact with—my panties, which tear just a little under the pressure. As I slide down in front of him, he cups my face between his hands. "I want you to use your mouth," he says. "You get right to the point."

"Always."

He wraps my fingers firmly around his cock, squeezing and moving my closed hand up and down his shaft until he's rock hard. When I bow my head to circle the tip of my tongue slowly around his crown, my hair goes everywhere—against the sides of my face, in his lap, on either side of his thighs. He strokes the nape of my neck, his touch encouraging, so I lick him once more. And again, when he mutters a sharp curse.

He gathers my hair up and holds it in his fist. "Don't tease." His voice is seventy-five percent commanding, the other twenty-five percent pleading.

I wrap my lips around his erection, keeping my gaze focused on his hazel eyes as I move my mouth and fingers from the head of his cock to the base, taking him completely into my mouth.

"Ah, shit, Sienna." He sounds surprised. Another flash of pleasure takes over me.

"Do that again."

My "yes" is nothing more than a little moan that causes a vibration against his flesh. I drag my mouth back up his length, running the hard tip of my tongue along it, and then draw him deep into my mouth again.

I don't want to lose this moment, to lose him, but when I start to repeat, he stops me by tugging roughly on my red hair. "Put your hands down flat." His tone is dangerously low. "No hands. Just that beautiful mouth of yours."

His words send a shiver through me, but I nod, my mouth bobbing against his cock in the process. I splay my palms flat on the polished wood of the bottom step, my movements slow and a little exaggerated, earning a slow smile from Lucas.

"You beautiful, intoxicating woman." He guides my head down as far as it will go and his hardness is pressing against the back of my throat. We both release a broken moan, seconds apart. "What are you doing to me? It's so good. You're so fucking good."

Whatever it is that I'm doing to him, he's done to me times two. Because as I use my tongue and mouth to drive him to the point of breaking—and as he stares down at me with one of those looks that twists the pit of my stomach into a million and one knots—I feel like I'm the first woman he's ever stared at.

The first woman to do *this* to him.

The first woman for him, period.

"You were fucking made for me, Si." This time, after my tongue traces a path up his cock, he draws all the way back, releasing his hold on my hair. "I'm going to fuck you." His breath is coming out in uneven bursts, but so is mine.

"Upstairs?" I ask, but he moves his head from side to side.

I barely have time to react before he guides me to my feet. I'm shaking as he hooks his hands behind my knees, urging me to come to him. I nearly lose my breath when he guides my legs on either side of his body. And as he pulls me down, his thumb gliding beneath my panties to shove the damp scrap of fabric at the juncture of my thighs to the side, I cry out. Because I'm not sure what to do with my hands—my brain is putty right now—I dig my fingers into his taut shoulders while his thick erection presses against my tightness.

"I'm safe. I'm not going to come in you unless it's safe," he promises against the crook of my neck. He strokes my clit once, twice. Without warning, he lifts his hips, easing his cock into the warmth of my body bit by bit, slowly filling me. It's agonizing. And it's bliss. Dragging my fingernails across his shoulders, I push my hips down, pulling him all the way in and clenching myself around him. He shudders and mutters a curse. "I'll pull out if you say the word."

His hands are gripping my ass now, moving my body back and forth, up and down. The sensation is so dizzying that it takes me a moment to clear my head enough to realize what he's asking.

"The shot," I gasp as he buries himself inside of me. "Last time was a month ago.

I never skip."

"Fuck, that's good to hear," he growls.

He leans back against the steps, and I follow suit, pressing my face against the tattoos on his chest as I rock my hips against him.

"Look at me," he says. When I don't, shaking my head because the feeling of him has officially fucked my head in the best way imaginable, he gives my ass a hard smack that seems to echo through the open foyer and off the high ceiling. "Look at me, Sienna."

I lift my head and stare him in the eye. "Happy? Do you see what you do—" My breath catches, and his lips move into a grin. He understands. He knows exactly what he does to me.

"I see." He circles his thumb urgently around my clit, causing my whole body to throb, and I cry out. "That's why I want to watch you when you come. I want you to look at me when I come in you."

"Please," I whisper, though I'm not sure what I'm begging for. He's giving me everything that I want right now, everything my body craves. "God, Lucas…"

He moves faster, harder, his free hand making rough contact with my ass once more when I squeeze my eyes together. "Let me see you," he repeats, and I nod, sweat-dampened strands of my red hair falling into his face.

"I want to—" I begin, but then the orgasm comes. It doesn't build slowly so that I have enough time to warn him. It rips through me, making me clench my teeth as my body tightens around his. I keep my gaze trained on the hazel eyes in front of me as the waves of pleasure send a painful shudder rushing through my body.

Then, he releases a low sound, and I feel him let go. It's a first for me, but I'm sure he already knows that, too.

Afterward, as we lay against each other at the bottom of his staircase, breathing heavily with our arms and legs and the sweat from our bodies intermingling, he finally announces that we're going upstairs.

CHAPTER EIGHT

After he reintroduces me to his vivid black and red bedroom upstairs, and as promised, to his kitchen where he cooks filet mignon and roasted asparagus for me,

Lucas takes me to his music room. Just like the infamous piano room from the house in Nashville, this room is on the bottom level of the house. But with its butter-yellow painted walls and light hardwood floors, it's a complete one-eighty from the moody, dark décor in the rest of the house.

While he sits strumming his guitar on the couch, I pace around the room, studying the collection of guitars—acoustic and electric—hanging on the walls the same way an average person would hang family photos and whimsical art featuring little quotes.

"These are amazing," I whisper under my breath.

"Kylie's idea." He smirks as I run my fingertips along the smooth surface of a vintage red and white Fender Stratocaster. It boasts a signature across its sleek body that I can't quite make out, not even when I trace my fingertip along the sloppy scrawl. Lucas changes the key of the song he's playing. "I would have just left the damn walls bare. And I would've left them painted black, but I've got to let her win sometimes."

"I like her ideas, makes the room feel … homey. Do the brighter colors help you write?"

"Good inspiration helps me write." He winks, and I feel my skin begin to warm up.

"The walls are just there."

I make my way over to the piano, and automatically, my gaze zeroes in on the notebook on top of it. Lucas' lyrics. As I absentmindedly tap out a few keys—which ends up sounding like the opening of "You're So Vain"—I can't quite pull my eyes away from the lyric book.

The Gibson squeaks loudly, and a moment later, I feel the long muscular lines of his body against my backside. I flatten my fingers on the piano keys, not caring that they make an awful screech as his warm breath fans my neck. "You're welcome to look through it. You're welcome to everything I have. I want you to know that."

I lift my chin, turning my face so I can look him in the eye. "I feel like I'm invading your privacy," I protest. He brushes his lips over my temple, back and forth, moving the tiniest strand of hair across my skin in the process. "Even if you do tell me I'm allowed."

Still, I can't help thinking about his ex and the hold she has over him. I can't help the part of me that doesn't buy into Lucas promising me that I have all of him. How can I when there's still so much about this man that's still a complete mystery?

His rough voice breaks through the toxicity of my thoughts. "I want you to look."

Taking my hand, and the notebook, he guides me over to the couch. For a few minutes, I remain hesitant to look at the lyrics. Clutching the notebook tightly, I listen to him play a song I've not heard before—probably something from Your Toxic Sequel or his new solo album—but halfway through he pauses.

Exasperated, he says, "Open the damn book."

Glaring at him from beneath my long lashes, I finally flip the front cover to reveal a full page of his handwriting. "Satisfied?" I ask, and he nods.

Many of the songs follow Your Toxic Sequel's usual style—raunchy, sexy, clever lyrics that make me blush from the top of my red head to the tips of my scarlet-painted toenails. But there are also lyrics with so much emotion that I feel rusted barbs shoving through my chest. These words are not about sex, but about pain and loss, about heartbreak and betrayal. About regret.

And then, several pages through the book, I find the original drafts of "Ten Days."

These lyrics range from moody and dark to downright depressing, but I read them all and I realize that he was feeling just as screwed up, just as alone, as I was during our time apart. When I get to the version that I've heard, I smile softly.

"I'm glad this was the one." I rub my thumb over the sloppy words on the page.

Crazy, heartbreaking, beautiful words written solely with me on his mind.

"Me too. It sure as fuck took a long time to do it." He starts playing another song on his guitar—"Ten Days." "As you can see, it was hard for me."

"Lucas Wolfe admitting that something was difficult?" I feign surprise as I flip backward to one of the initial drafts. "Glad you kept going. The other ones are just as beautiful, don't get me wrong, but a little…"

"Emo? Completely fucked up? That's what Kylie called me the entire time you were gone." I scrunch my nose and shake my head, but he laughs. He inclines his chin down to the page that I'm on right now—one that's talking about a ripped open and bleeding heart. "I, ah, wrote that particular one after seeing you out one night."

Stunned, I jerk my gaze up to his. "What?"

"At Sunny's. Little bar downtown. Cheap beer and absolute shit for lighting."

I know the place, but I can't remember the last time I went to it. Self-consciously, I close Lucas' notebook and set it down on the couch between us. "When did you see me there?"

"About a month after Atlanta. Wanted to get you out of my mind, and sure as fuck you were right there in that damn bar looking as beautiful and forbidden as ever."

And instead of coming to talk to me, instead of ending both of our misery a few months in advance, he'd come back here and wrote about angst?

He plucks a flat note and gives me a grim look. "You were with another man— some blond motherfucker—and a few of your friends. And as much as I wanted to beat the shit out of him simply for being with you, going after him would have made me a douche." He thumbs a few additional notes and then lifts his eyebrows in a look that screams guilt. "Well, a bigger douche than I already was."

Some blond guy? Facing the piano, I squeeze my eyes together. Who the hell is he talking about? The only men I've had continuous contact with who could be a match for Lucas' vague description would be my brother and my former roommate's boyfriend.

Micah.

Of course.

Laughter bubbles from my chest. Before I have a chance to explain, Lucas leans forward. "And now you're laughing at me, Red?" he warns. "I should turn you over my knee right now."

I'm tempted to tell him to go ahead and do it, but then I force the breathlessness down as I skim my lips against his. "The blond you saw me with is Micah. Tori's boyfriend." And I remember the night now. They'd coaxed me out of the apartment because I spent the better part of a month moping around over Lucas. To him, I explain, "We went out as a group. And I sure as hell didn't go home with Micah, nor have I *ever* slept with him."

Lucas' full lips part into a silent "ah." He leans back on the couch and begins to play his guitar again. I can't deny the smug look of relief and satisfaction on his handsome face.

While the rest of our night goes smoothly, with Lucas playing me song after song on his Gibson, the next morning is a little chaotic. He wakes me up after sunrise, dressed in nothing but a pair of navy blue gym shorts that hang low on his hips. He's sweaty from working out and looking down at me wearing his typical cocky grin.

"Get up, Red. It's day one."

"The show isn't until late tonight," I point out, but Lucas yanks the sheets that I'm desperately trying to hold on to off the bed.

"We've got a lot of shit to do today. Get up."

Lucas' words remind of my short-lived days—eight in total—working as his personal assistant. He had, and I'm not even kidding, mandated that I be up at seven unless otherwise notified.

Sure enough, when I turn over to glance at the black Bose alarm clock on his nightstand, it's a few minutes after seven AM. "You've got to be screwing with me."

"Get used to it." He goes to the window and opens the darkening blinds, allowing the light in. "Our road manager tries to get our asses up much earlier than this." Groaning, I swing my legs over the side of the bed and place my feet on the floor. As I stretch my arms over my head and shake out some of the stiffness in my muscles, I ask him sarcastically, "Should I call you Mr. Wolfe and sir, then?"

He doesn't give me an answer until I walk across the room to the adjoining bathroom. "Only in private."

Smiling to myself, I shower quickly, wondering if he was serious about me calling him Mr. Wolfe, which had been another stipulation of the old contract. Once I towel off, I return to the bedroom. He's nowhere to be found, but I can hear a shower running in the bathroom down the hall.

Humming softly—an incredibly offbeat version of "Rill Rill" by Sleigh Bells—I rummage through my suitcase. Since I'm limited by my lack of shoes, I dress in a fun, multi-colored Betsey Johnson sundress, which is the only item of clothing I have that matches my bright yellow flats. By the time Lucas returns, I'm leaning against his dresser, my face close to the mirror as I concentrate on wrapping my slightly damp hair in a messy bun.

"Leave it down." I look past my reflection, dragging in the sight of him with beads of moisture trickling down his muscular chest. Dear God, the man should have fan pages just for how beautiful his body is. Come to think of it, he probably does. "You know what seeing your hair like that does to me," he adds with a hungry grin.

Despite the fact it'll just get in the way, I release my grip on my hair, letting the updo down in one swift motion. I start to rake my hand through the tangled mess, but Lucas jerks his head from side to side.

"Just like that, so I can think about fucking you while I go through bullshit all day."

The first order of "bullshit" turns out to be a meeting here with Your Toxic Sequel's tour manager—a short, strawberry blond guy with one of those tans that, as a fellow redhead, makes me envious. Dressed in a citrus-colored polo, Tyler looks like he's about to head into a day at the office, or to flag down a caddy, instead of on a rock tour. At first, he stares me down with undisguised curiosity, taking every opportunity to study me as we go through the house and out to the backyard. Once we're on the patio overlooking the pool though, Lucas introduces me as his girlfriend.

Admittedly, hearing him do so makes me flush like a seventh grader at her first dance, but I hold out my hand to Tyler. "Good to meet you."

Flashing a wide grin, Tyler gives my hand three hard pumps. "Just wanted to make sure you were the right one," he says with a wink as he sits down in one of the outdoor chairs that are situated around a circular fire pit.

If there were an award given for the most awkward, dumbass introduction, Tyler would easily take it. I force a smile and dig my fingernails into my palms. "Oh boy, thanks for being considerate," I force out through clenched teeth.

Lucas slams down in the seat across from Tyler, the muscles in his tattooed arms tense as he places them on the armrests. "You know exactly who the fuck she is." He glances over at his manager, and I feel the punch behind every word. "And you also know how I already feel about this tour. Don't think you're irreplaceable, Tyler. There are thousands of motherfuckers out there who'd kill to have your job."

Like most people—except for the truly masochistic—I hate situations like this, so when Tyler squeezes the bridge of his freckled nose and winces, I look away for a moment. "Ah hell, I didn't mean to imply that...." Cocking his head, he gives me a quick, apologetic grimace. "Sorry, Sienna."

Lucas' hazel eyes silently challenge his manager for a moment longer and then he turns his gaze on me, his expression relaxing. "I've got to go over tickets sales and business stuff, I'll be—"

"I need to go call my brother and Tori." At this point, I'd be willing to deal with a prison call from my mother to get away from this tension. "See you in a little while?" He nods and kisses my wrist before I leave.

As I walk away, I hear his manager say in a low voice, "She's sure as fuck prettier than what Cilla said. Did you talk to her about the NDA?"

Lucas' icy retort is the last thing I hear before I step inside the sliding doors. "That's because Cilla's a fucking bitch. And no need for a disclosure agreement. She's not the type."

He doesn't come back into the house for nearly an hour, and in that time I manage to confirm with Seth that my shoes will be arriving today, speak to Tori who promises me that we'll still get to see each other tonight, and make myself breakfast—a whole grain bagel, a few pieces of fruit, and a large glass of orange juice.

When Lucas strides into the kitchen and finds me eating, he immediately apologizes for Tyler, but I wave it off and force out a laugh. "I mean, I didn't think you were celibate or anything while we were apart."

"I was," he says simply, taking my breath away. He slides onto the bar stool beside me at the center island, the fabric of his jeans brushing up against my bare knee in the process. "Tyler was a dick. It won't happen on the tour, and if it does, you come to me. I'm not going to let him play games with your head to cause problems. I won't do that kind of shit just for the sake of record sales and media plugs."

"Will that actually sell records?" I ask, shocked, as he takes a drink of my orange juice. "You and I getting into it?"

He coughs on the juice, sets the glass down on the counter, and then takes my chin in his hand. "People always give a bigger fuck about you when your life is in ruins; I thought you knew that already, Red."

Oh, I do. I learned that firsthand after my mother got arrested for drug trafficking just before I graduated high school. I'd gone from just another face in the hall to the most talked about girl on campus. Still, it doesn't mean that I have to accept how screwed up and vicious some people can be.

Lucas glances down at his watch. "It's after ten, we need to get going."

I chug the rest of my juice and take my soiled dishes to the dishwasher. "By the way, how'd things go? With your road manager, I mean." For the first time since he came back into the house, I notice how drawn his expression is.

"Sinjin had a fucking moment. Tyler swears it's been worked out, but I won't believe it until I see it. Sin's not answering my texts." He slides off the barstool as I come around the counter and places his hand on the small of my back.

Though I'm not too sure what a "moment" for Sinjin entails, it's a no-brainer that it's bad news for Sin and something that could possibly be detrimental to the tour. Though he doesn't mention Sinjin again while we take care of last minute details around the city, I know that whatever is going on with the drummer is bothering Lucas.

By the time 4:30 rolls around, and the band has their sound check at the venue in Pomona, even I'm worried like crazy over Sinjin, especially when it becomes clear that he likely forgot about the rehearsal this afternoon. Or as Cal puts it, "Just brushed the shit off." As Lucas and the rest of the band speak to each other backstage in angry, hushed tones, I excuse myself to tour the venue.

This place is less than a quarter of the size of the Staples Center, which is where Your Toxic Sequel will perform the final show of the tour in September, forty-five days from now, but Lucas had told me earlier that playing here was a given. It's where the band played their first "big" show, so there's a sentimental tug.

Plus, with its intricate design and artsy atmosphere, this place is absolutely gorgeous, and I'm kicking myself for never attending a show here while I was living in Los Angeles.

I'm in the lobby looking at posters for upcoming shows happening this month when I feel a hand on my shoulder. Expecting to see Lucas, I put on my warmest smile before facing him.

"Did he show—" The words catch in my throat when I come face to face with

Sinjin. Thank God I hadn't turned and immediately groped his junk. "Sorry."

"You shouldn't be." He looks better than he did the last time I saw him. Still skinny, but so much better. Dressed in dark jeans, a black shirt that says *Stranger (With Benefits)*, and a black and white Atlanta Braves baseball cap, there's no wild look in his green eyes. No disdain. Only amusement. "I'm touched that you're worried about me."

I hit the home key on my phone and check the time. "You're twenty minutes late."

He drags off his hat, revealing a mess of short, jet-black hair. It's a complete change from the blond he sported the last time I saw him. "Not sure what those fucks in there told you, but I'm always late. Can't manage time to save my life."

I wait for him to show any sign of what Lucas had alluded to in the car, but if he's high, I can't tell. And after living with my mother and stepfather, I've spent more than my fair share of time around screwed up people to be able to read the signs. There were always

105

addicts around our house, which is why Gram's home became a place of solace for Seth and me.

Sinjin continues to look at me intensely, so I glance away and break the silence.

"So I'm guessing Tyler getting you up at an ungodly hour won't go over well on the tour."

He sneers. "Tell Tyler to eat a dick."

Why am I not surprised to hear him say this? "I'm sure you'll be telling him yourself."

"No doubt. He's already heard it from me more than once today." Giving me an unapologetic look, he shrugs. "He started with the shit early this morning, I let him know

I don't give a fuck and that he's more than welcome to find another drummer."

So that was Sinjin's "moment" this afternoon? An argument with Tyler? There's no way he'd tell me if I asked him, so I say, "I see."

"*Sure* you do." As he heads toward the grand hall's double doors, he calls out to me, "Lucas told me to apologize. Thing is, I don't like *sorry*. It's just a word, and it doesn't mean shit. So, I'll have to figure out a way to make it up to you." He doesn't look back at me, but I wish he would so I could at least read the expression on his face.

"I can't sing, so this might take some time."

There it is again—one of those white flags that I'm a sucker for. "That was a good enough apology," I tell him softly, but he's already gone into the grand hall.

A few minutes later when I hear Cal, the lead guitarist, rip into the beginning of

106

"Handcuffs," I walk through the double doors, too.

CHAPTER NINE

"This is amazing," Tori shouts out several hours later over the buzz of the backstage crowd. She tilts her head to one side, sending her dark waves cascading over the single strap that holds her little black dress from taking a nip-slip dive. "No, this is beyond amazing. It's insane."

"Nah, this is nothing." My words cause Tori's eyes to narrow as she mouths a "what-the-fuck-ever."

Earlier this evening, when I'd offered to bring her with me to the concert over drinks, she accepted my invitation without a moment of hesitation, cancelling her late nightclub plans with a group of her co-workers on the way to Pomona.

"I bet it's just going to get crazier," she muses.

I move out of the way of a sound guy who's too busy talking on a headset to notice me before giving Tori my thoughts. "I'm still trying to catch my breath." I have been ever since late this afternoon when I was reintroduced to each member of the band and to various roadies, including the wardrobe crew, which consisted of one woman. Maggie had come right out and told me that dressing YTS was the easiest and most laid back gig she's ever had.

Shooting a skeptical look in my direction, Tori nibbles her bottom lip between her teeth, smudging her ruby red lipstick slightly. "And you're sure he doesn't care if I'm back here?"

"I swear it's fine. Now stop, your lips are not a damn stress ball, and you're getting lipstick all over your teeth." I press my back flat against the wall to avoid a couple of giggling women dancing past us. Liquid sloshes out of the bottles held closely to their chests and falls on the concrete floor, leaving behind the scent of whipped cream vodka. Once they disappear around a corner, I motion for Tori to follow me.

"I've got to admit, even my desire to kick Lucas in the balls ninety-five percent of the time wouldn't have stopped me from seeing *that* show." She easily catches up to me, even with her mile high pumps. "And I don't even like rock music," she confides in a low whisper.

Yeah, sure. For someone who doesn't like this type of music, she sure as hell knew enough YTS lyrics to scream them out along with everyone else during the concert.

"Finally." I point to the only door backstage with swarms of barely clothed women, and several men, hanging around it. "This has to be it."

There's a bodyguard—an enormous mixed guy who makes Lucas, in all of his six-foot-four, muscular glory, seem fun-sized—guarding the entrance. He's in the middle of an argument with a woman claiming to be there for Wyatt. She's red-faced, seething, but the bodyguard doesn't seem fazed.

"What fucking list are you talking about?" she demands. "This isn't a nightclub. Just let me in—Violet Dawson." She says her name slowly, emphasizing it into five, drawn-out syllables. Admittedly, hearing her do so makes me want to kick her in kneecap. There's a special word for those who are asshats to people just trying to do their job, and Vi-o-let Daw-son definitely meets the requirements.

I wait for the bodyguard to tell her off, but he seems completely at ease when he responds. "Only the band and guests are in there right now. Press and *Brenley in the Morning* contest winners get inside in half an hour. You're not on either list."

Violet heaves a frustrated sigh. "Look, I hung out with him and Cal after their show here a year and a half ago. He'll *want* to see me. They'll both want to."

Wonderful. Now I won't be able to look at Cal or Wyatt without thinking of this woman.

"The band that plays together—" another woman standing close by begins, but Violet shoots her a withering look. The bodyguard leans over to tell Violet something discreetly, and Tori motions for me to bend down a little, too.

Once her mouth is close to my ear, she whispers, "Just think, when Mr.

Bodyguard over there actually lets you in, all these bitches are going to want to beat the crap out of you."

"Thanks for—" I pull Tori out of the way before Violet can plow her over as she flounces off in a blur of highlighted hair and floral perfume "—making me feel better about being alone for the rest of this tour."

"Just stating the obvious." She steps in front of another woman and her boyfriend so that we're first in line to talk to the doorman and jabs her manicured index finger in my direction. "She's on the list."

The bodyguard gives me a long stare, from my black fringe sandals, to my ripped skinny jeans and loose black high-low tank, and finally up to my blue eyes and red hair.

By the time he says, "Name and ID," I feel thoroughly undressed. He lifts an eyebrow at

Tori. "You too."

Lowering my head, I look through my bag for my license and say as quietly as possible, "Sienna Jensen and Tori Abrams. We should both be on the list." I suddenly feel like all conversation around me has come to a standstill. As the security guard looks at his iPhone for confirmation, the door behind him opens a few inches. Sinjin pops his head out, and the squeals around us are deafening.

He soaks it all in for several seconds and then winks a green eye at his admirers before addressing the bodyguard. "Fuck the list. These two are in, David," he says. The bodyguard returns his gaze to Tori and me, his lips curled into a suggestive grin.

I know what he's thinking. Hell, it's obvious, especially after hearing Violet try to get access to the band just a couple minutes ago.

And I feel my blood begin to boil.

I open my mouth, ready to let him know I'm not what he thinks I am, but Sinjin's one step ahead of me. "And just so we're clear, the redhead will be around for the rest of the tour. Lucas' new girl." Sin smirks, and it looks so natural on his face that I'm sure he was born wearing a mocking grin. "So giving her shit is a real quick way to wind up jobless."

As David moves aside for us to go into the lounge, a flush creeps past his neck and up to his face, and he mutters a slew of hasty apologies. Once I'm inside the room, which is nearly filled to capacity with members of the crew and the lead guitarist and drummer of Wicked Lambs, I give him a reassuring smile. He tips his head in embarrassment.

Even before the door is securely closed, the women in the hallway begin whispering. Words like "Lucas" and "bitch" and "lucky" jump out to me. My teeth are clenched when I meet Sinjin's amused gaze.

"You didn't have to do that," I say, embarrassment skulking into my voice.

He shrugs, wiping sweat and short strands of black hair off his forehead with the red and black striped towel draped around his shoulders. "Might as well make it clear now before David looks at you like you're nothing but a piece of ass in front of Lucas."

He throws himself down on a plush loveseat, between two women dressed in Your Toxic Sequel tanks that they've customized by strategically ripping them up to show off their boobs and flat stomachs and not much else. "Besides, none of us wants our guests being treated like shit."

"He's got a point," my best friend pipes up loudly from beside me, and I roll my eyes.

Et tu, Tori?

Okay, maybe Sinjin does have a good point, but I don't want to start off on the wrong foot with any of the crew, specifically one of the bodyguards. Nodding stiffly at Sin, I debate on whether I should look away or keep staring as one of the women—the one with the auburn pixie cut—openly slides her fingertips inside of his jeans. She winks up at me.

Screw it, there's no way I'm looking away now.

"I'm sure I'll be able to handle it on my own from now on, but thanks for the help." I start to walk off, but I stop, earning a wide grin from Sinjin. "Do you know where Lucas is?"

He moves his head to the left, where there's a separate room with the door wide open. "In there. But he's doing an interview. Might as well help yourself to some food while you wait." He inclines his head to a long table of refreshments and drinks on the right side of the room.

"Thanks," I acknowledge, steering Tori left when she heads toward the food. We find Lucas in a separate lounge area. He's on a black leather couch with Cilla, sitting entirely too close for my comfort, and talking to a pretty journalist I'd seen on set a few times during my days working on the set of *Echo Falls*. On the opposite side of the room, a cameraman is snapping photos rapidly, so I back out of the room.

"Who the hell does she think she is?" Tori hisses, her eyebrows furrowed as she stares at Lucas and Cilla.

"That's Cilla." I can't keep the worry out of my voice, and Tori gives me a sympathetic expression, which I quickly look away from. "I'm hoping that—"

I swallow my words when someone wraps an arm around my shoulder. I immediately recognize the barbed treble and bass clefs on his forearm, so I turn my head, coming eye to eye with Cal. Like Sinjin, he's lean and pretty close to my height, but Cal is also ripped for a skinny guy.

"Enjoying the circus?" he asks, glancing from side to side at Tori and me, earning nods from both of us. "I'm Cal, by the way," he tells Tori, as if she doesn't already know.

Once they're formally introduced, and she's told him about her co-worker's Calvin Romero cubicle shrine, he turns to me, his lips spreading into an easy smile. "Crazy shit, huh?"

I'm not sure if he's talking about Tori's co-worker or *this*—being backstage at a rock show—but I bob my head. Because seven feet in front of me, Cilla tries to put her hand on Lucas' thigh again, but he shoves it away and shoots her a disgusted look that the journalist fails to notice because she's looking down. Cilla tilts her head back to laugh at something, but his expression remains aloof and irritated. Sinjin is seven feet behind me, and by now, there's a 50/50 chance he's talked one of his fan girls (or both) into giving him a blowjob.

My blue eyes never break focus with Cal's dark brown eyes. "Yeah, crazy." I start to ask where Wyatt is, but then I shake my head. Right now, I'm not sure I want to know. "Is there—will *they* always do interviews after the shows like this?"

Looking into the other lounge, he cringes. And to my mortification, he gives my shoulder a small, reassuring squeeze. When he answers, he avoids my question, but I can't blame him. "Got a bottle of Jager and Lucas' Red Bull. Shots before fans and press come in?"

Though Tori's a peppermint schnapps and sugar-free chocolate syrup type of girl, she quickly agrees, so I have no other choice but to go along with them. But as Cal guides us away from the doorway of the lounge, I can't help but glimpse one more time at Cilla and Lucas. I can't help but see how easily their bodies respond to each other as they discuss the tour, despite how all of Lucas' answers seem to be sarcastic and snippy. And I can't help but feel a painful pressure in my ribcage as I force a smile at Sinjin, who joins us once Cal starts doling out the Jager and Red Bull.

The two women who were with him have disappeared, and Sin doesn't mention them as he sits next to me. "Get used to it," he snaps into my ear.

I furrow my eyebrows in confusion, but I already know what he's talking about. I'd be naïve not to. "What?"

"Don't play dumb. You're going to have to suck it the fuck up if you're going to get through this tour. Jealous, pissy girlfriends and wives don't last long. Why do you think Kylie's not around? And Cal's last girlfriend only stuck around for a few months?"

He doesn't mention Lucas or himself, and I don't think he will, even if I press the subject. I paste on a smile that makes my face feel like it's cracking and grab my drink, holding the highball glass a little too roughly.

"And here I was thinking you were going to be all sweet to me."

"Fuck being sweet." Sinjin pries the Jagerbomb from my fingers and downs the drink for me, ignoring my protests. "But I'll be truthful. And at the end of the day, being around all this shit, honesty is what you'll want more than anything."

Sinjin's words about honesty bother me well after Lucas' interview is done. For the rest of the night, there's little contact between us—in fact, I fade into the background to spend time with Tori as he

116

greets the press and his fans. Every few minutes, his hazel eyes lift away from whomever he's talking with to find me. His gaze is intense— like I'm the only person in this small room full of people who worship him and the rest of the band—but it's also questioning.

The reassuring smile I manage to muster does nothing to wipe that look from his face.

We don't get back to his house until close to three, and since the buses are rolling out in just a few hours, we immediately climb into bed. He's silent for a long time—so quiet I begin to think he's asleep—so I'm startled when he speaks up.

"What'd you think?"

"Your show?" I glance over at him in the dark to see his head bobbing up and down. "Incredible. But why wouldn't it be?"

"You were fucking out of it backstage."

I clutch the black sheets tightly. "I'm not going to say it's not overwhelming— because it is—but I'll get used to it. Eventually."

"You've been doing shit like this for a long time, Sienna," he points out skeptically. "And I've seen you make that face before. Look, let's get something straight right here, right now. There is nothing, and I do mean abso-fucking-lutely *nothing*, between me and Cilla. I'm not going to lie and tell you there never was, but I can tell you it was never anything more than sex. She and I haven't happened since long before you came back into the picture earlier this year."

If that's supposed to make me feel better, it doesn't. I had figured out that Cilla and Lucas had been together at some point after I had to sit through lunch with them several months before.

And then she'd drunkenly admitted to me that she loved him during her birthday party, just after getting into a verbal altercation with Lucas' crazy ass ex-wife.

I sink my teeth down on the inside of my cheek because thinking about Sam is a whole new level of irritating.

"Alright, since we're being honest, tell me about your ex," I implore.

The silence comes back in full force, and that constriction in my throat just gets worse, squeezing until it's hard to breathe and I have to sit up in the bed. "You're better off not knowing."

"I would tell you."

He releases a bitter laugh. "I doubt that. We're not getting into this shit, Sienna."

"Why not?" I whisper, my face burning like hell. "Why can't we talk about it?"

"I love you too goddamn much for you to leave again, so let it go. I've taken care of it. That's all you need to know."

He thinks that whatever he's hiding is so bad I might leave him? Or is he threatening to tell me to go again if I don't stop probing? Either way, I'm not done with this subject. "Then you should know that I'll ask you again."

"And I'll say no again," he replies coldly.

"And then what? We'll go through this? You'll tell me to drop it? Threaten to spank me if I don't let it go."

"I should." The king-size bed squeaks as he leans in close to me and places his hand firmly on my bare knee. His hazel eyes are full of passion—lust and anger—as he stares down at me, and my breath skips. "I should say fuck sleep and spend my last few hours in my

118

bed buried inside of you instead of arguing over shit I can't change. It fucks with my head enough as it is without you reminding me."

I cover his hand with mine, entwining our fingers as he gives the sensitive spot on my kneecap a little squeeze. "I don't want that."

But I do want honesty.

And the way I see it, that should be one of the easiest things to give to someone you love.

He inhales harshly, but when he continues, his voice is calmer. "All you need to know about Sam is that we're done. That thinking about her is bad for music. Bad for this tour. Shit for me."

Once, he told me I was bad for music, but I understand how his ex-wife could screw with his productivity. Even if I don't understand the reason behind all of his evasiveness. Scooting away from him, I slide off the edge of the bed.

"Si—" he starts, but I shake my head.

"I'm fine," I snap and walk through pitch black to the bedroom door and twist the dimmer switch just enough to get a good look at his face. His dark eyebrows are pulled tightly together, and he's dragging the palm of his hand across the dagger-filled heart tattoo covering his chest. "I'm going to grab a water, need anything?"

He shakes his head, and as I go into the hallway, his voice freezes me. "This is still fucking new to me."

Tension pulls my shoulder blades together. "I know it is. Be back in a few."

I don't want to go back to bed frustrated, so I spend longer than a few minutes downstairs. I grab my laptop from the huge pile of luggage waiting in Lucas' foyer and march into the living room, where I begin checking my messages. Three Google alerts have made it into my inbox since the last time I checked several hours ago.

Each notification leads me to an article that connects me with Lucas Wolfe and

Your Toxic Sequel.

"Nashville-Based Designer Consumes the Wolfe," I whisper, reading one of the gossip titles aloud. Beneath the caption is a photo—one that I hadn't realized was being taken because it's of me from behind—of Lucas and me earlier this evening during one of our rare moments alone. His hand is resting on the small of my back, and he's leaned in close to me, his full lips worked up into a sexy grin.

Already, eighty-seven comments have been posted. Shit. I've dealt with Lucas' fans before, after a video of him singing to me in Ashley's parents' bar surfaced on the Internet. Don't get me wrong; I don't shy away from criticism. Working with some of the people I've encountered both in L.A. and Nashville, getting ripped a new one isn't uncommon. But there's something screwed up about someone who's never met me, who doesn't know a thing about me, tearing me apart for no reason other than their discontent with my love life. I'm not quite ready to take another massive blow to my confidence, so instead of scrolling down to the comments, I exit out of the website completely and rest my chin in my hands for a moment.

I knew this was bound to happen. Eventually. I just hadn't realized that the press would climb onto it so soon.

I start to sign out of my email, but a new message at the top of my inbox stops me. It's an inquiry form sent directly from the website I had a friend create for my wardrobe consulting. I click on it, expecting a request for a price quote or a query from one of my clients.

Instead, it's a short message that has absolutely nothing to do with my job. Four sentences, but enough to send my world spinning.

He didn't waste any time getting back with you. I had hoped he would be smarter than this, but Lucas always did do stupid shit when tits and ass were involved. Hope you enjoy it, Sienna Jensen. I just wonder will you still want him when I'm done.

-S.W.

Samantha Wolfe. Speak of the crap-for-music devil. The devil who has now personally sought me out on my business website just to send me a passive-aggressive message. With my fingers and hands tingling, I close my laptop, shove it back into its bag, and return it to the foyer. I tiptoe upstairs feeling even more restless than before.

To my irritation, I find Lucas facedown, sleeping soundly.

Standing on my side of the bed, I open and close my fists, wanting to wake him up though I know it's pointless. Telling him that his ex has electronically threatened me—if I can even call it that—will do nothing but piss him off. And besides, it'll just make me sound like I can't handle my shit—the exact thing that Sinjin had warned me about earlier.

He doesn't budge when I stretch out beside him, or when I clear my throat.

"When this is all over, you, Lucas-fucking-Wolfe, will tell me everything."

122

CHAPTER TEN

Lucas

The blaring of my phone, and not my alarm clock, jerks me out of bed first thing the next morning. Sienna is sleeping peacefully in the bed next to me. The room is still dark, but I already know we're running late. I accept the call, knowing damn well who's waiting on the other line without having to look at the screen. My sister is the most predictable person I've ever met.

"Wake up," Kylie sings. "And don't give me that crap about already being up. I can practically hear the yawn in your heavy breathing."

Groaning, I turn on the bedside lamp. "Why the fuck do I feel like you'll be doing this more than Tyler for the next month and a half?"

"I may not be going on tour, but I'm still your assistant. It's my job to make sure you're doing what's right. Including waking up on time and not missing the bus," she says, sounding like she fell out of an after school special.

"One, they won't leave me, and two, if you keep bitching at me, I won't ever make it there. I'll call you once we get on." We end the wakeup call on that note. When I finally look at the screen, I realize that Kylie's calling me from Wyatt McCrae's local number and not her cell or the landline at the apartment they've been staying at in New Orleans—besides our parents, Kylie is the only person I know who uses a landline.

Still, this solves the mystery of why Wyatt was nowhere to be found last night. It's a relief. Nothing would ruin this tour, our collaborative future, and Wyatt's pretty face faster than him fucking up by refusing to keep his dick in his pants and stay faithful to my kid sister.

"Guess you weren't lying about this early morning thing," Sienna complains. I look back to see her sitting up, her red hair flying in every different direction, looking like the best kind of trouble. "Do I have time to shower or are we too late?"

I search her face for any of the emotions that were there last night before she stormed off downstairs, but none of it's there. Suppressing a yawn, she self-consciously smooths her hands through her hair and runs her tongue over her lips. "Why are you looking at me like that?"

"Because you're beautiful." I trace my knuckles down the side of her face, and she shivers. "Also because Tyler will just have to deal with us being late. There's no way you're going into that shower without me."

A half an hour later when we go downstairs, there's already a car waiting out front for us—this must be Kylie's doing because she's the only person besides my housekeeper and myself with the code to the gate. As soon as I'm settled in on the bus, I'll have to order her a big ass bouquet of her favorite flowers and some of those cupcakes

124

she's always going on about. Once the car starts to move, I sink back in the black leather seat, squeeze my eyes shut, and let my head fall back on the headrest.

Anyone close to me knows I don't oversleep. This is the first time in months that it's happened to me, but not for a good reason. I've got one motherfucker of a headache. The little bit of sleep I managed to get last night was screwed over by shitty dreams. The only bright side is the twenty minutes I spent in the shower with Sienna, with my cock pushed balls deep inside her pussy, and her fingernails raking a crisscross pattern across my back as we fucked against the slate tile wall.

But even after letting go, that tension from last night came back. Not just for me, but for Sienna, too. Guess I was wrong when I let myself believe she was over it. The muscles in the back of my neck tighten. Fucking Samantha. She's kept her promise to leave me alone, and yet she's still causing me problems.

Sienna rests her hand on my chest. "Are you alright?" Her voice is worried. Even when she's frustrated with me—with anyone—my needs are still first and foremost to her.

Opening my eyes, I take in the sight of her—loose red hair, delicate oval-shaped face, and soft pink lips, the bottom of which is currently being pulled between her teeth.

"How many of these cities have you been to before?"

Her eyebrows knit together over her piercing blue eyes. "Did you know that you're the most evasive, infuriating man that I've ever known?"

"There you go again." I brush my thumb over her cheek, and her shoulder lifts a little. "Answer the question, Sienna. How many?"

125

She draws in a breath and then lets it out. "A handful." I trail my finger around the scooped neck of her tight t-shirt, and her skin gradually changes to the sexiest shade of red. Staring down at her thighs, she continues, "We didn't go on many vacations when my parents were still together. Once they got divorced, traveling all but stopped. Unless you count my dad's half-assed attempt to get Seth and me to move to Maine. Obviously it was out of the question because we both decided to stay with Gram."

"You ever regret that?"

"Absolutely not, but...."

My hand freezes on her breast and I cock my head to look into her eyes. "Tell me, Red."

"The thing is, I *do* wish I had a relationship with my dad, you know? We talk every few weeks or so, but it's awkward and frustrating. Back when my mom first went to prison, and she'd play her little games with my head, she used to remind me that my dad left long before she screwed up. But then I think of Gram, and I realize that I'm lucky. There are kids who are dealt a hand that's so much worse." Glancing down again, she fusses with pushing a lock of hair behind her ears as she runs her tongue over her lips. "I sound like a crazy bitch with daddy issues, don't I?"

"Never." I don't know much about Sienna's childhood, but the few times she's mentioned it, she's almost immediately changed the subject. Hearing the disappointment in her voice just now—it just makes me want to give her even more. "I'm going to take you everywhere—all over the goddamn world." To drive my point home, I take her hands, holding her long, slim fingers between mine. "You'll eventually get tired of it and tell me to fuck off."

126

Dipping her head, she presses her lips to the side of my wrist closest to her face.

"I'm a travel virgin. I won't get tired."

Glancing up at the driver whose eyes keep looking at the rearview mirror, I flash him a warning look before I let go of her hands and touch my mouth to her ear. "Don't worry, I'll—" I begin, but then I realize she's not wearing her usual apple-scented perfume today, but something else with a hint of cherry. "You smell good enough to eat."

"Good luck with that on the bus." She inclines her head to five parked buses coming into view, and immediately does a double take. "Holy shit … you never said it was that many."

"It's a big tour, Red. Two buses for us, one for Wicked Lambs, and two more for the crew. We've moved past the days of the one bus shit."

"That sounds so unbelievably cocky."

"Just being honest." I regret those words the moment I say them. Irritation flashes in her blue eyes, but she blinks, and it's gone just as quickly. Our driver slows the car to a park, and as soon as he gets out to grab our things, I take the conversation back to where I was intending to go before her scent fucked me up. To a place that's far away from words like past and truth and honesty.

"Just so you know, your ass is mine as soon as we get on that bus, and I'm going to enjoy breaking you in to each and every new city."

She races her tongue over her lips. I can't decide if it's just nerves or to test me. "I'm guessing that has nothing to do with

127

sightseeing," she laughs nervously as the driver opens the door for her.

I'm right behind her, steadying her by gripping her hips so she doesn't fall over on the bright wedge sandals that make her legs seem even longer. As I stand up, my cock brushes up against her ass, and she jerks forward, taking in a sharp gasp of air.

"That was on purpose, Red." Wyatt is approaching us and grinning like a dumbass, so I keep my voice low enough for only her to hear me. "Like I told you in there, your ass is mine." Her mouth is parted when she whips her head around to look at me. "You can take that however you want for now."

"Honestly, I'm afraid to take it any way."

"I'll be gentle," I promise.

Our conversation is cut short after that because of Wyatt, who gives me about ten excuses on why he bailed after the show last night until he finally fesses up and admits that Kylie flew in from New Orleans to spend the night with him. I smirk when he's done. "I already know where you were," I say before leading Sienna away from him in the direction of the bus.

"You could've just told him that from the beginning," she points out, the corners of her lips shaking, and I shrug.

When Wyatt catches up to us a few seconds later, he's shoving a cigarette into his mouth. His response is the same as Sienna's. "Then why the fuck did you let me go through all that?"

"Unlike my sister, I'm not against watching you fuck yourself into a corner every once in a while." We reach the second black bus with Sequel's logo—a heart full of daggers—emblazoned on the

128

side. I run my hand down Sienna's forearm and stare down at her. "This is ours. Give me five and I'll be up, too."

"Ours alone?

"Wouldn't that be convenient," Wyatt mutters under his breath. Pressing his fist to his mouth, he clears his throat, and adds aloud, "You and Lucas. Whichever bus driver is on the rotation that day. Sinjin. Whoever Sin's fucking."

Sienna's pink lips drag into a tight smile, causing me to debate whether or not I should punch McCrae in the mouth right here and now. "Good to see you again, Wyatt," she says brightly, right before she climbs the bus steps. Once I hear her introducing herself to the bus driver, I face Wyatt.

"I'm bigger than you."

Stuffing his hands into his pockets, he nods. "Yep."

"And you don't need teeth to play your fucking guitar."

He claps me on the shoulder, but I don't budge. "I'm envious of you." He stares up the bus stairs. "We all are. Now pipe the fuck down and enjoy what you have. Even if she is here to—" he grins broadly and clears his throat "—work."

"Don't go fucking everything with a pussy and maybe, just maybe, Kylie'll come around too." In the past, I played ignorance and didn't step into their relationship. That changed when they got married. "You fuck my sister over and you'll wish you never met me."

Wyatt's still stunned into silence as I get onto the bus, but he speaks up before I'm completely out of earshot. I don't hear his exact words because my attention is drawn to Sinjin, who's giving

Sienna his hung-over version of a grand tour of the bus, but I know what he's saying.

I need to follow my own advice.

I'm not going to bullshit and say that it's not a little rocky, but the first couple of days on the bus aren't the potential clusterfuck I had prepared myself for. Sinjin's not walking around screwed up out of his mind, so he's decent company. Because we have no other damn choice, we fall into a quick routine. Sienna focuses a lot of her attention on wardrobe, while Sinjin and I work on music, with David the bodyguard coming on briefly after shows just to keep an eye out for stray sets of tits and ass trying to find their way onto the bus. They want a lucky break—a night with one of us with hopes of something more.

The something more part almost never happens.

I'm sick of the bus—with its full-sized master bedroom and cramped standup shower—by the time we check into our Denver hotel mid-afternoon on the third day of the tour. Sienna's obviously ready for a break too. Even before the door closes in our executive suite, she falls down on the bed, curling her bare toes into the crisp white sheets and grinning with glee.

"I thought I never wanted to see another Four Seasons again, but this is heavenly," she sighs happily.

Fuck.

Since I'm on the other side of the hotel room and her eyes are squeezed together in pleasure, she doesn't see my muscles tighten up at the mention of what happened in the Atlanta hotel. I'd treated her like shit. And I feel like shit just thinking about it.

By the time she sits up, raking her fingers through her hair, I'm back in control. I cross the room slowly, allowing myself a little grin as her chest rises and falls faster and faster with each of my steps.

"It's a good break from Sin's goddamn drumming, huh?" I ask.

"Ugh. The guy makes a drum set out of everything he sees." But she's smiling. She moves those sexy legs, pulling her knees up to her chest, and I follow the path her red toenails make up the bedspreads, imagining how they'll look on my shoulders a little later. "How long are we staying for?"

"Tomorrow morning. Next city is only a few hours away." The need to be inside of her is a second away from trumping everything else I've got planned, and I know I've got to leave this room before that happens. I've already told Tyler that I would stop by his hotel for a meeting, and even now my phone is going off in my pocket. "Rest. I've got some band shit to take care of and then I'm yours."

She starts to protest, but I bend my face to hers and cover her soft lips. "Here I was thinking I'd managed to break that annoying habit of yours. Why do you have to argue with me at every turn, Si?"

It takes her a second to answer, and when she does, she traces her tongue around my lips every couple of words. "Isn't my"—she clears her throat and when she continues, her voice is a little lower—"habit of being infuriatingly compliant to everyone but you what drew you to me in the first place?"

She starts the rotation of her tongue once more, but I pull it into my mouth. She moans softly, pleadingly as our mouths crush together. The moment her fingers touch my cock, I jerk away from her.

"Get some rest," I tell her again. "You're sure as fuck going to need it." The look she gives me is just about enough to break through my thin layer of self-control, but I turn abruptly and stalk from the room.

Because Tyler's staying in a different hotel, Wyatt and I walk over together with David, from security, following several paces behind us. The Embassy Suites is about five blocks away, and Wyatt bitches all seven minutes about how Cal and one of my sister's friends have been keeping him awake with their loud ass phone sex.

"I'm just waiting for the *really* weird fetishes. Balloon popping bullshit or—" Wyatt pauses when a woman pushing her kids in a double stroller turns and glares him down.

"I know what you're thinking," he says to me, dropping his volume.

"Why the fuck would I think you have too much time on your hands?"

"Fuck you, Lucas."

I go inside of the hotel lobby with my head down. Even though it's only just after two, women are already mulling around the lobby, earning pissed-off stares from the hotel staff. With one of the tour buses stupidly parked at the side of the building, it doesn't take a goddamn genius to figure out what they're here for.

Luckily for Wyatt and me, Brady Callahan, Wicked Lambs' lead guitarist is already in the lobby signing tits, back dimples—whatever he can without getting tossed out of the building by hotel security.

Once we're away from the fray and almost to the elevators, I speak to Wyatt under my breath. "If it'll help, I'll buy you some earplugs. Then you won't be able to hear Cal and Heidi's balloon popping, and I won't have to hear you bitch and moan like a little bitch."

Lowering his eyes to the floor, he grins. "Nah ... but I do feel bad for Sin. Has to fucking blow living with the king of ropes and handcuffs. " Before I can respond he makes a face at the crowd waiting at the elevator. "Taking the stairs. See you lazy fucks at the top."

Almost immediately after he turns the corner in the direction of the staircase signs, the elevator doors open, and the line starts to die down. Figures. I wait until there's nobody left to catch a ride up.

As soon as David and I step inside, we get company, and I suck a frustrated breath in through my teeth.

A couple of women—both dressed in little black shorts that show off their ass cheeks and tight t-shirts—trip all over themselves to rush inside. They look like they're minutes away from lining up outside the venue despite having several hours to go. They also know exactly who I am. That much is obvious by the flushed skin and nervous fumbling for cell phones.

I'm grateful, don't get me wrong, but there's also a limit.

"I've seen you on tour four times." The woman speaking to me is redheaded—not natural, but it's close to the same fiery shade as Sienna's. I can't help but wonder if she colored it on purpose—like my ex-wife had earlier this year. "I love your music. Love 'Handcuffs' and 'Ten Days' and—" She moves forward, but David steps between her and me, shaking his head to each side.

133

"Ma'am, you're going to need to take a step back."

Normally, I wouldn't give a shit. I guess it makes me a dick to admit that, but I wouldn't. I would step off this elevator at the very next floor, and there wouldn't be a doubt in my mind that the redhead and her friend would still come to my show tonight. It was a control thing.

It was also fucked up.

Rubbing the pad of my thumb across my chin thoughtfully, I lean against the elevator wall. "Which shows?" I ask. David's eyebrow jerks up, but I ignore his surprise.

The redhead looks momentarily stunned and her mouth hangs open for a long time. Finally, her friend answers for her. "Two years ago. Los Angeles, Vegas, and Salt Lake City." The brunette stretches her arms out against the railing surrounding the elevator and shakes her head. "Teresa runs *Everything YTS*."

I have no fucking clue what *Everything YTS* is, but I nod and make a mental note to Google it once I'm done with Tyler. "Okay, so only three shows so far. But I'm seeing you tonight," Teresa gushes.

Hearing her say that makes me realize why I haven't gotten off this elevator yet, despite having just missed Tyler's floor. These women haven't come on to me, or offered to fuck me in a three way in the first floor laundry room, or even spoke to me with a hint of invitation in their voices.

"Then I guess I better sing my fucking ass off, huh?" I ask, and Teresa snorts.

"Lucas Wolfe doesn't disappoint. Ever."

"No." With a grin, I turn my head slightly. "I sure as fuck don't."

We hold up the elevator for another minute, and by the time we get off, I've taken a photo with both women. David gives me a funny look when we finally head left to room 708—Tyler's room.

Everyone but Sinjin is already here, and after Cilla shows up shortly thereafter, smelling like booze with bloodshot eyes, Tyler's important meeting takes a total of fifteen minutes. Sin's birthday is next week, and Tyler wants to make sure we'll stop by the surprise party after the St. Louis show, which is the night after one of our days off. It's something that could've been done by text or email, and when I let Tyler know as I start to leave, he gives me a cool smile.

"I take it you won't be coming to Sin's party?"

His tone irks me. This is the second tour that I've done with Tyler, but this is the first time I've butted heads with him. I close the door and some of the generic paintings on the wall shake as I sit down in the chair across from it. "Actually, I can keep my dick dry longer than you give me credit for, so I'll be there."

Tyler opens the mini-bar. "I've been hearing good things about your girl from

Maggie." The tail end of his statement is emphasized, and I know he's got more to say. And I probably won't like it. He holds out a Red Bull, which I decline. "I'm going to cut to the chase here, Luke. Her being with you on this tour is making things hard for Cilla."

Hard for Cilla?

"Sienna's not going anywhere, so Cilla can either accept that or leave. Guess you're forgetting that none of us wanted Wicked Lambs on this tour in the first fucking place."

Sinjin had gone as far as threatening to pull out the day of our first show in

Pomona. He had told me that being around her messes with him—that she's his "Sam."

I don't think it's as deep as that, but he still deserved better than Cilla's shit.

Downing a shot of vodka straight out of the miniature Skyy bottle, Tyler slams the glass on the countertop. "She's drinking heavily."

I'm not surprised, but my breath is coming out in rapid bursts through my nostrils when I comment. "Like I said, if Cilla's got a problem with Sienna, or with anything else, tell her to get the fuck out."

Tyler holds up his hands defensively. "Hey, calm down, alright? Last thing we need is for you to go off on her and ruin things. I thought you were ... friends."

"We are." Standing, I stride over to the door. "That still doesn't change the fact that none of us wanted to tour with Cilla." Tyler starts to protest, but I won't hear it. "And the last fucking thing I need is you trying to make me feel responsible for her."

I slam the door behind me so hard that David, who's waiting for me in the hallway, flinches. "Let's get the fuck out of this place," I growl.

When we come off the elevator, the crowd in the lobby has multiplied, and I can see why. Cilla's joined Brady, and she's posing for pictures with their fans. She spots me immediately. She throws her long black hair over her shoulder before leaning in to open mouth kiss one of her fans for a photo, but her heavily lined eyes are pleading with me when she pulls away from the other woman.

"Boss?" David jerks his head to the exit sign ten feet from the elevator. "You don't want to walk through that."

No, I don't.

My mood is dark as we walk back to our hotel. My history—hell, the band's history—with Cilla is twisted, complicated. She's dangled Sinjin around for years. And then there was the last time we all toured together several years back. For eleven months after that, I hadn't been able to look at Cilla, talk to her, or return the messages she left for me. Then again, I was too busy dealing with Sam.

I truly am fucked up to have agreed to this tour.

The only thing that helps me is the way Sienna molds against me seconds after I open the door to our room.

CHAPTER ELEVEN

Sienna

After Lucas returns, giving me the news that his road manager is planning a surprise party for Sinjin's twenty-ninth birthday next week, I look past his flared nostrils and hard hazel eyes. I pretend that he's not distant and completely distracted for the rest of the day, after his show that night, and even throughout the next day. But by the time the loud beeping noise of the bus pulling into its parking spot for the day wakes me up first thing Friday morning, I'm frustrated and tired. Since neither has anything to do with my being up late for last night's show, and everything to do with my crappy mood, I begrudgingly convince myself to ask some questions.

Instead of approaching Lucas directly, or calling Kylie to pick her brain, I decide to ask Sinjin. He's a man of few words—which are almost always sarcastic and usually offensive—but he notices everything.

I finally get my chance shortly before noon, when Lucas leaves our parked bus to go speak with Tyler about a stage concern. Once I hear the bus door clang shut, I wait a couple of minutes before putting the book I've been reading aside. The scent of what Sinjin swears are homemade cigarettes—because he must confuse my being slightly naïve for incredibly stupid—immediately hits me in the face the second I step outside the back compartment. I follow the smell down the carpeted aisle and into the galley.

I find Sinjin at the table, smoking and looking at something on his computer screen. He's shirtless and barefoot, wearing only jeans, and his black hair is damp.

After spending nearly a week on the bus with him, I've come to realize that this look is the norm for him.

Tentatively, I slide into the seat across from him. "How's it going?"

One of his eyebrows jerks up. He makes a few more pecks on his netbook before he finally decides to acknowledge me. "Either you have a question about your loud boyfriend—yeah, I fucking heard *everything* this morning, and I honestly feel well acquainted with your pussy—or you've decided that you can't resist my charm. If that's the case then I can't say I blame you." He lifts his green eyes to mine and winks. "I'm pretty fucking charming."

Ugh.

In an effort to hide the flames crawling up my face, I focus my eyes on the cuffed hem of my black shorts and fidget with the scooped neck of my gray burnout t-shirt. My silence is met with Sin's chuckling. *Asshole.* "Am I making you nervous?" he teases. When I neither confirm nor deny, he sighs and leans back, tilting his head to the side to regard me cynically. "Alright, Sienna, get whatever the hell it is out there. I'm all yours."

Forcing the thought of him listening in on what had gone on in the back compartment, I clear my throat, square my shoulders, and peer across the table at him.

"Do you know what's going on with him? Why he's been so—"

"Let me guess: Why he's been so *Lucas*?" At the sight of me rolling my eyes, Sinjin smirks. "Makes me feel all warm and fuzzy inside that you're coming to me for answers that just about everyone on this tour already knows."

"Just like they all know you're an asshat?"

Laughing, Sinjin shakes his head from side to side. "Use your brain, gorgeous. He's got you here with him. He's got that bitch Cilla trying to jump on his dick at every turn." He takes a drag from his joint and exhales. The smoke whispers into my face, and

I draw back, waving it away. "Look, the only break that motherfucker is getting is that

Sam hasn't popped up with the bullshit she usually brings to every tour."

Sam. Hearing her name makes me curl my fingernails painfully into my palm. Sinjin obviously notices this because he tilts his body forward and stares down at my clenched hands, his eyes suddenly curious. I spring to my feet and grab a Coke from the fridge adjacent to us. When I return to my spot, the sneer has returned to his face.

"Way to make me feel better about Cilla," I throw back at him, opening my drink.

"What the hell's your deal with her?"

Besides the fact that her mood is all over the place. Suddenly, thinking about Cilla makes me feel like an idiot for even asking that last question. So far she's alternated between being reasonably cordial to

141

me and ignoring my existence. Just two nights ago she was drunkenly arguing with David backstage that I was definitely not on the after show list.

I haven't witnessed very much interaction between Cilla and Sinjin, but if the way she treats me is any indication … well, I guess I can see why she's on his shit list.

He sucks his cheeks in, making his face look even thinner. "What, you want me to tell you it's complicated?"

"Is it?"

"Not really. I gave a shit about her, she chased Lucas even after he made it clear he wasn't interested." He thinks on that for a moment and then snorts dismissively. "Correction, she's still chasing Lucas. You know, she swears she's not like the groupies. Ironic that she thinks she's so special, isn't it?"

Why does he seem so absolutely gleeful when he tells me that?

As if he can read my mind, he winks a grass green eye at me. "You'll be alright. Even if she weren't a drunken bitch, Lucas still wouldn't want her. Not his type. Not *you*." He's quiet, and just when I begin to think we're done talking, he slams his netbook shut. "Watch out for Cilla. And stop staring at me like I'm stupid—I'm looking out for you."

A coarse laugh that burns the back of my throat bubbles up from my chest. "Is there *any* woman from Lucas' past that I shouldn't keep an eye out for?"

"Kylie. She's the only one who's not going to try to drive a fucking dagger into your back."

I massage my temples. "Good to know."

Fortunately, his phone begins to vibrate on the table between us. I manage to make out the name "Zoe" before he gives me a withering glare and swipes the iPhone up. He stalks off toward his section of the bus—the four bunks in the middle, right before the compartment I've been sharing with Lucas—leaving behind the strong scent of smoke mixed with Ivory soap.

Running my fingertip around the cold rim of my drink can, I close my eyes and scan my brain for ways to solve the Cilla problem. To be honest, I can't come up with a single solution that doesn't involve us getting into a verbal—or hell, even a physical—altercation.

She sees me as a threat. I just want her to leave Lucas alone. There's enough static between us without having to deal with Cilla.

I don't realize that I'm no longer alone until I hear the distinct sound of a man clearing his throat slowly. I open my eyes, expecting to find Sinjin or even Lucas, but Wyatt's tanned face is grinning down at me.

Seeing that he has my attention, he leans his tall, toned body back against the counter in the tiny kitchen behind him. "You alright?"

I rake my hand through my red locks and lift my shoulders indifferently. "I'm decent. You over here to see Sinjin?"

"What can I say? I was good with one bus, but Lucas likes his space." His midnight blue eyes dart around the kitchen and lounge. "Is Sin even around?"

I jab my index finger to the other half of the bus, which is closed off. "He's back there on the phone."

"Ah, I see." Instead of taking Sin's unavailability as his cue to leave, Wyatt pulls a packet of cigarettes from his back pocket. He shakes one free but then pauses and gives me a questioning look. "You—"

I shake my head. "No, I don't mind." He gives me an appreciative smile. As he cups his hand over the cigarette and his New Orleans Saints lighter, my thoughts go to

Kylie. "Guess you can't wait until the New Orleans show, huh?" I ask.

He shakes his head briskly and mumbles an "Mmm hmm."

"Do you think she'll come around and change her mind?" After tonight's show, there will be a little less than forty days left in the tour, but I'd be lying if I didn't admit how ecstatic I would be if Kylie was around.

Wyatt blows out a long breath and rolls his eyes up toward the recessed lighting in the roof of the bus. "Who knows with Kylie— she's stubborn as hell. It's … hard." He offers me a strained smile that I try to return. But all I can think of is the little bit of Kylie and Wyatt's history that I know about, and I can't help but wonder if this tour has been too hard for him to stay faithful to her.

We're barely a week in.

"Right," I say in a drawn-out voice.

Bending forward, he crushes the remains of his cigarette in Sinjin's ashtray and shoots me a sheepish look. "Anyone ever tell you that you wear your emotions on your face?" At these words, I glance down at my lap, causing him to laugh bitterly. "For the record I'm not messing around on my wife."

144

"And for the record, I swear I'm not thinking about the assistant at that recording studio back in February," I reply sweetly. He grabs his chest as if he's wounded, and I narrow my eyes.

"I didn't fuck her." Releasing his chest, he rubs the palm of his hand over the top of his forehead, messing his short dirty blond hair with his musical-note-tattooed fingers. "What I let her do wasn't right, especially since it was fueled by my anger at Ky for not coming to Nashville, but I did not fuck that woman."

"I swear this sounds like something I've heard before on old political documentaries," I respond quickly, not wanting to hear any more details, and the left corner of his lip quirks up. "But, really, don't have to explain anything to me."

"'Course I do."

A few feet away from us, Sinjin groans loudly about how sentimental stuff turns his stomach, and Wyatt and I both turn our bodies toward him. He's shed a layer of clothes—now he's only wearing baggy plaid boxers—and I twist my lips to the side to hold back any type of reaction. Though he's looking at Wyatt, his words are aimed at me. "Fuck you, Sienna, it's not even what you think it is."

This is the second time in the last twenty minutes that I've heard this, and I roll my eyes. I slide my butt across the leather dinette seat and stand. "I wasn't even going to accuse you of phone sex behind that curtain, but whatever."

Sinjin laughs—one of those rare, genuine ones that seem strange coming from him—as I maneuver past Wyatt and stumble off the bus. Early August sunlight beams against my face, hot and blinding. Squinting, I consider going back in to find my sunglasses, but then I decide against it. For starters, I don't want to interrupt their conversation. And secondly, I don't necessarily want to hear whatever that conversation may entail.

Easing down on the last bus step, I pull my phone out of my pocket and call Gram. I haven't spoken to her since Wednesday. Even though I'll be seeing her at the end of next week when I fly back home for a job I have lined up, I've missed her like crazy and I'm dying to hear the sound of her voice.

When I don't reach her at home, I try her cell number. She picks up after a few rings, and I can hear the pleasure in her voice. It's impossible for me not to smile. "We were just talking about you this morning! Are you having a good time?"

Since I assume "we" refers to her and my brother, I answer honestly, "It's really different."

"Not the bad different, I hope?"

"No, no, it's good," I reassure her. "Of course, by the time I get used to it all, the tour will be over."

"Have you been working much?"

Holding my phone between my ear and the crook of my neck, I rub my damp palms down the front of my shorts. So far, working as Lucas' wardrobe consultant has consisted of very little consulting and limited wardrobe. Literally. No doubt Gram's already aware of that, but she's too classy to say anything that will embarrass me.

"Not as much as I would at home."

Because that's a safe answer, right?

"Well, I can't wait to have you back here."

"It'll only be for a couple of days." Most of which will be spent helping out on the set of a new Nashville-based reality show. Better to prepare her for not seeing me around much now, so she's not disappointed next week. "There's a lot of work to be done while I'm at home."

She pulls in a breath to speak, but she's cut off by what sounds like a man telling her something in a soft, professional-sounding voice. "Sienna, honey, I'm going to have to call you back. I've got an appointment that—"

Since she's been my biggest supporter for as long as I can remember, shielding Seth and me from whatever bullshit my mother threw our way, I've always been protective of my grandmother. Hearing the word "appointment" instantly makes the tiny hairs on the back of my neck stand on end.

"Is everything alright? You're not sick, are you?" I question, my voice going up an octave.

"Calm down." She pushes out a shaky laugh. "I've got an appointment with a lawyer."

And without having to ask, I know this has something to do with Mom. Anytime the words lawyer or bank or loan come out of my grandmother's mouth, it has to do with that woman. The question is, what are the reasons behind my mother trying to use Gram this time? I bring my hand back up to my phone and grip it with all my might. "I hope she's not asking you to spend your money on hiring someone for her."

"It's just a consultation. I can promise you that I haven't spent a penny."

"Sorry, I just ..."

When she interrupts me, her voice is soothing. "I know, and I love you so much for who you are. I'll call you when I get home, alright?"

I find myself nodding; despite the fact that the only people nearby are a couple of roadies walking past who are in a heated debate about bass guitars.

"I love you, too," I whisper.

After she hangs up, I set my phone in my lap and stare down at the beach inspired wallpaper until the screen goes black. There's a part of me that's dying to know why my mom has Gram going to an attorney, but the other part—that's completely wary of any of any of Mom's motives—trumps that. She's caused so much heartbreak for my grandmother, so much stress, that I can barely think of her without feeling a bitter twist in the pit of my belly.

I start to head back inside the bus but then I see Lucas and Cal coming off the one parked on the other side of the venue's back lot. Lucas' hazel eyes lock with mine and his lips lift slightly. Though he seems to be in an intense conversation with Cal, he motions me to him. Pushing myself to my feet, I slip my phone back into my pocket and head over to them.

Cal turns his Monster can up to his lips, and when he lowers it, his dark eyes are dancing with laughter. "Sinjin scare you away?"

Shaking my head, I stop beside Lucas. Without looking at me, he works his arm around my waist, pulling me to his side. Like always, his touch is magnetic, and I melt against him, not caring that it's as hot as the depths of Hades in Houston right now. "I can handle Sinjin. Even if he is pants-less at the moment."

"Sounds about right." Cal offers me a flash of his straight white teeth. "I think this means she's inviting herself over to our bus."

"Over my dead fucking body." Lucas grins down at me, looking more relaxed than I've seen him in the past few days. "Sin is tame compared to Cal."

"Wyatt balances me," Cal argues, placing his palm flat against the side of the bus to support his weight. "He's been as virginal as—" He runs his gaze over the length of me before cocking his head to one side. "Well, shit, he's just been virginal."

I bite my lip to keep from smiling. There's a sound against a window inside of the bus, and I tilt my head back to see a pink-manicured finger tapping a rhythmic beat on the glass. "I think you're being summoned."

Looking behind him, Cal waves at the woman inside the bus before turning back to Lucas and me. "Looks like I am. God, I love Houston." He shoots us a wicked grin as he heads up the bus steps. After stepping inside, he grabs something from behind the door. I'm caught by surprise when he thrusts a guitar in front of me, wiggling it around until I accept.

"Enjoy," Cal tells me. "Lucas-Fucking-Wolfe has good taste."

I don't get a chance to respond before the door slams in my face. I draw away from Lucas, running my fingertips along the body of the acoustic Gibson guitar. It's beautiful—with a mahogany back and sides. "You plan on teaching me how to play this thing?" I ask gently, stunned, and he nods.

"I missed your birthday in June." He takes the guitar out of my hands, holding it effortlessly as he leads me back to our bus.

149

"Figured if you can play a piano like that, you can do some creative things with this, too."

Twisting my face, I study his expression carefully, searching for any of the stress that's been there the last few days. It's not there, but then again, Lucas is good at hiding his emotions. I press my palm to his hard chest, letting the steady beat of his heart drum against my hand.

"It's perfect." I smile. As he walks up the steps of the bus, I curl my fingers into the hem of his t-shirt, stopping him from going inside.

"There's that look, Red," he teases. "What is it?"

I pinch my lips together and then relax my mouth. "Is everything okay?"

He gives me one of those soft looks that pulls me apart, piece-by-piece. "Never been better."

CHAPTER TWELVE

One thing I quickly realized about being on the road is just how much I prefer the outdoor concert venues. Sure it's the second week of August, which means it's unforgivingly hot and nearly all my clothes cling to my body—and the Dallas show on Sunday night is only the second one that I've attended outside—but there's something magical about listening to Your Toxic Sequel's delicious brand of angst and debauchery beneath a bed of stars.

Thinking about tonight's show, a rush of adrenaline speeds through me as I leave our bus for the backstage area—a gray-painted building that's located directly behind the venue.

A beefy guy wearing a baseball cap and a black Security t-shirt that hugs his broad muscles guards the entrance to the backstage. "Do you have a crew pass?" he asks, skimming his eyes over me when I walk up. I lift my wrist and hold it close to his face. Once he examines my black and red wristband that reads *YTS VIP-AUG 12*, he lets me in. "Have a good one, ma'am."

"You too." Dragging in a nervous lungful of air, I step forward into the chaos that is backstage. As I force my way through the crewmembers moving around busily in the wide hallways, I hear a female voice shouting my name.

Spinning around, I use my height to scan my eyes over the crowd. At last I spot Maggie, the wardrobe director, cupping her hands over her pierced lips. Noticing that she's caught my attention, her shoulders slump a little.

She crooks one of her fingers at me. "I need you," she mouths before disappearing inside the room she stood in front of. I follow close behind her, barely missing two stocky roadies who are lugging a wide black box of equipment. Inside of the dressing room, Maggie is accompanied by a few other people that I've yet to meet. Still, it's nowhere near as chaotic in here, so I rush inside.

As soon as I close the door, pressing my shoulders against it, I lift my gaze to Maggie. She's leaned over a vanity table, making hasty scribbles on a bright pink clipboard.

"Please tell me you're not busy," she pleads in a strained voice.

I rock back on the heels of my nautical-inspired espadrille flats. "Only if you need me to be."

Her head pops up, and under the harsh vanity lighting, I notice how freckled she is. "Where have you been all my life?" She doesn't wait for me to answer. "The boys have agreed to let these wonderful folks film tonight's show." She gestures around the room, and for the first time, I notice that one of the guys has a giant camera hoisted on his shoulder. He wiggles his fingers at me, so I incline my head in acknowledgment.

"What do you need me to do?" I question Maggie.

She swipes one of her wrists across her forehead, leaving a light sheen of sweat on the pinup tattoos that extend from her wrist to the inside of her thin elbow. "They want to do a quick interview with me. God knows why, but whatever, right?" She points to the wardrobe rack that's against the wall on the side of the room. "And I'm already a little behind because I had to hunt down some purple fishnets for Cilla. Can you finish this up for me for the guys?"

I stride over to the garment rack. "Of course." Turning a little, I take in how flustered she looks and offer her an encouraging smile. "You'll do fine. Just don't tell them this is the easiest job ever."

She scrapes her hands through her short mess of black and blond curls. "I'll keep that in mind. Thanks, Sienna." She darts away, muttering about her hatred for all things camera related.

The camera crew follows right on the heels of her gladiator sandals.

Pinching my bottom lip between my teeth, I race my hands across the bounty of jeans and t-shirts hanging just a few inches from my face. It feels like it's been an eternity since I've gotten to do work—even though I have spent a good deal of my bus time focusing on my job back in Nashville. Of course, checking and responding to emails has absolutely nothing on being hands-on.

Call me silly, but having Maggie ask me to help out right now makes me feel a little giddy.

Maggie's already gone so far as to separate everything on the rack with colored dividers for each member of the band, so most of my work has already been done for me. I can hear Wicked Lambs running through their set on stage, so I go as fast as I can, humming a Queens of the Stone Age song that Sinjin had been listening to this morning on our bus.

Less than ten minutes later, I've made selections for Your Toxic Sequel that's suitable for the dry summer night.

I load everything onto a shorter wardrobe cart that I find in the back of the closet and then roll it down the hall to Your Toxic Sequel's dressing room. Because this is a smaller venue, they're sharing a space that David is standing in front of. His arms are crossed over his chest, making him look every bit the part of badass bodyguard.

As soon as he spots me, he offers me the same unsure look—crooked grin and hesitant deep brown eyes—that he's been sending my way ever since Sinjin told him I was Lucas' girlfriend. "Maggie put you to work?"

"*Finally.*" I jerk my head to the closed room behind him, making my long red ponytail swing around one of my shoulders. David's gaze follows my hair where it lingers a little longer than necessary on my boobs. I clear my throat. "Um, is it safe for me to go in?"

Yanking his dark eyes up to mine, he lifts his shoulders and reaches back to knock several times on the heavy metal door. "As safe as it's gonna get." The door swings open, and David holds it wide for me as I shove my cart through the entranceway. "Watching the show tonight?" he asks.

I peek back at him. "Are you kidding me? The outside ones are the best."

He nods in agreement before returning to the hallway and letting the door clank shut.

Stopping in the center of the room a few feet away from a beverage table, I sniff the air. And once my brain processes just how good this room smells, I inhale again.

The scent is vanilla and something citrusy. I spot three candles—one on each of the side tables and the last positioned in the center of

154

the coffee table. On the other side of that table, Tyler is on the couch next to Cal. Their heads lean close together as they talk.

"You put scented candles on your rider?" I ask, stretching my arms out in front of me.

"The candles are Sin's new thing," Wyatt answers. I look around the garment rack to find him sitting on a stool in the opposite corner of the room. No surprise, he's smoking like a freight train, but luckily, Sinjin's candles pretty much cancel out the odor. I wrinkle my nose as Wyatt stubs it out and immediately fires up another. "Helps him relax."

I follow Wyatt's gaze until it lands on Sinjin, who's stretched out on the loveseat. There's a folded cloth covering his eyes and a bottle of Southern Comfort within reaching distance on the floor.

"How's that coming along for you, Sin?" I tease. He answers by giving me the finger. Laughing, I begin to distribute everything from my cart. When I get to Wyatt, and he lifts the hangers out of my arms, I arch my eyebrows together. "So what weird shit do *you* have on there?"

"On what?"

"The rider for the dressing room. Sin's got his candles and booze. I'm not even sure I *want* to know what Cal asked for. What about you?"

Wyatt tosses his clothes on the back of the armchair that's closest to him. "Gum.

Cigarettes. Energy drinks. I'm simple as hell compared to the rest of these fuckers."

Cal snorts loudly, dragging my attention back to him and Tyler. "You should tell her how all the weird shit on the dinner and lunch

155

menus belong to you." Tyler remains wordless—he's literally said a total of twenty words to me since the tour kicked off—but he nods his strawberry blond head in amusement.

Wyatt changes the subject. "How are the guitar lessons going?"

Twisting my lips, I wobble my hand from side to side. Lucas has been teaching me a little each day since he surprised me with the mahogany Gibson. When I throw that in with the few chords I learned from my grandfather as a kid, I'm average. "It'll take some time."

"Takes some getting used to," Wyatt says, "but you'll pick it up. I taught Ky in about a week."

He doesn't say another word about the food rider, and I make a mental note to pay better attention to what we're served during the next couple of days. Spinning around, I pace back to the wardrobe rack, which is empty except for a pair of Diesel jeans, a black, short sleeve Henley tee, and black and white Converse. For Lucas. Who is nowhere to be found.

Rubbing my hands down the back of my tight, navy blue skinny jeans, I glance around at the rest of the band. "Do y'all know where—?"

"Don't worry, you'll have him all to yourself after the show," Sinjin says, sitting upright. He tosses the cloth that was over his eyes behind him, where it lands a few inches from the candle burning on the end table. "But if it makes you feel better, he's on the phone in the bathroom." He shoots two fingers at the restroom in the back of the room. Sure enough the door is closed.

"Look at you cooperating," I say sarcastically. "Was that so hard?"

Cal gets up from the couch, his straight black hair swinging around his shoulders. "He's twitching from having to be a good boy," he states dryly. "Oh, and your ass better come back here tonight after the show." He winks theatrically. "I heard a rumor you're supposed to do body-shots. What I want to know is if it's supposed to be with me or off of me? Or off of you? And how Lucas feels about that?"

I shoot a hell-freezing look at Sinjin who's the only person aside from Lucas that I've mentioned Ashley's YTS bucket list to. He smiles like the Cheshire cat and then stretches back out on the loveseat, rolling over on his side so that his face is turned away from us. When he speaks, his voice is low, but it's quiet enough in the dressing room for everyone to hear what he's saying loud and clear.

"Lucas will break the fucking bottle over your head if her lips even come close to you."

Ignoring Sin, I address Wyatt. "Can you let Lucas know that I'm putting his wardrobe for tonight in that closet over there?" He confirms that he will, and after I take Lucas' belongings off the rack and hang them neatly in the dressing room closet, I pull my garment cart toward the door.

Before I leave, I pause.

My gaze flit to the restroom door once again, and I narrow my eyes at it. I try to convince myself that it's not Sam he's talking to and that she hasn't tried to snake her way back into his life. I haven't heard from her since the night before we left, and I've almost talked myself into believing that she won't send another message. That she wanted to retaliate against Lucas after reading an article about us being together and the easiest way for her to do so was to reach out to me.

Ripping my gaze away from the door, I give the band—minus Sinjin, whose back is still turned—an upbeat smile. "Good luck. Or break a leg."

After I return the rack to the crew dressing room, I make it a third of the way up the hall before I hear yet another voice shouting my name. This time it's a shirtless

Wyatt McCrae.

I meet him halfway. "Yes?" I ask.

He rubs his hand across his shoulder, pulling my attention to the intense bluebird tattoo that runs to the center of his chest. "Can you stick around for a few minutes?"

"Do you need me to come back for something?" I start to return to the band's dressing room, but he stops me.

"No, trust me, we're good. But Sin and I thought it would be a good idea to get someone to escort you to the stage?"

I fold my arms over my stomach. "I know how to find it."

"I bet you do, but you're on a lot of women's shit lists because you're with Lucas. Believe me, I would do the same thing if Kylie was here." When I try to get a word in, he continues, "And she wouldn't give me shit over something like this. Give David ten minutes, okay?"

"He's walking with me?"

Wyatt rolls his blue eyes, obviously irritated with all of my questions, but his voice is patient when he answers, "No, but he's calling someone on the radio to do it for him."

David ends up taking less than five minutes to find me an escort. The man introduces himself as Aaron, but after that, he's silent as he walks with me out of the backstage building toward the sound of Cilla Craig yelling into a microphone. Aaron doesn't leave until the security crew near the stage has cleared me to enter the pit, and I'm immersed in the crowd that's rocking out and screaming their heads off along with

Cilla.

Even though it's jam-packed out here, with sweaty bodies rubbing against me at every angle, I turn my face up to the stage and watch as she struts around and goes through the chorus of one of Wicked Lambs' more popular songs.

No matter how much I want to head-butt that woman 95% of the time, there's no denying just how talented she is, or how amazing she looks on stage in a lace-up corset top, tiny black shorts, purple fishnets stockings, and tall black leather boots. She doesn't seem to notice the groupies pressing themselves against the stage, shrieking her name at the top of their lungs, or how all around, there are cameras flaring as they snap photo after photo of her.

Toward the end of the song, as she scans the crowd, her blue-green eyes lower into the pit and lock with mine. At first, shock registers in her expression—this is the first time I've come out to see Wicked Lambs—but then a grin sweeps across her face. She winks at me before flipping her shock of black hair back and crooning the last line of

"Let's Get Messy."

The crowd goes crazy. As she catches her breath, Cilla seems to soak it all in, reveling in the worship. Once the thunderous applause begins to die down, she brings the mic up to her lips. "Wow," she sighs, her gritty voice sounding full of surprise. It sounds so genuine that I almost believe she is. "Can I just say that Dallas makes me so stupidly happy?"

"I fucking love you, Cilla," a girl screeches from nearby, and Cilla blows a kiss down to the pit before pulling in another long breath.

"Here's what's going on." Eyeing the crowd carefully, she begins to pace the width of the stage. "My manager is going to have my head for this shit, but I wanted to give you beautiful people an exclusive listen to something that hasn't quite made its way onto one of our albums."

Once again the audience erupts. A bulky guy standing nearby pitches into me, knocking me forward into two skinny blondes who cast me withering glares before refocusing on what Cilla has to say.

"Me and Brady sat down to write this back in—" She spins around for just a moment to face Brady, her lead guitarist, who mouths "March," before continuing, "Back in March. I'd just broken up with my cheating motherfucker of a boyfriend."

Somehow hearing those words come from a woman who's been slinking around with her lip poked out because of a man who's involved with another woman is ironic.

"So, let's go out with a bang." Cilla widens her stance. "This one's called 'Second

Best.'"

Crossing my arms over my chest, I listen as Brady plays the opening. The melody falls in line with most of Wicked Lambs' ballads, but the lyrics are just as punchy and cutting as the last song.

Other woman who needs to fuck off, check.

A man that the heroine scorns and yet, absolutely adores, check.

An entire verse dedicated to how, eventually, he's going to crawl back to her?

Yeah, that crap's there, too.

I know the song is about Lucas—I would be a fool not to figure that out—but it's not until she croons the final line that my slight irritation takes a giant leap over the line into pissed off. Her shimmery-lined eyes locate my blue eyes in the crowd again, and she leans into the microphone almost seductively. "I fucked him first," Cilla sings.

She holds my gaze for so long that the big guy next to me stares over and draws back, as if seeing me in a new light—a light that also turns Cilla into a victim. My skin feels like it's crawling as I watch her take a dramatic bow.

Then she puckers her red-painted lips at her fans. "Thank you, Dallas."

CHAPTER THIRTEEN

I feel like I'm on fire during the brief transition from Wicked Lambs to Your Toxic

Sequel, and I barely hear a word the emcee says.

Rather than leave and go backstage to where I'll most definitely run into Cilla, I stick around in the pit for Lucas' show. I don't feel any of that under-the-stars magic I was so excited about earlier this evening. Instead, I notice the bad and the ugly. Like when a drunk, red and black bikini-clad girl gets knocked into the stage. I flinch when she finally manages to pick herself up, and the entire lower portion of her face is covered in blood. Or when two men get into a shoving match over god knows what or who and security has to intervene and drag them away as they threaten to beat each other's ass.

The band doesn't seem the least bit phased by the pandemonium or the naked breasts, thong straps, and ass cheeks being flashed at them at every turn.

After the second to last song on the set is performed—which is one of their newer tracks called "Tumbles Down"—I start to leave the pit to avoid the flood of departing fans that will happen in about fifteen minutes.

It takes me twice as long as it did before to get backstage, and I find myself flashing my wrist more than normal until I've secured my spot in the VIP area. Tonight, both Wicked Lambs and Your Toxic Sequel are supposed be doing interviews with the press and then an acoustic show for a handful of their fans who upgraded their tickets to include the backstage pass.

As I push through the crowd to get to the hospitality room, I make up my mind not to say anything to Cilla. First, I've had an hour and a half to get some of my anger at her "I fucked him first" line out of my system. And second? It's not like this is something new to me. Still, admitting that makes my stomach feel like it's swallowing my chest.

But my resolve to stay quiet changes a few seconds after I enter the packed room.

Cilla's perched on the side of the plush armchair that Brady's sitting in, a red Solo cup tipped up to her mouth, and her face turned toward the entrance to the room. When her gaze lands on me—her prey—a satisfied gleam crawls into her eyes. She moves her lips, mouthing something slowly, but it's impossible for me to decipher it through the haze.

It's probably best I can't.

I have never wanted to hit someone so badly.

No, correction: I've never wanted to repetitively throat chop someone this much.

Her red lips widen as I stalk across the room to her. "Did you like the song?"

"Loved it." My voice is higher-pitched than normal, and I pray she doesn't notice.

"Especially the part where you seemed like a desperate bitch."

Cilla's lips flatten into a sneer. "You're really coming in here with that bullshit?" She glances back, probably to get some type of confirmation from Brady, but he's staring down at what's probably a non-existent message on his phone. Grunting in disgust, she scoots her butt off the chair. "I'm getting a drink."

If she thinks I'm anywhere near finished speaking to her, then she's sadly mistaken.

I'm right behind her as she makes a beeline to the adjoining room. There's a couple of crewmembers in here grabbing food, but Cilla pays them no mind as she slinks over to the refreshment table that holds the liquor. She snatches a plastic cup from the stack on the corner of the table and places the rim of it against her lips in amusement, her nails like talons against the plastic.

"Are you following me, Pepper? I guess this tour isn't complete without me getting a brand new stalker."

Cilla would say something so conceited.

"Trust me, you are the last person I'd ever want to stalk," I bite out through clenched teeth, earning a dramatic pout from her. "And if you think being a bitch, or letting me know that you've fucked my boyfriend in the past is going to make me turn around and go home, then you have another thing coming." With each word, I move closer to her until I'm standing less than six inches from her face. Up close, I can see that her lips are trembling.

She races her tongue over the center of them. "Mmm, the submissive has a backbone. You must drive Lucas up the wall with that type of shit." She reaches for a bottle of top shelf vodka, but I grab it first. She laughs coldly. "Just so you know, I don't give a shit if you're here or not."

"Right." I tilt my head to the side, sizing her up from the heels of her black, lace up boots to the strands of dark hair damp against her high forehead. "I'm sure you don't.

But just so *you* know, I'm not going anywhere unless Lucas asks me to."

She pries the bottle of vodka out of my grip, sloshing some on the front of my white strapless shirt. "Well if that's what you're waiting for, I guess you know exactly what to expect then, don't you? The only question you should have is when."

The only thing that stops me from flinching is just how hard I poke my nails into the palms of my hands. Cilla is watching me carefully for a reaction, trying to find my weak spot, and I refuse to give her the satisfaction of knowing that her bitter reminder of what happened in the past has stung me. I give her nothing but a distant smile that only confuses her and makes her shoulders hunch forward in defeat. Sometimes, the prey doesn't get eaten. Sometimes, the prey wins.

"Guess we both know our roles," I retort.

Her face flushed, she finishes pouring her drink in sharp, jerky movements. As soon as she's done, she raises the plastic cup in a shaky toast. "Enjoy the after-party, bitch."

I wait until she's gone to move even an inch. My hands are completely numb as I grab myself a miniature bottle of Coke from one of the side tables. Every muscle in my body feels taut, and I'm unable to keep from working my teeth together. For a long time, I stand by the spread of refreshments, clenching and unclenching my hand around the cold plastic, oblivious to the comings and goings of the band and crewmembers.

Finally, I feel a familiar, possessive touch flare across my hip. I inhale, drawing

Lucas in, but I don't dare look at him. Not just yet when I'm still seething.

"The show was incredible," I say flatly.

"Fuck the show, I care more about you stabbing someone in the eye with this thing." He plucks the bottle out of my hand and places it on the table. "Look at me, Sienna."

I'm reluctant to face him, but he pulls me around anyway. His look of concern changes the moment he's able to study my face. Lifting his head to the handful of people coming into this room, he barks, "Get the fuck out and close the door."

Like always, they comply, racing away to do his bidding.

And like always, I'm a little envious at how much control Lucas has over everyone around him.

He cradles my face between his long fingers and gives me a deep stare that causes my throat to go dry. "Tell me what the fuck is going on, Sienna."

I rake my bottom teeth over the corner of my lip. "I see why Sinjin thinks Cilla's the devil."

"Is she fucking with you?"

"Apparently I'm her new stalker."

Dropping his hands from my face, he draws back several inches. His breath bursts in and out until he demands, "She told you that?"

"Oh, and she wrote a song about screwing you, too." I duck away from him because I can't think clearly with him looking at me like this. With my back turned to him, I add, "Not sure if you've heard it yet, but yeah, you're kind of a big deal."

I brush past him, determined to be anywhere but in here, but he stops me before

I can leave the room, pinning me against the door. Before I can stop myself, I breathe in his scent, a seductive mix of cologne and the sweat still clinging to his skin from performing.

"Do you hold all your girlfriends hostage?"

"Only you. And trust me, Red, this isn't hostage. You would know if that were the case."

"I swear I'm fine, Lucas," I reassure him a little too loudly, because in the other room, Sinjin yells something about not being fine and dying of thirst.

"Don't stand there and try to feed me bullshit," Lucas says.

He attempts to draw me to him again, but I press my palms flat against his chest. He pulls them away easily, holding my wrists to my sides. "You are the only thing that matters to me," he growls against my lips, and I squeeze my eyes together tightly. "You are mine, and anything that hurts you, fucks with me."

Everything burns—my chest, the inside of my eyes from the tears that I'm trying desperately to hold back—but I nod anyway. "You have no idea how hearing that makes me feel. But, Lucas, I can hold my own."

Pressing his fingertips to the outer corners of my eyes, he exhales. "I know you can. But I'm still going to talk to Cilla." I open my mouth to protest, but he covers my lips with the tip of his finger. "I don't care if she's pissed off at me or not—she's not going to bring up old shit just to get a rise out of you. And me, too."

Jabbing my tongue into my cheek, I glare up at him. "That's probably what she wants, you know? For you to confront her."

"You're a perceptive little thing."

Once again he releases me, and I widen my eyes just in time to see him kissing the tip of his thumb. Before I can react, he leans into me, his mouth coming down on mine. I'm still frustrated, as I taste the salt from the tears he caught, and I push myself angrily against him. He lets out a rough groan as his lips hungrily devour mine.

"Oh, Sienna," he breathes. "What am I going to do with you?"

"I draw the line at sex in the refreshment room."

He strokes the backs of his fingers along the curve of my cheek. "I want to take you back to the bus and spend every moment from here until we get to Chicago tomorrow in that back room with you."

I shake my head. "And Sin would hear—and comment—on everything he hears."

He takes a step backward and then another, offering me a miserable, forced smile. "Exactly. And nobody else will give us a moment of peace either." As if to reiterate his point, someone bangs on the door. Groaning, Lucas shoots me an apologetic look. "When this is all over, I'm taking you home with me, and there won't be a thing that will pull me away from you."

Ugh. Only Lucas could confront me while I'm angry, diffuse the situation (sort of, at least) and end the conversation by leaving me anxious and anticipating our future.

"You done in there?" Sinjin yells, and for the first time, I witness Lucas gritting his teeth together.

"Frustrated, Mr. Wolfe?" I flick my nail over his nipple through his damp black Henley tee. He grabs my hand, sucking the tip of my

169

finger into his mouth, sucking my ability to breathe just right away from me.

"You'll find out when we get to St. Louis on Wednesday."

Shooting my eyebrow up, I step aside so he can open the door. A dozen flashes and voices seem to greet him all at once, but he's still able to hear me when I ask,

"What about Sinjin's party?"

Giving the crowd a cocky grin, he responds to me in a low voice. "We'll go. After I'm finished with you. I'll show you why it's impossible for me to even think of another woman, much less fuck her."

With those words, he steps into the hospitality room, his stride confident and sexy. I stay put for a couple minutes to calm my breath. Once I'm no longer so flustered, and my face is cool to the touch, I walk out after Lucas. He's in the center of the room, signing autographs and talking to the press, so I find a place in the corner away from the camera flashes.

When I scan my eyes around the room, I'm not shocked to see that Cilla has left early. Nor am I surprised that when Sinjin and I lock eyes, he's wearing the most satisfied expression that I've seen him manage so far this tour.

For the next forty-eight hours, Cilla steers clear of me, and I can't help but feel like that's a minor victory of its own. The only close encounter that we have is backstage in Chicago, when Maggie asks for my help again. After I pick out and deliver wardrobe to Your

Toxic Sequel, she tasks me with taking a box of vintage-looking necklaces to

Cilla's dressing room.

I dread doing it.

I loathe conflict—I witnessed enough arguments growing up to not want any of that in my adult life. And people like Samantha and Cilla—they're the type I've always avoided under any and all circumstances.

But surprisingly, when Cilla throws her door open, she's somewhat civil. She's wearing nothing but a strapless bra and lace boy shorts and has no problem showing off her curvy body as she poses in the doorway giving me a pointed stare. "Yes, Pepper?" she drawls.

I hold the box out to her, and she looks at it skeptically. "Maggie wanted you to have these. She said you wanted to wear them tonight." As soon as I say that, she snatches the package out of my hands, opens it up, and squeals like a little girl.

"Etsy is my crack." She dismisses me with a flick of her hand, but before she slams the door in my face, she pokes her head out and says, "Tell Maggie I said thanks."

"Yeah," I mutter. "You're welcome."

"You know," a voice says from beside me, and I look over at Cal who's guzzling an energy drink, "She's not the norm for female musicians."

Of course, I already know this, but I drop my mouth open in mock surprise. "So, you're telling me I shouldn't expect passive-aggressiveness and crazy mood swings?"

"Only if you're Cilla Craig."

"You sound almost as negative as Sinjin when it comes to her."

"No, not negative. But there are—and I shit you not—diseases that I'm more drawn to than Cilla."

Not negative my ass.

"Gross," I mumble.

Opening the door to the band's dressing room, he motions for me to go inside. "I speak nothing but the truth. She and I've never gotten along. She thinks I have a smart mouth," he continues, following behind me. He stops short as soon as he sees Lucas on the couch.

"I swear if you're still on her about that fucking body shot—" Lucas growls, but Cal quickly disappears inside of the restroom before he can finish. Lifting his hazel eyes to me, Lucas jerks his head slightly, motioning for me to come over. As soon as I reach him, he pulls me onto his lap so that we're facing each other, and I can feel his heartbeat drumming against my chest.

"Sin and Wyatt could come in at any moment," I point out. "And there's Cal, too."

He gives the sensitive spot on my sides a sharp squeeze, and I move my hips against him. He groans. "God, you better be ready for St. Louis tomorrow."

"No show, hotel bed, and a giant tub? Yes, yes I am."

"Remember what I told you in Dallas?" He massages his thumb against the side of my breast. It feels agonizingly amazing, and I suck in a little breath between my teeth. "About the thoughts running through my head?"

"Yes."

"Good."

172

Lifting me off of him, he gets up, and I slide back against the couch cushions. He walks out of the room, singing "Handcuffs"—one of the YTS songs I was introduced to earlier this year that had been written about my first encounter with Lucas. I'm glad Cal's in the bathroom, and Sinjin and Wyatt are nowhere to be found, so they can't see how hot my face is.

When Lucas returns, he's carrying a large vase of flowers—pink lilies, and red and white roses. "Funny." I bring my knees up to my chest. "I didn't take you for a flowers and candy type of guy."

He sets the vase down on the coffee table in front of me and then bends over me. Heat pools in the pit of my stomach, and I grip the seat cushions as he traces my features, each flick of his thumb drawn out and teasing. When he pulls away, he's wearing a knowing smile, and he dips his gaze between my legs.

He knows just how wet he's managed to get me in such a short amount of time.

Before he leaves the room again, he winks at me. "While I would love the credit, and the reward, those flowers are from my sister."

Pretending that every nerve in my body isn't on fire, I slide forward on the couch and pick the large white envelope from the cardholder addressed from Kylie Wolfe.

"Kylie, you are absolutely amazing—"

I stop speaking, though, the moment my eyes land on the words written in messy red ink on the crisp white card that I find inside of the envelope.

Sienna-

Congratulations, you're STILL with him. Maybe you're more of an idiot than I thought you were. At the end of the day, he will always be tied to me. It's just a matter of time before he crashes and you go down with him. Have you even asked him what it is he's keeping from you? Has he offered to tell you? S.W.

PS: Good luck with this.

Directly beside the last word, there's a crookedly drawn arrow, and I feel my stomach clench for a brand new reason as I shakily flip the card over. Written on the back of the note is a long website address, and I scan it carefully, committing it to memory.

It's for a YTS fan forum, and scribbled directly below it are the words **THIS SITE IS MY FAVORITE** written in all capital letters and underlined several times.

"That face, Red." Lucas' voice makes me start, and I fold the card back up, sliding it hastily into the envelope. "Didn't think Kylie would write something deep enough to make you look like that."

"It's not—" I begin, but then I stop myself. What good would giving this to Lucas do? If it were a letter from any crazy other than Sam, I would say something about it.

But the envelope sitting on my lap? This would only take us several steps backwards. Aside from his usual spurts of moodiness, Lucas has been happy for the most part during this tour. And that means that Sam hasn't been sending him shit like this.

Grasping the envelope, I clear my throat.

"It's not necessarily deep," I breathe. "She just made a really awkward sex joke."

To my own ears, the lie sounds obvious.

He seems to take me at my word, but as soon as Cal comes out the restroom, wet and in nothing but a towel, I lock myself inside. I stare at the note for a long time, my face burning, until I finally snap a photo of it, front and back, with my phone. Then, I rip the paper into the tiniest shreds my shaking fingers will allow. When I'm done, I flush the pieces down the toilet, determined to put it out of my mind.

But much later, when thoughts of Sam's cryptic message and her creepy gift of flowers keep me awake hours after the bus rolls out of Chicago, I find myself looking at the picture I took earlier. I take my laptop to the galley of the bus and start to Google the forum that Sam had mentioned, but then I freeze.

A few seconds later, I have Facebook pulled up on my screen and my fingers are flying across the keys as I search for Samantha Wolfe. There are several—looks like it's a common name—but after scrolling down a few times, I see her gray eyes and her sneer staring back at me. I'm not the least bit surprised to find that her profile is private, but it doesn't stop me from opening a new message window.

The second I hit send, guilt rushes over me, cold and numbing, and I glare at my message on the screen—a message that she's probably expecting—until the words meld together.

Samantha … Tell me the truth. Why are you doing this to him?

Taking a deep breath, I logout and finally look up the fan page. I last for a total of five minutes reading posts in a sub forum entitled "The Toxic Cunt" before I'm sick to my stomach. When Lucas finds me kneeling over the toilet in the tiny restroom stall dry heaving, he comes onto the floor next to me, his gorgeous face frowning in concern.

"You're sick?" he asks, but I splay my palm out on his chest and shake my head.

For the second time this evening, I have a chance to tell him exactly what's going on, but I can't bring myself to do it. Instead, I let him help me up and wrap my arms tightly around his neck when he lifts me up in his bare, tattooed arms.

He takes me back to our small bed, whispering into the crook of my neck, and I say nothing.

CHAPTER FOURTEEN

By the time we reach St. Louis this morning, Samantha hasn't responded to my message, so I push her note and the discovery of how fiercely some of Lucas' fans hate me to a dark corner in the back of my mind. I make myself a promise that I won't drag out the picture I took of the note for the next twenty-four hours or worry over whether Sam will message me back. Just thinking about Lucas' ex is toxic for me, and after witnessing only a glimmer of Sam's idea of communication, I'm starting to understand why Lucas chooses to avoid talking about her.

Today, I'll do my best to focus on the good.

As I peek out the blinds in the galley, I'm practically bouncing on the balls of my feet in anticipation of getting off our bus. Two of the other drivers have already maneuvered their respective buses into parking places. I watch as the rest of Your Toxic Sequel and Cilla's group start to unload. There's a white shuttle parked in between the buses and Wyatt ducks inside of it, lugging a giant green duffel bag.

Lucas slides up behind me, bending his head to tickle my shoulder with his full lips. "Are we taking the shuttle too?" I ask, shivering.

"We're not even staying at the same hotel. When I told you I wanted you all to myself, I had no intention of half-assing it." His voice slides over me like velvet. I turn my face sideways, and he strokes the outline of my face before nodding to the far end of the parking lot where a sleek, black 7-series BMW is parked. "I've dealt with the manager at the rental company—well, Kylie has on behalf of me—so they pulled some strings and made sure it was here for our arrival."

Our bus starts to beep, indicating that we're safely parked. In the center compartment, I hear a loud bang followed by an even louder string of curse words from Sinjin. As soon as I yell to ask him if he's okay and he snaps that he is, I meet Lucas' amused eyes. "So what about the key? Even Lucas-Fucking-Wolfe can't pull off driving a car with no key."

He smirks. "Since you have to know—they overnighted it to me." To prove his point, he pulls me by the wrist out into the aisle of the bus and dangles a key fob over the tip of my nose.

My thoughts shift to a few nights ago, at the Dallas show when he had locked himself in the restroom for the sake of a call. "How long have you been planning this?"

"A while."

I shake my head incredulously. "Do you always have to be difficult?"

"Always." He pulls me up against him, grinding his cock against the palm of my hand so I can feel his desire for me. The motion is rough, animalistic, and it makes me feel like the bus is spinning around. "Do you have to ask so many fucking questions?"

Breathlessly, I nod. "Always."

Our mouths inch closer together, but as soon as his lips begin to skim mine, Sinjin coughs loudly. He's bleary-eyed with his short black hair poking up all over the place. "It's six o'clock in the morning," he complains, yawning. "All I want is a real bed, not to watch you two about to fuck on the table I eat on."

Sin's interruption gives us the much-needed boost to grab our stuff so we can leave. I've packed an overnight bag with enough clothing to last me through tomorrow night. It's small in comparison to Lucas' enormous suitcase, but he carries both as we exit the bus. I tote my purse along with my Gibson guitar and my laptop, though I have no plans for music or work.

Or checking up on what's being said about me via the Internet, for that matter.

I shudder. "I will not think about that shit during this break," I repeat as I slowly follow behind Lucas across the parking lot. "I will not think about Sa—"

"If you click your heels together, Kansas, it might come true," Sinjin's teasing voice says from beside me, and I yelp.

Once my heart has calmed down enough for me to speak, I turn and jab him in his bony chest. "Don't. Do. That. And it's Tennessee."

Wincing, he runs his hand across the area my fingers poked. "You're abusive, but I've got to say, I'm going to miss you while we're on this break." By the look on his face, I don't exactly buy that, but I give him a sweet smile nonetheless.

"You'll get to see me tomorrow night. And besides, I'm sure you have plans tonight."

He waggles his jet-black eyebrows suggestively. "Two actually. Scarlet and

Bella."

My arm has started to get numb, so I rotate the guitar to my other side. "You do know that the way you just said their names makes them sound like strippers."

"Did you ever stop to think that maybe they *are* strippers?" His gaze slides past me to Lucas, who's closing the trunk of his BMW rental. Sinjin cups his hands over his mouth. "Don't do anything I wouldn't do," he shouts, and Lucas yells back for him to screw himself. When Sin looks at me again, he looks pleased with himself.

"Be careful, Sinjin. And be ... *safe*." I start for the rental car, but he hooks his fingers around my shoulder. He nudges me around to face him, his green eyes suddenly serious and no longer teasing. "Okay, you're freaking me out," I say.

"Then I guess I'll cut through the bull and give it to you straight. I'm not going to play dumb like I haven't seen some of the shit that's been posted online about you."

Shuffling my feet on the asphalt, I release a laugh that feels and sounds like jagged nails being scraped over a chalkboard. "Scouring the gossip sites to look for yourself, Sin? You've been an angel on this tour, so you probably won't find anything until after tonight."

The corners of his lips tighten into a line. "Cute, but no. You left your computer open in the galley last night." When my mouth drops open, he rolls his green eyes and huffs, "Look, it was a fucking invitation to snoop, and besides, I didn't click on anything."

I believe him when he says that. He'd probably seen what was pulled up and turned around to research that awful website on his own computer. It still doesn't make me any less annoyed.

"Thanks for going through my personal stuff," I snap. Across the parking lot, Lucas honks the BMW's horn, and I spin around halfway to hold up my finger. Sinjin responds with an entirely different finger. "Okay, so what's your point? Aren't you the one who told me I needed to suck it the fuck up?"

"I told you that you needed to suck the jealousy up. Dealing with crazy fucks is a whole new ball game. Whenever we have a beautiful woman around, we'll always have the crazies coming out right behind her. Case in point, Cilla's alleged stalker several years ago." He doesn't expand on Cilla but instead shoves his hand into his back pocket. When he withdraws it, he slips something short and slim that feels like a miniature flashlight into the palm of my hand.

"Bitches are crazy. Especially bitches that think they're in love with Lucas," he says.

Opening my hand, I look down. "You want me to pepper spray someone?"

He smiles serenely. "Like I said, lots of crazy people out there. They know Lucas is in town, and they will seek him out."

Gripping the pepper spray, I run my teeth over my bottom lip. This ... *gift* from

Sinjin tells me two things: That, even though it's highly unlikely, the shit talking on the YTS message boards could always take a nasty turn into real life. And that Sinjin, in all of his sulky glares and rude comments, has been worrying about me.

When I open my mouth to speak, I choose to focus on the latter. "I'm touched."

Narrowing his green eyes, Sin snorts. "If you get all sentimental on me, I'll skip the hotel and take both Scarlet and Bella to your compartment on the bus."

"Ugh." I drop the pepper spray into the bag that's slung around my shoulder. "You are foul." But then I clear my throat and in a sincere voice add, "Have an amazing day off, Sinjin."

His expression goes slack, depressed, and I pull back in surprise. "It'll be the best birthday eve I've ever had."

As I back up to the BMW, which Lucas has driven closer to us, I can't help but watch Sin as he returns to the bus for his belongings with a stooped posture. I'm quiet as we leave the parking lot, but after driving for a few minutes, Lucas' hand slides across my thigh, stopping to rest between my legs.

"Tell me about Sinjin," I ask, genuine curiosity behind the question.

"What about him?"

"Why he's so...."

"Tortured?" Lucas asks, a little too sarcastically.

Rubbing my hand over the delicate column of my throat, I nod. "It sounds so cliché, but yes, I guess that's the best way to put it."

The corners of Lucas' mouth curl down. "Because he came from a fucked-up family. An abusive stepfather. A drug addict mom." He pauses as the dashboard GPS tells him to take a left. "He didn't have someone like your grandmother to look out for him. Even after his parents lost custody, shit didn't get any better for him or his sisters."

"Is Zoe one of his sisters?"

Lucas' head whips around, startling me. "Why do you ask that?" When I don't immediately answer, he shakes his head slowly. "She's a woman he met in rehab."

My mouth drops open. "So, she's still there, then?"

Lucas grips the steering wheel until his knuckles turn white. "She's not a drug addict," he explains in a low voice. "She's his therapist's nineteen-year-old daughter. To say that Sinjin is conflicted about it is an understatement. But I'm starting to think it's the best goddamn conflict he's ever faced. He's clean."

Yes, but Sinjin is also unhappy.

Resting back against the seat, I turn my head to the side, staring out at the

Gateway Arch and the buildings beyond it until they all become one massive blur. I don't speak again until Lucas pulls the rental car up to the front of our hotel, and that's to thank the valet who holds my door open for me. Someone from concierge greets us almost as soon as we walk inside, and instead of the elevators just off of the right of the lobby, we're directed to a separate part of the hotel, to the penthouse elevator.

"If there's anything that I, or the rest of the staff here at The Avery, can do to make your stay more enjoyable than the last time, please don't hesitate to let us know," the short, balding man acting as our escort says before Lucas and I step onto the elevator.

As soon as the doors slide closed, I lean back against the corner, cocking an eyebrow at Lucas who's swiping his keycard to start the elevator car. "More enjoyable than the last time," I repeat.

"Do you know how sexy you look when you make that face?" he demands, taking slow steps toward me. I wrap my fingers around the cold metal bar behind my body. "And before that beautiful head of yours starts to wonder, no. No other woman has ever been inside of this box with me since you and I reconnected."

"I wasn't going to ask," I whisper. He pins me against the elevator wall, and I let out a moan of pleasure as he skims his teeth over my earlobe. "I mean, I don't care.

And we shouldn't do this here—there are cameras."

"There you go with the lying again," he growls. "And do you think I give a fuck about the cameras?" He kisses around the outline of my face until he finds the sensitive flesh at my throat, and I swallow hard. "You taste so good. So sweet. All I can think about is tasting more of you."

Without warning, he hooks his hands under my thighs and lifts me up. I let out a shriek and straddle my legs around his waist. "Of course you care about cameras," I whisper, as he glides his tongue over the delicate bones of my shoulder blades. "You of all people *should* care about them."

My head is spinning and if not for the loud warning noise, I wouldn't have even noticed that the elevator has stopped on the top floor of the building.

"When I take you into this room, you are completely mine," he says, his voice rough and intense. "No tour talk, no Cilla. Just me and you."

He doesn't mention Sam, but I think of her for the briefest moment. Once again, I vow not to let the little bit of contact she's had with me ruin my time with Lucas. I'll be home in Nashville this weekend, and I want to savor every moment I have with him alone.

"Alright. I promise."

"I'm going to hold you to that, Red," he tells me in a dangerous voice.

He carries me inside the penthouse, not setting me down until we reach the large, circular couch in the middle of the room. It's a rich, mahogany brown leather sectional where each piece has been slid together to make one round surface. Scooting myself back, I look around, trying to become better acquainted with where I'll be staying for the next thirty-six hours.

As always, Lucas sprung for the best, and the room looks more like an upscale apartment than a hotel room. There's a neutral color scheme going on in here—rich shades of brown, tan, and cream. Directly across from the couch is a bar with a gleaming sand-colored granite countertop. To my left, closed French doors are bordered by ornate molding, leading to what I assume is the bedroom. And to my right sits the centerpiece of the room. A Steinway piano. Memories of the night in Nashville when he bent me over the same model claws its way into my thoughts.

Memories of his cocky grin and the way he pressed his body up against mine, daring me to beg him to take me to bed.

"Take me all the way, Lucas," he'd said to me, as my palms pressed against the piano keys. *"And that's what you're going to say the first time we fuck. My name. Just Lucas."*

"This feels familiar." I try to keep my tone teasing and light, but my words come out husky and laced with need. "Lucas, I—"

"It's supposed to." Taking my hands in his, he pulls me up until I'm sitting on my knees and our bodies are rubbing together. He frames my face with his hands, his calloused thumbs stroking my cheeks. "Play for me."

185

I feel his hot gaze following me as I walk to the piano, and a shiver of anticipation creeps through my body as I sit down at the bench. I haven't taken lessons in years— since I was a child—but I still have a decent ear and a good memory. I play the first three chords of "Crave It," one of Your Toxic Sequel's most popular songs, but Lucas immediately stops me by lightly clearing his throat.

"Something else. Something I don't have to hear every night."

Hovering clenched fingers over the keys for a moment, I scan my brain for the perfect song to perform for him. Finally, I close my eyes and play the opening notes of

"Fade Into You." He listens in absolute silence, though when I reach the second verse, I feel his touch on my shoulders and I move my head to the side until my cheek brushes the back of his hand.

Before I can play the final chords for the chorus, his hands slide down my arms, until they cover mine, and he links our fingers together. He bends, brushing my ear with his lips as he whispers, "The couch, Sienna. I want you on the couch."

"And if I say no? If I told you—"

Carefully, he pulls me up and around to face him. Pinning my arms over my head, he covers my mouth with his, kissing me hard, rough, and fast until it's hard for me to catch my breath. I stumble backwards, the backs of my legs hitting the bench behind me once he lets my arms go, but he shakes his head. "No questions, Sienna."

I could argue with him. I could ask him *why* just to see what inventive punishment he'll come up with this time, but I don't. Keeping my eyes trained on his, I comply, walking around him. I climb on slowly and scoot forward until the front of my body is touching the backrest of the couch.

"Do you know what I realized?" His fingertips slip beneath the soft cotton of my shirt, and I hold my breath as he urges me to raise my arms so he can draw it over my head. "I was wrong about the bus."

I look back at him. "What?"

"I can't touch you like I want. Can't drive you crazy every time you grind those damn teeth of yours." He spins his fingers in a circular motion, and I turn back around to face the floor-to-ceiling windows that extend along the entire back wall of our suite. "I'm going to spend this entire fucking day inside of you, tasting you, touching you. Do you understand?"

I nod, gasping a moment later when he unhooks my bra with one well maneuvered snap of his fingers. "If you rip another bra, I'll have your—"

"God, you talk too much." When he comes up behind me on the couch, I slide forward until my bare breasts are pushed flat against the cushions. He drapes my bra— which is still completely intact—over the back of the couch. "See, no rips."

Pushing my hair away from the nape of my neck, he runs his straight nose along the sensitive area between my shoulder blades. "You smell so good—so right. Did you know that?" When I make a movement with my head that's neither acknowledgment nor denial, he chuckles against my skin. "I'm going to finish undressing you now."

"Yes, please."

As he removes the rest of my clothes, his touch varies. He's gentle when he unfastens my shorts, his fingertips careful and soft as they run along the inside of my thighs, but then when he reaches my panties, he's rough. He rips them into two uneven pieces as soon as his thumb makes contact with the dampness in the center.

By the time I'm naked, gripping the back of the couch hard, I'm trembling. He slides off of the couch, and when I try to see what he's doing, he gives me a rough slap on my ass.

"Turn around, Sienna."

Sinking my teeth into my lip, I whip my head back around, staring out the window as the first drops of sunrise splash across the sky. He rummages through his luggage for a few minutes, and when I hear him zip everything closed, my body shivers in anticipation.

When he returns, he's naked, and he drops something on the couch before touching my shoulders. His hands trails down my arms until he reaches my wrists and has brought my hands together behind my back

I wait for him to bind my hands.

Then, he surprises me.

Releasing my wrists, he grabs whatever it is he brought back to the couch. When he touches me again, cold leather wraps around my right thigh. I glance down my body just in time to see him hook the cuff, using the metal clasp found on the inside of my leg to stretch it taut across my skin.

"What is this?" I gasp, as he does the same thing to my left thigh.

"These," he starts, taking my right wrist and placing it against the outside of my leg, "are bondage cuffs." To demonstrate, he unhooks a separate, smaller cuff that's attached to the outside of the leather. I try to slow my erratic breathing as he tightens it around my wrist and secures it. "Because you couldn't keep those hands of yours out of my fucking hair the last time I had you all to myself."

I give his leather contraption a test as soon as he's secured my left wrist, and sure enough, I can't move my arms.

A heavy wave of desire rolls through me, and when I drop my head forward so that my forehead rests against the back of the couch, he gives my ass another tap.

"Stand up," he orders, moving away from me.

Carefully, I slide backwards. When I nearly lose my footing getting up, he reaches out and grabs me. "Thank you," I whisper.

"Turn around."

As soon as we're facing each other, he cups my breast, rubbing my sensitive nipple between his thumb and forefinger until my breasts are tight and heavy. "You are the most beautiful thing I've ever seen. The most beautiful thing that's ever happened to me."

"So are you," I murmur, gaining a tiny smile from him, and he kisses my forehead. When he leans back, his lips move into a wicked smile that shakes me to my core.

"I want you everywhere, every way." The emphasis he puts on those last two words makes me gulp.

"Every way," I repeat, and he paces around me in a slow circle, giving my ass a harsh squeeze on the way.

"I'm your first," he says, and it's more a statement than a question. Of course, he is. Before him, I would have never let the thought cross my mind because it felt like forbidden territory.

But now...

"Yes," I reply breathlessly.

"Good." As he comes around in front of me, running his hand along my flat stomach, he gives me a serious look. "You have to tell me it's what you want. Just say the word, Sienna."

This is similar to the game he played in February. He had seduced me to the point of distraction, and the only way he would make love to me was for me to beg. Back then, I had waited too long, played too hard, and I'm not in the mood for any of those games today.

I keep my eyes on his, too shaken to risk a glance at his cock—if I do, I'll never have the nerve to go through with this. "I want you to fuck me everywhere," I whisper.

He runs his tongue over his perfectly straight teeth. "Hearing you say that makes me want to start right here."

"Then you should follow through."

He shakes his head as he kneels in front of me, running his hands down the outsides of my legs until he reaches my ankles and then back up the insides. When he comes to the leather strapped to my thighs, he nudges my legs apart. Wider and wider—so far that I have to arch against him to hold myself upright.

Without warning, two of his long fingers delve inside of me, testing my wetness. He pushes them in and out, not stopping until I'm shaking, and my long red hair is falling over both of our faces.

"Please," I cry out, and he turns his face to kiss the soft flesh between my legs.

"Please, Lucas."

He touches my clit, working it back and forth between the two fingers that were just inside me. "You've never been this wet."

No, I haven't been, and I feel like I'm on fire as he teases me even more.

"Ah fuck," he growls at last. In one swift motion, he has me on my back on the couch. Urgently, he slides my feet backward until my legs are bent at the knees. He dips his head between my thighs and licks me hard. "Your body drives me crazy, you beautiful girl. You taste like..." Instead of choosing a word of praise, he uses his mouth, hungrily plunging his tongue deep inside of me.

A moan of pleasure tears from the back of my throat.

"God, Lucas." I shudder as he replaces his tongue with two of his fingers. He pumps them frantically in and out of my body as his teeth find my clit. When he sucks me into his mouth, I buck my hips wildly against his face.

I can feel the orgasm building, can feel the frenzy shifting through me, and then I feel something new. Gasping, I start to sit up as his thumb presses against my ass.

"Do you still want this?" he demands roughly, and I nod in a mixture of fear and frustration.

"Just ... please."

He's careful, but I still cry out in pain and pleasure as his finger slides inside of me, and a moment later, I feel his chest against mine and his shaggy, dark hair falls into my face. Spreading my slick folds apart with his erection, he fills me, muffling my moans with his lips, his tongue. Letting me taste myself on him.

I meet each of his thrusts, rocking my hips against his as his fingers and cock move greedily within me. When I reach up to grip his shoulders, my hands don't move, and I scratch the outside of my own thighs instead.

"You tricky bastard," I gasp, and he laughs wickedly against my mouth.

"I love you, Sienna," he growls. "I love you more than I've ever loved anything in my goddamn life."

When we let go together, and he pulls and unhooks the straps around my thighs, I wrap my arms around his shoulders and bury my face into his neck. "God, I love you, too."

CHAPTER FIFTEEN

Lucas

It takes a great deal of self-control not to wake Sienna the next morning, just so I can feel her once more before going to our sound check. Yesterday and last night weren't nearly enough. After I've showered and dressed, I sit beside her on the bed in the master bedroom. She's lying flat on her stomach, with the silky white bedspreads wrapped messily around her naked body.

I touch the small of her back, roaming my fingers over her soft skin. She whispers something incoherent that makes me smile. That's one of the things about Si that makes her so irresistible, so different from any other woman I've ever been with. She always makes me smile. Gives me a touch of that warmth that I'm still getting used to. Makes me want to come into the light.

Finding a pen and a pad of paper in the nightstand drawer, I write her a quick note:

Sound check at the venue. Order anything you want.

Then, kissing her smooth shoulder, I force myself to leave her there. As I take the elevator down to the lobby, I make a vow to spend as much of this afternoon as possible in that bed before I have to go back on the road, and she has to fly home to

Nashville.

To my surprise, I'm the last one to make it to the venue. My bandmates give me knowing looks as I walk onto the stage, and I shake my head. "If you say a goddamn word, I'll throw you into the pit," I threaten, causing Wyatt to snort.

"Looks like your night wasn't shit," he mutters as he slings his blue Kramer around the front of him. His nostrils flare. "Getting your sister to give me a break is like talking to a brick fucking wall."

Throwing my head back, I laugh. He doesn't know it yet, but Kylie's already decided to meet up with us in a few stops. I'd talked to her at the end of last week, right before the Dallas show, and had convinced her to give it a shot. She claimed her decision was mainly because she wants to see our parents when we play in Atlanta, but she's not fooling me with any of that bullshit. She can see our mother and father at any time.

She's drawn to everything about being on tour—the venues, the crowded bus,

Wyatt McCrae.

Fear of coming on this tour just to see Wyatt stepping out on her is what held her back in New Orleans in the first place. And now that word has gotten back to her from her friends on the crew that McCrae is succeeding at keeping his dick in his pants, she wants to be around again.

Sinjin stalks between Wyatt and me, whipping a set of his drumsticks from the back pocket of his jeans. "Let's do this shit so I can get back to my room."

"Rough night?" I ask, and he twists in a complete circle, shrugging.

"Spent too much money on booze and ended up kicking two drunk bitches out of my room." He slams down behind his drums and scratches one of the sticks across his temple. It draws my attention to his bloodshot eyes. "So, I'd say it was shit."

Since we're all tired and desperate to get back to our hotels, this is the first time since the start of the tour that one of our sound checks goes down without a single hitch. As soon as we're done, and I've let Tyler know I'll be around backstage for Sin's party tonight, I leave the building with David trailing a few steps behind me. Just before I reach my rental car in the parking lot, Wyatt yells for me to slow the hell down.

He's never been one to beat around the bush, so when he starts off the conversation hesitantly by asking David to leave, I know it's going nowhere good. Once

David's gone, Wyatt looks at me and says, "Cal and me were talking about stopping in

Louisville before we go to—"

"Louisville's not on the tour schedule," I say. "Last minute shit never works out."

He sits down on the front of the black BMW. "Are you fucking with me? Tyler could call any venue in this country right this goddamn minute, and we'd be booked before he finished the pitch."

There's no doubt in my mind about that. Still, I'm not going to Louisville. I had stayed the fuck away from that place the last time we went on tour two years ago, and I have no intention of making an effort this time. "Then you, Cal, and Tyler go. I won't."

"Cilla was all for it."

Hearing that doesn't do anything but make me see even more red. She spent most of her time drunk so why the hell would she remember anything that happened the last time we were in Louisville. Which to me, is frustrating, considering there's a video of her online from four years ago, bitching at the audience of the venue we played in that night.

Wyatt moves his head expectantly, and I give a tight smile.

"Then, let me rephrase that: You, Cal, and Tyler go and take Wicked Lambs with you."

It wouldn't be the first time he and Cal took off to do shit with another band, and

I'm sure as hell it won't be the last.

Wyatt holds up his hands defensively. "It's not a big deal so pipe the fuck down."

But it is. And I need to get out of here because I can feel my head starting to pound. This entire conversation is about to rip apart the rest of my day. Without another word, I stalk around to the driver's door of the BMW.

Wyatt has the good sense to jump off the front of the rental. He backs away, hooking his hands behind his head. I don't spare him a second glance as I speed out of the parking lot.

I don't know St. Louis as well as I do some of the other cities I've toured in, but that doesn't stop me from driving around with the GPS turned off. I won't go back to The Avery—not just yet— because I refuse to treat Sienna like shit just because I'm pissed off. I

drive through the city until I'm as relaxed as I'll ever be today. Because of a traffic jam, I get back to the hotel later than I planned.

Concierge stops me in the lobby to inform me that I've missed checkout, so I sign the paperwork to authorize another night's stay on my credit card (and sign an autograph for the attendant's son) before taking the penthouse elevator up to the top floor.

"I'm back," I yell as soon as I walk into our suite, but she doesn't respond. Dragging my t-shirt over my head, I toss it on top of the rich brown granite counter of the bar along with the keys to my rental car. "Sienna?" When she still doesn't say anything, I figure she's still asleep. I make my way across the penthouse quietly.

But as I stride past the French doors leading to the bedroom, I freeze up because of the noise coming from inside the slightly cracked doors.

It's the sound of music—more specifically my music, "All Over You"— being strummed painstakingly on an acoustic guitar. Carefully, I push the left side of the doors open. She's sitting up against the headboard with the guitar in her lap, covering her beautiful naked body. She doesn't realize that I'm standing here, and I'm not prepared to let her know that I am just yet.

Watching her is much too tempting.

The way she grinds her teeth in irritation when she attempts to master a difficult chord. How her long red hair falls over her pink cheeks and lips and the front of the Gibson when she manages to play for longer than fifteen seconds without making a mistake. And the way she sighs and closes her blue eyes right before she does it all over again.

I watch her, and I feel my cock harden at the sight of this incredibly sexy creature that is completely naked in my temporary bed, playing the guitar that I had given her.

"Did you know," I start, and her head flips up. Her eyes widen with surprise that, only a moment later, morphs into shyness—one of those unsure looks that dragged me to her in the first place. She brushes her hand back through her hair self-consciously, and my gaze zeroes in on her flushed neck. "That I could have the shittiest day, and then I come within a hundred feet of you and everything changes?"

Flicking her tongue over her lips, she bounces the guitar nervously on her knee.

"You're having a bad day? Is everything alright?"

"It's perfect now." Making myself relax, I reach the bed in three long strides where she presses her hand to my chest, scraping her fingernails softly over the tattoo in the center. "Wyatt wanted to hit a city that's not on the tour. We won't be going."

She lays her red guitar pick on the nightstand next to a tray of half-eaten food.

"So, why don't you want to go to—?"

"Louisville," I growl, even though she's the last person I want to bring it up to. The only reason I tell her now is because she can easily ask Cal or Wyatt or even Sinjin, and they would gladly tell her that I've been avoiding that place like the plague since we toured there several years ago. "And I abso-fucking-lutely won't go."

Dipping her head down, she seems to digest this for a moment before she gives me a questioning stare. "Why not? I love Louisville."

"Because we've got plenty of cities lined up already, Red." My voice is harsher than I intend it to be, and she recoils sharply. "Look, Si, this tour is getting to me. I'm not going to add more stress to it," I reply, my tone softer.

Sitting next to her, I run my gaze up her smooth, bare legs as she fidgets with the neck of the guitar. "What about the tour is getting to you?" she asks hesitantly.

I cup her cheek, and she rubs her face back and forth across the heel of my palm, her slight movement causing a jolt in my arm. Touching her always feels so fucking right for me.

"Lucas?"

"Mmm, let's see. Not getting to do what we did last night." A flush warms up her body, from the inside of her pale thighs to her tits, and I take the guitar and put it aside. I allow myself to drink in the sight of her delicious body before I say, "Being on that damn bus." Dampening the tip of my thumb with my tongue, I rub it over one of her nipples until it hardens.

She sucks her breath between her teeth. "The bus is like a luxury home on wheels," she reminds me.

"A luxury home on wheels we have to share with someone who drums on everything he passes by," I add, focusing my attention on her other nipple. "Then there's the shit food."

Turning her head to the side, she struggles to keep up a straight face as I squeeze her soft flesh hard, rolling it between the tips of my fingers. "Most of the venues serve you guys amazing food." When I give her a skeptical look, her lips part into a tortured smile. "I didn't say all, just most." Pushing her body closer to mine so that I'm able to smell the sweet scent of the soap she used, her eyes search mine. "Is that it?"

I drop my hand from her breast. "Yeah, that's all."

"Are you … sure?"

It's almost like she wants to say something herself, and I feel a sharp pain in my chest because I think I know what it is. Sinjin had pulled me aside the other day about some of the shit being written about her online. I've been able to get a lot of it taken down, but there will be more to come. There always is. More than anything, I want to shield her from it and all of the other negativity that comes with what I do.

What I've done.

But I also don't want to push her away by flying off the handle.

When she speaks, her voice has dropped an octave, and it's seductive, teasing.

Caressing all over me like a naked body, which is what follows a few seconds later. "Then let me love you, Lucas."

After our show that night, Sinjin's new record of being on time is shot all to hell when he fails to show up backstage to the party that Tyler and the publicity director for the venue are co-hosting for his birthday. Just about everyone is in here—both bands and most of the crew (minus the few that Sin's cussed out and blew up on during the pill-popping days)—and Tyler's went all out with one of those big ass cakes that make me think a stripper is going to pop out at any second.

Knowing Sin, a stripper probably will, and he'll bring her back to the bus with him in hopes that she'll make him forget Zoe—a girl he refuses to let himself have.

"Should you call him?" Sienna asks nervously, after she comes back from the restroom. I know she's been out in the hallways looking for him, and I've got to admit it's a relief she gets along with him after the bad blood between them earlier this year. He's been treating her with the same protective ferocity that he shows my sister since the first week of the tour, and I don't think it has anything to do with me threatening him anymore. "Should *I* call him?"

"It's Sin." I drag her down onto my lap. Her face reddens, and she glances around to see if anyone is looking at us on the couch. I touch her chin to turn her gaze back to mine. "Relax. They all know you're with me, and I don't give a fuck what any of these people think. About what *anyone* thinks. Let them talk."

"*We* were talking about Sinjin," she points out, awkwardly putting her hands against my shoulders.

Casting an amused look at her wrists on each side of my chest, I grin. "He'll show," I promise.

When he does show up a half an hour later—which is after Tyler blows up his phone with text messages—Sin's got a short, cute blonde on his arm. Her brown eyes dart around the crowded room anxiously. She looks familiar, though I can't place her, and when Sienna asks me if it's one of the women he was talking about taking to his hotel last night, I shrug.

"I think things went to shit with them, but this wouldn't be the first time he changed his mind." And it wouldn't be the first time a woman came right back to him after he acted like a dick.

Maybe, and I feel like a piece of shit for admitting this, that's why Sin and I understand each other so much.

Sinjin makes the rounds of the room to talk to everyone. When he gets to Cilla and Brady, who are a few feet away from us talking to Maggie in wardrobe, Cilla stops her conversation. Holding up her hand in front of Brady's face to silence him, she blurts,

"So which one is this, Sin?"

"None of your fucking business." Realizing his mistake, Sin attempts to lead the blonde away from the situation. "Come on, let's—"

She shrugs out of his grip and faces Cilla. "I'm sorry, what?"

Cilla cocks her head to the side, sizing the other woman up with narrowed blue-green eyes. "I met you and your roommate in the lobby last night, right?" She snorts.

"Did *not* think you'd be around tonight."

"I don't think we've met," the blonde states in a cool voice. Her chest is rising and falling quickly, and beside her, Sin's face is unreadable. "I'm Zoe Whitlow—one of

Sinjin's friends from back home."

Sienna sucks in a sharp intake of air just as I jump up from my seat. He's about to lose it.

"Give me a sec," I tell Sienna. She's nodding as I take off toward Sinjin, and when I reach them, instead of speaking to him or Zoe, I place my hand on the middle of

Cilla's back.

"What are you doing?" she demands as I lead her from the room and into the hallway.

"Keeping you from making a bigger ass of yourself."

"See, you do care." She struggles to lean against me, and I'm surprised when I don't smell any alcohol on her breath. And I'm disappointed, too. She knew exactly what she was doing back in there with Sin. "Ask Pepper to leave yet?" I grip her shoulders to hold her at bay. "Afraid not."

"Then what the hell do you want?" she shouts.

I lean back angrily. The thing is, Cilla wasn't always like this—she was vain and a little erratic, but never like this. The last several years she's gotten worse. Bitter. I regret letting her beg me into coming to her own birthday party early this year because it had put an end to my long break from her.

I need that space again.

When I speak, I grind the words out, "Stay the fuck away from Sinjin tonight."

She's mastered the art of bullshitting so well that she's able to quickly slap a blank look on her face—from her vacant bluish-green eyes to her parted lips. She blinks a few times. "What?"

I don't have the patience to do this shit with her today or any other day.

"I'm done with you," I say, disgusted.

I drop my hands away from her shoulders and turn to leave, but she digs her fingers into my shirt frantically. "What is that supposed to mean?"

Removing her hand, I sneer at her. "I don't know how to make it any clearer. Personally. Professionally. I can't do this shit with you."

She swallows hard and rakes her hands over her face. "All because I made a little joke and screwed around with Sinjin's little girlfriend?"

"Because if not every man in the room that you've ever fucked doesn't throw themselves at your feet, you go on a path of destruction. Because you enjoy misery. I think that's the worst part, because it reminds me of my ex-wife." I quirk my lips into an angry smile. "And I try to stay away from all things Samantha."

Tears pool at the inside corners of Cilla's eyes, ruining her makeup, but I don't buy her act for a second. "Look, I'm sorry."

"Don't tell me that." Leaning into her again, I jab my finger toward the entrance of the room. Even from out here, I can see that Zoe's not standing as close to Sinjin. That he looks like he's just a moment away from a breakdown that would set him back months, years. "Take your destructive ass in there and tell it to him or her."

She gives me that skittish look she gets whenever she's confronted, and I almost think she's going to do the right thing and speak to Sin to make everything right. But instead, she spins around on her heels and stalks off in the other direction toward the dressing room she used earlier tonight.

"Tell Tyler to text me when my bus is ready to roll out," she shouts.

CHAPTER SIXTEEN

Sienna

"Okay, spill, how much of that stuff have you done already?" my friend Ashley demands, popping the top off of a beer with the bottle opener attached to the world's largest set of keys.

It's Saturday night, and I've been back in Nashville since yesterday afternoon. Ashley had texted me right at 10:30—while I was in the shower—to ask if I wanted to come to karaoke night at her parents' downtown bar, The Beacon. Since Gram had gone to bed an hour earlier, and I haven't seen Ashley in a few weeks, I immediately accepted the invitation.

After the day I've had, I needed to do this for myself.

I had worked for twelve hours only to come home and find that not only had Lucas' ex sent me a one-worded letter—"Cunt"—to my *house* and she'd responded to my Facebook message by reporting it, but I also had an email from one of my clients asking me to cancel all of her upcoming appointments indefinitely.

"Sienna?" Ashley jerks my thoughts away from the note and back into the jam-packed bar and bad singing—a high-pitched rendition of Florence Welch's "Howl" at the moment.

"How much of what stuff?" I ask, mustering a teasing grin.

She rolls her eyes up toward the exposed piped ceiling that gives the small bar an industrial feel. "You know exactly what I'm talking about." When I say nothing, she groans and rests her chin on her closed fist. "Oh come on, don't tell me you haven't done any of them."

I think of the list she gave to me before I left Nashville a few weeks ago and how many items I've scratched off so far. "I have about four or five to go—and no, I'm not doing a body shot off Cal." When Ashley's lips purse into a thin, disappointed line, I hold out my hands in defense. "I *think* I'll get through them before the tour is over. I mean, there are three weeks left. And don't forget, they'll be here in twelve days."

Just as I hope, mentioning Your Toxic Sequel's upcoming show in Nashville shifts the conversation. Ashley casts me a grin and claps her hands excitedly. "I have a countdown on my phone." She shakes her head. "Ugh, I know. I'm pathetic—I'm the biggest fangirl who ever lived."

After seeing some of the band's other fangirls in action, I seriously doubt that, but I don't say that to Ashley. "And maybe while they're here, you can finish up your own damn bucket list," I tell her in a low voice.

Running her hands through her multi-colored hair, she rolls her eyes dramatically. "Where's the fun in that?"

My phone buzzes once in the center of the table, alerting me to a new message.

I flip it over to reveal a text from Lucas. I've been waiting for him to respond to me since I came home from my job, and my smile must give me away as I open it. Ashley lets out a low whistle.

"I could ask you so many questions, but you're already bright red, so I'll bug you more about your job today. Inquiring minds want to know, will this new reality show be worth watching? Is it the Jersey Shore of Music City?"

"It was … boring. Well, the job was. I'm not sure what the show will be like." I don't say anything about my other client's cancellation. I've been working with this woman, a politician's wife, since I started my wardrobe consulting business. Her email had been two lines, mostly stating that due to my "other work in the public eye," she saw it fit to discontinue her association with me.

It stung enough for me to sit staring at my computer screen for several minutes afterward.

I had started to message her back to ask if it was because of the hundreds of pictures of Lucas and me circulating the Internet, or if she took a peek into the various YTS fan sites that have smeared my name with every lie imaginable.

Like an idiot, I took a look at one of the websites—*Everything YTS*—after dinner tonight to discover that there's a good chance I'm pregnant. I'm positive that by tomorrow morning, that will have changed, and I'll have betrayed Lucas with a secret abortion. Or that the baby will turn out to be Cal's or Sin's, or hell, maybe even Kylie's.

If it wasn't so sad, and undeniably scary, I would probably laugh.

"God, girl, you've been spacing out since you walked in here tonight," Ashley complains. "I just said that boring is good, but I'm sure there's none of that being on the road." She fidgets anxiously with the rim of her beer bottle, and it's obvious that she has a question about Your Toxic Sequel and the tour.

Since I feel like crap for being such awful company tonight, I wait until a couple passes by to say to her, "Okay, shoot."

Plunking her hands down flat on the table, she leans in close. "Cilla Craig?"

I consider my words carefully, but then I shake my head. Screw being nice. "The devil in fishnets and MAC lipstick."

"I knew it. I *knew* it!" Ashley sits up straight and takes a sip of her beer, wrinkling her pierced nose at the taste. "Ugh, we're never ordering this crap again. It's like cold piss." She slides the nearly full bottle to the edge of the table. "So, this will be the first time I've actually seen the Lambs live because I've been scared Cilla would throw a mic off stage or some other equally crazy crap."

When my eyebrows furrow, and I motion for her to keep talking, she says, "There's a video of her on YouTube at a show in Louisville when she toured with YTS a few years back. She went *off* on that audience. Like throwing ice cubes, screaming, and threatening."

I still have a vivid image in my head of Cilla calling Sinjin out in front of Zoe two nights ago, and the back of my throat burns. "Why am I not surprised?"

"Anyway, I—" Ashley's cut off when Nick, one of the doormen, drops by our table and whispers something into her ear. When he leaves, her lips are twisted to one corner. "Shit, one of the bartender's kids is sick, so she's got to leave early. Give me twenty, okay? I'm going to try to see if someone else will come in."

But I move my head from side to side and scoot off the barstool. "I need to get home. I fly out tomorrow morning, and I've got an early breakfast with Seth and Gram."

Ashley hops off of her own seat. "Have fun," she says loud enough to drown out the sound of the tipsy guy slaughtering a Kesha song on stage. She makes it two steps before she whips back around, tapping her finger against her lips. "Before I forget, when will you be back in town again?"

"Five days from now." I would be sticking around in Nashville until Your Toxic Sequel brought their show to town because I've been lucky enough to contract more work with the crew I dealt with today. I have a private client too, but after the email from earlier, who knows if that will pan out. "We'll have to make plans to do something."

Ashley gives me a very 80s-inspired fist pump. "Alright, it's a date. I'll see you then, and if the only thing left on that list isn't involving Cal's belly button... So help me, Sienna."

Forcing a laugh, I promise that I'll do my best to deliver.

Fifteen minutes later, after I step into Gram's house and lock up the door behind me, a chill hits me at full force when I think about something Ashley had said tonight. I creep quietly up the stairs. As soon as I duck into my sweltering bedroom, I kick off my jeans and head straight to my computer to Google Cilla's Louisville rant.

It's the second item that pops up on the search engine—right under an article about a man who was mugged in the parking lot during the Wicked Lambs show in

Louisville.

I click on the video.

For a total of five minutes and thirty-nine seconds, I watch in horror as Cilla sobs her way through a song before telling the audience to go fuck themselves and finally douses them with a small bucket of ice cubes.

It leaves a sick taste in my mouth.

The sound of an incoming message startles me, and I glance up at an open tab at the top of my screen. I've got a new Facebook message from Kylie, who's finally changed the last name on her profile from Wolfe to McCrae.

Kylie McCrae: *Guess who will be seeing you soon?*

Biting the inside of my cheek, I type out a response. *Let me guess, she's short, amazing, and she has incredible blue hair?*

Kylie McCrae: *Yes, yes, but NO. I dyed it again. I think I love it.*

I wince. Kylie had tried platinum and cherry red several months back, and it had looked like a candy striper threw-up in her hair. Before I ask what color she went with this time, she uploads a photo of herself. It loads slowly, thank to our agonizingly slow Internet connection, so I'm able to view a little at a time until I'm finally staring at the full image: a surprised looking Kylie who's pointing at the top of her head. Which is now an utterly plain shade of dark brown.

Kylie McCrae: *Since I've rendered you speechless (wordless?), I can tell you adore it. And to answer your next question, my normal hair and I will be on the bus from Atlanta to New Orleans.*

That means she'll be around for just about the rest of the tour, except for Phoenix and Los Angeles. When I ask her why she doesn't want to go to the last two shows, she immediately responds that it's still high up in the air.

Whatever that's supposed to mean.

Grinning at my screen, I start to let her know that I can't wait to see her, but then I erase that message. That video of Cilla is still bothering me, and what better person to ask than Kylie, who was probably around at the time.

Hey, weird question, but what was Cilla's deal at that Louisville show?

For the first time since we started chatting on Facebook months ago, Kylie answers me almost immediately, which is a shock.

Kylie McCrae: *She thought she was being stalked. Someone was sending her letters and gifts. She got one right before the show and LOST it. It was ... sad. I felt awful for her.*

Letters and gifts. This sounds so much like the crap Sam has been pulling with me that I want to hurl. It also forces a few things into a clear focus. Like Cilla calling me her newest stalker. Or why Lucas wants to avoid Louisville—Cilla's rant had to have come with some backlash for Your Toxic Sequel.

Still, like Kylie, I genuinely feel sorry for Cilla. Nobody deserves to be scared to the point of breaking.

Kylie McCrae: *Okay, I hate to do this, babe, but I've got to run—I'm exhausted!*

Putting my fingers back to the keyboard, this time I actually do tell Kylie that I'm excited to see her before closing my computer screen. Frustrated, I climb onto my bed. When I spot the letter Sam had sent to me lying face down on my nightstand, I flick it into the drawer. Even if I don't want to see it, there's no way I'm getting rid of that thing—not after what Kylie just told me.

Letters and gifts.

No, I absolutely wouldn't be surprised if Cilla's "stalker" was Lucas' ex-wife just trying to screw with her, but it still doesn't make it any less disturbing.

Instead of me leaving my car at the airport again, and having to face the outrageous long-term parking fees upon my return next week, Gram offers to drop me off the next morning for my flight to South Carolina. During the drive, I finally bring up the attorney appointment she'd mentioned to me a couple weeks ago.

I've avoided mentioning all things related to my mother during the last two days, but now that I'm leaving, I feel like I don't exactly have a choice. I can either say something now or suck it up and wait until I get home next week.

After I ask her, Gram squints at the road. "Rebecca's trying to push for an early release," she explains.

For good behavior, no doubt. I grunt at the thought. I won't say anything about all the fights my mom has been involved in during just this past year alone. "And this attorney's not going to do it for free, is he?" My grandmother is not a wealthy woman, and the last thing I want is for her to get herself in a bad situation again just because she wants to help my mom.

Gram is silent for a couple minutes, and the only sound in the car is the soft whoosh of the air conditioner. At last, she says, "Not even close to it, sweetheart." The corner of her lip trembles, leaving me to believe that there's something she's not telling me.

I can easily guess what that is.

"She wanted you to talk to me about paying for it?"

"She knows you can't do it. She wanted you to talk to Lucas," Gram corrects me, and I narrow my eyes into thin blue slits.

"How does she even know about him?"

My grandmother shakes her head, the air conditioner blowing thin strands of her gray hair around her face. "I'm not sure. I imagined that it was in one of those entertainment magazines they pass around in there." She pulls around to the airport's drop off section and puts her old Mercedes sedan in park. "I told her I wouldn't ask you." And chances are my mother had gone ballistic on her, calling her every name conceivable. That's how it usually goes, so why would this time be any different? My body tenses up, but I give Gram a smile that I hope tells her just how much I adore her.

"I love you." I lean over and kiss her cheek. "I love you so much."

"You too, sweetheart. Have a safe trip."

As I grab my belongings from the backseat, I add, "And if Mom calls you again, tell her that even though the answer is no, she could at least have the balls to ask me herself. In fact, she can call me anytime and take it up with me."

My grandmother's cornflower blue eyes twinkle in amusement. "I will. You take care of yourself. I'll see you in a week, Sienna."

Unlike the last time I flew out of Nashville, my flight to Greenville is short—a total of three hours, and that's including a brief layover in Charlotte where I grab a sandwich from a bagel shop. I'm almost too excited to eat, but I force myself to anyway.

Despite the client cancellation and the Sam letter, I'm more anxious than before to get to the band—no, to Lucas. Part of it's that almost painful need to be near him and the other part is pride. If I stay by his side, maybe it'll prove a point. That I'm loyal, unbreakable. That I love him more than being an anonymous face in the crowd that nobody knows and free from the harsh opinions of other people.

Instead of sending someone to pick me up, he's waiting for me in the terminal when my flight touches down in Greenville. Before I can get out a single word, his mouth slants down over mine, and he kisses me like we've been apart for years and not just two days. I'm left dizzy, with my heartbeat racing wildly against the wall of my chest, when he sets me away from him.

"I've been thinking about this ever since you left," he says in a low voice.

"I've been gone for two days," I point out, although I feel the same way he does. This thing between us—it's crazy, consuming. Even here it makes us nearly oblivious to the world around us. I don't notice the three women a few feet away from us until after he leaves me to grab my luggage from the carousel. The women have out their camera phones, snapping pictures of Lucas, and I can almost guarantee that I was also the focus of their rapidly moving fingers only moments before.

One of them gives me a look that throws daggers into my chest. She leans toward one of her friends and says something behind her hand. But as Lucas calls my name—and I see him coming toward me holding my duffel bag with a look in his eyes that screams desire and love and want—I couldn't care less.

Let them talk.

CHAPTER SEVENTEEN

After the Greenville concert, next comes Charlotte, North Carolina on Tuesday night, followed by Charlottesville, Virginia on Wednesday evening. Even though I'm exhausted from walking around downtown Charlottesville after the show last night, I drag myself out of our compartment Thursday morning when the bus parks behind the venue in Virginia Beach.

As I walk to the front of the bus to grab myself a glass of orange juice from the galley kitchen, I'm surprised to find that Sinjin is already up. He's in the lounge area, playing a video game on his PS3 and cursing at the screen.

"Good morning, Sunshine," I say cheerfully, pouring my drink. When I face him, he runs his gaze up from my bare feet to my shorts and ratty tee shirt and finally to my messy flame-colored hair.

"You look like shit," he says.

Sliding down on the couch next to him, I polish off the rest of my orange juice and lean over to place the glass on the dinette table across the aisle. "Your honesty makes my life complete."

"I told you, I'll always tell you the truth. Even when you don't want to hear it." He tosses the controller between us and rakes his hands over his face. "God, I'm half tempted to go with you to Nashville tomorrow and skip this shit for a while."

Rolling my eyes, I pick up the remote and restart his game. Once I manage to get myself killed, and then brutally eaten by a zombie, within the first thirty seconds, he jerks the controller out of my hands. "If you come with me, who'll play your drum solos?" I ask sweetly.

"Your fucking boyfriend." He survives slightly longer than I did—a grand total of about three minutes—before *Game Over* flashes across the small flat screen in blood-drenched letters.

"What the hell do you have that thing set on?" I ask as he shoves the game remote back in my direction.

He gives me a sarcastic flash of his teeth. "Carnage."

We do this for a good thirty minutes, making small talk about video games and passing the controller back and forth as soon as we're killed off. Finally, I work up the nerve to ask him about Zoe.

His thin face clouds over, but he quickly swaps it with a look of indifference and lifts his shoulders. "Cilla pissed her off, but she said she expects shit like that from me, so I don't know." I don't miss the way his voice quivers or how tightly he's gripping the remote. "The fucked-up thing is that I didn't fuck either of those girls."

"Did you tell *her* that?" I ask quietly.

"Why would I? It was doomed from the start."

Hearing Sinjin say those words—doomed from the start—puts a sour taste in the back of my mouth, and I'm determined to prove him wrong. The worst part is … I'm not sure if what I say next is meant more for him or as a pep talk for myself.

"Then maybe that means it's supposed to work?" Drawing my knees up to my chest, I wrap my arms around my legs. "You know, like all those epic romances."

He grants me a sideways glance, like he's really considering my words. Then the consideration changes to a sneer, and I realize that I've lost him. Sometimes with Sinjin, it doesn't take much. "Epic romances are always fucking doomed. That's why they're epic."

The sound of Lucas shuffling noisily down the bus aisle puts an end to our conversation, and Sinjin hands me the game remote for good. "I'm going to catch some shut-eye before sound check." His green eyes flash a warning at Lucas. "Meaning don't wake me with any of that bullshit before then."

Scratching his head so that his shaggy dark hair falls into his eyes, Lucas gives his bandmate a cocky smile. He turns that look on me for just a moment, and something flutters in the pit of my stomach.

"I'll do my best to go as loudly as possible, Sin," Lucas promises.

Making a growling sound in the back of his throat, Sinjin disappears to the back of the bus, but a few second later, he peeks his head out into the lounge. "Before I forget." He holds up a set of drumsticks. I catch them, one at a time, when he tosses them in my direction. "Signed and all that good stuff." Before I can offer him a word of thanks, he's gone, and I can hear the sound of Puddle of Mudd's "Famous" playing loudly inside of his compartment.

"Okay, he's scaring me. He's being way too … nice." I lift my gaze to Lucas who's leaning against the galley counter with a Red Bull in his hand. "You look … well rested."

He pops the tab of his energy drink. "I've got two weeks left on the road. Fuck yes, I'm rested." Giving me an animalistic grin, he throws himself onto the couch with me, grabbing my leg and pulling me on him so that I straddle him. I muffle my shriek of delight with the back of my hand as he grinds my hips against his cock and leans me backward so he can kiss my breast through my tee shirt. "God, you look like—"

My phone vibrates on the table, interrupting him, but I'm positive he wasn't going to tell me I look like shit—like Sinjin did.

At first, I have no intention of answering it, but then he gives my thigh an encouraging squeeze. Reaching over, I begrudgingly grab my phone and turn it over to reveal a call from an unknown number. A sliver of anxiety coils through me as I stare down at the flashing screen because the first possible person my mind goes is to Sam.

So far, she's only used words to screw with me. As much as I hate to admit it, my address was probably easy to find because I had once included it in the *Contact Me* section on my website. It had been a dumb move on my part, but I had gotten rid of it fast, knowing that nothing ever really disappears from the Internet.

But still, the thought of Sam going through all the frustration of digging up my phone number, especially after refusing to reply to my message to her?

Calm down, I warn myself. *Stop getting ahead of yourself and just answer the damn thing.*

"Just pick up the phone, Red," Lucas murmurs into my ear, "Then we can get back to what we were doing."

Giving him a trembling shake of my head, I swipe my finger across the bottom of the phone's screen to accept the call. The person on the other line is already talking before I put my ear to the speaker, and I'm relieved to discover that the voice is automated.

Well, sort of relieved.

"… A collect call from Rebecca Previn."

It's my mother.

I don't know how many times I've received similar calls in the past, but they've been few and far between over the last year. I had run out of things to give her, and that meant my use ran out too.

I'm not sure if it's my anger at her sending Gram to that attorney's office or my old desire to make my mom happy that drives me to accept the call, but I do. She doesn't start the conversation like she normally would—in that soft, sweet voice she uses whenever she wants something from me.

No, she's already advanced to spitting fire and brimstone.

"You stupid little bitch," she yells. "How dare you try to turn my momma against me?"

Scrambling off of Lucas' lap, I frantically work my finger over the volume button so the conversation isn't as loud. Lucas is already leaning forward, working his long fingers over his bottom lip in concern.

Turning my back to him so he can't see my face, I take a cleansing breath. "I don't know what you're talking about."

She releases a guttural growl. "Don't try that with me, Sienna, I see right through you. Always have. You're trying to warp her mind against me, and it's not right."

I pinch my fingers over the bridge of my nose. It's been a long time since I had a headache that burned the backs of my eyes. Leave it to my mom to immediately bring one on. "What exactly did I *do?*" I ask in a muffled voice.

"She told me she was ashamed that I wanted your boyfriend to help me out. Ashamed of me. I don't think she's ever said anything like that to me. She said she won't ever—"

"No." I shake my head. "Gram shouldn't feel even an ounce of shame over that. You should. You don't even talk to me, and the first thing you do after reading something in a gossip article about me is call me expecting—"

Now it's my mother's turn to cut me off, and when she does, she's bellowing into the phone. "You wrote me a letter *offering* to help me, not the other way around."

"Mom," I breathe, hating the way my chest burns when I call her that. "Don't do this crap."

There's the sound of shuffling paper on her end of the line, and then, in a clipped, shaking voice, she reads the letter aloud for me. It's short and to the point, telling her that I would have Lucas pay for her lawyer if she wanted to take me up on the offer.

Even for my mom, making up something like this is a little far-fetched.

Once she's done reading, Mom says something that wraps a layer of ice around my heart. "Sent three weeks ago—postmarked from Atlanta, Georgia—so don't sit there and lie to me. You owe me more than lies."

My body goes numb. "Where did you say it came from?"

"Are you deaf? You heard me the first time." She makes a strangled noise. "Don't worry, I don't want or need you or your boyfriend's help. But let me tell you something. If you ever, ever, try to turn my mother against me again, I'll knock you on your ass the second I get out of this place."

She hangs up then, not giving me the chance to get in another word—but really, what the hell would I say after everything she's just told me? Placing my phone on the countertop, I stare down at it blankly until I feel strong arms wrapping around me.

"Your mother?" he asks, and I nod slowly, trying to catch my breath. "You didn't let her push you around, Red. I'm impressed."

But all I can focus on is what she had said to me. That I had sent her a letter postmarked from Atlanta.

Atlanta.

Where Samantha Wolfe, Lucas' ex-wife, lives.

Lucas spins me around to look at him, turning his head to the side so he can examine my expression. "What the fuck did she want?"

"She wanted something from me that I can't give her."

Because he knows that the phone call had at least something to do with him, he holds my face between his hands. "Let me help you, Si."

A bubble of hysterical laughter rises in my chest. "No. Absolutely ... no. I don't want to give my mother anything."

"She was that bad?" There's no scorn or negativity in his tone, just gentle curiosity. I shake my head.

"Not always. I mean, she was on and off. One minute, she was crazy about Seth and me, and the next she was pretty much telling us

221

to fuck off or trying to manipulate us. I guess I have mommy and daddy issues because I…"

When I don't continue, Lucas' eyebrows tug together. "What?" he implores.

Closing my eyes, I take a deep breath. "Even though I had Gram, I was always jealous of all my friends whose parents were around. I mean, I speak to my dad as often as most people talk to their great-uncle and you see how it is with my mother. Hell, I was even a little bitter seeing you around your parents earlier this year." Saying that last part out loud causes my chest to seize up.

Yanking me to him, he holds me against his toned chest for a long time until my breathing has calmed down. By the time he lets me go, and I sink down on the couch, I've managed to regain some semblance of control.

Lucas kneels down in front of me, massaging his thumbs against the backs of my calves. "Look, I've got an errand I need to run with David, but if I need to—"

I shake my head quickly. "No, you do what you need to do. If I shut down every time my mom ripped into me, I'd still be twitching on the floor by now."

As he gets dressed, I pace the aisle of the bus, anxious for him to leave. The moment he's gone, I grab my phone and go outside so Sin won't be able to hear me. As I wait for Gram to pick up my call, I wrap my arms tightly around myself, afraid that if I let go, I'll fall apart.

"This is early for you," Gram answers warmly.

Pulling in a harsh breath, I cut to the chase. "Have you gotten anything strange about me?"

"Sienna, what's this—?"

"Have you? Any letters or *anything* since I came out here for this tour?"

Gram's silence is deafening, and it tells me everything I want to know. I feel like the breath has been ripped out of my chest. "Why didn't you say anything?"

"Because it just came yesterday," she says, her voice defensive. She takes a tremulous breath before continuing. "I ripped that cruel trash up and threw it away right after I read the first line. Do you think I'm going to tell you when someone sends a nasty note to tell me what they think of you, just because they don't agree with whom you're dating?"

"I—" I look down at the asphalt, glaring at a piece of broken glass a few inches away from my flip-flopped feet. "Gram, I'm so sorry someone was hateful enough to send something like that to you."

Not just someone. Samantha. I am almost one hundred percent sure that she is behind the note both Gram and my mother received.

As my grandmother tries to assure me that everything will be fine, I come to a conclusion that makes me feel nauseous.

Now that my family has been dragged into this mess with Sam, my plan to keep

Lucas in the dark just flew out the window.

Because Lucas is gone right up to just before the band's late afternoon sound check, I decide to wait until after his show tonight

to say anything about what's been going on with his ex-wife. I can hardly focus on the concert—I spend most of my time nervously looking down at my phone, checking to see if Sam's sent me another message and wondering if Gram will call to say she's received yet another note.

I haven't been this nervous—this sick to my stomach—in a long time.

I've seen how Lucas reacts whenever his ex is mentioned—hell, I've stressed over that reaction. Asking questions about Samantha makes him automatically clam up.

This will result in the same, or maybe he'll finally hit the roof, like he had in our hotel room in Atlanta several months ago.

It's close to one in the morning when everything is said and done backstage. When Tyler lets the band know that we're facing a slight postponement due to a mechanical issue with a crew bus, Wyatt suggests we take the party back to the bus he shares with Cal.

Which puts yet another delay on my heart-to-heart talk with Lucas.

As we head from the backstage area of the venue toward the other Your Toxic Sequel bus, Lucas turns around and begins walking backwards. When I cock my eyebrow at him, he says, "I've got to run and talk to Tyler for a few minutes." His lips curl into a relaxed smile. "Go on ahead without me."

Pushing my hair away from my face, I bob my head. "But Lucas?" He stops walking and faces me, the look in his hazel eyes patient as he waits for me to say something. I turn toward him, wringing my hands together. "I've really got to talk to you before I leave to go home tomorrow, okay?"

224

And it abso-fucking-lutely cannot wait until I come back, I add silently.

Leaning down, he brushes his soft mouth over mine, raking his straight teeth over my bottom lip before backing away. "Good. There are a few things I need to say to you, too."

I watch him as he sprints to the crew bus that's still functioning. As soon as he goes inside, I climb the steps leading up to the bus right in front of me. I'm immediately greeted by the sound of Theory of a Deadman blasting loudly over the sound system.

This is the first time I've ever stepped foot inside Cal and Wyatt's space, but I quickly realize that it has a similar layout to ours.

"Hope you're ready to take that shot," Cal says from the kitchen. He looks over at me as I take a couple steps toward him, his dark brown eyes shining in amusement. He holds up two bottles—one of them vodka, the other spiced rum—and dips his head to the hem of my shirt. "You taking it off now or are we doing this shit later?"

"In your dreams, Calvin."

I walk down the aisle, passing through the small kitchen until I'm standing in the lounge area. When he spots me hovering near the kitchen table with my nose wrinkled up at the piles of laundry covering the couch, Cal downs his shot. "You can sit down. I swear the piles of junk won't bite you, so there's no need to be a snotty bitch," he teases sarcastically.

Ignoring the jibe, and knocking a lacy purple bra aside, I plop down on the couch. "I never took you for a D-cup, Cal," I say. "I thought your man boobs were much smaller."

To my surprise, he flushes beneath his darkly tanned skin.

"The infamous Heidi was here last week." I pop my head up to see Wyatt, shirtless and smoking, coming out of the other section of the bus. Heidi. That name sounds familiar. When I twist my lips, trying to figure out where I've heard it before, Wyatt says, "One of Kylie's friends. She went with her on that trip to New Orleans earlier this year."

"Ah, I see." Now, I can easily remember a conversation I had with Kylie on the front porch at my grandmother's house back in February. She had come to visit me to bring a peace offering after she helped Lucas trick me into having dinner with him and had mentioned Heidi. "Will she be tagging along with Kylie this weekend in Atlanta?" I ask, and Wyatt shakes his blond head quickly and mouths a dramatic "no."

"I can only handle being around Heidi in small doses," he explains, sitting down at the two-person table across the aisle from me. "As of right now, I've overdosed on her this year. Any more and I'll lose my goddamn mind."

The bus door swings open, but instead of Lucas, it's Sinjin who steps inside with his black hair still wet from a shower. When he catches the look on my face, he stops in the middle of the aisle, his exhausted green eyes challenging mine. "Yeah, happy to see your ass too." Grabbing a beer from the fridge, he takes a seat beside me, propping his feet up on the table that Wyatt's sitting at.

"You've looked like a damn deer in the headlights all night," Sin points out, and I tilt my head at him. "Hell, it's worse than a deer in the headlights."

That's because your leader's ex is playing games with my family.

To Sinjin, I say, "It creeps me out that you've been staring at me." He mutters something, but then I realize he's shifted his focus on Wyatt, whom he's now arguing loudly with.

Sliding a little further away from Sin, I pull my phone out of my pocket. There's a 5% battery warning displayed on the screen, and I groan. When I get up, I turn to Wyatt, whom I trust more with giving Lucas a message. "If Lucas comes in, can you tell him I went over to the other bus?"

After Wyatt promises that he will, I go outside. It's chilly tonight, and by the time I get inside of our bus, I'm shivering and hugging myself, rubbing my hands quickly over my upper arms. Leaving my phone to charge, I sift through my already-packed luggage until I find the only jacket that I brought with me—an *Echo Falls* hoodie I'd been given by my old boss at Christmas last year.

As I leave our bedroom and walk through Sinjin's section of bunks, the sound of rustling bedspreads stops me in my tracks. Turning around, I flip on the light by the door. When I see a body beneath the covers in Sinjin's bunk, I let out a snort.

"Did you give up on Cal and Wyatt already?" I tease.

When the body rolls over, though, long, shiny black hair tumbles over the side of the bed and blue-green eyes stare up at me.

"Is that where he is?" Cilla asks. She bats her eyes innocently. "Then you should go get him for me, Pepper. He and I need to have a little talk."

CHAPTER EIGHTEEN

For a long time, I stare at Cilla without uttering a single word. I take in the sight of this drunken woman who has made it perfectly clear time and time again just how much she dislikes me. It's not until my vision begins to blur that I glance away. I stare at the neatly tucked black comforter on the bunk right across from Sinjin's, forcing a few harsh breaths in through my nose.

Cilla Craig brings out emotions in me that I didn't even realize I had until I met her and Samantha.

When I return my gaze to her, she smirks up at me.

"What in the actual fuck are you doing in Sinjin's bunk?" I demand.

Planting her hands on the edge of the bunk, she pushes herself into a sitting position, flinging her curtain of black hair over her bare shoulder, and gives me a coy look from under her sooty lashes. Even wasted out of her mind, she manages to make every movement look sexy, which automatically tugs my mind to picture her waiting in Lucas' bed instead of Sinjin's.

I grind my teeth together. "I'm not in the mood to do this with you tonight. Does

Sinjin know you're in here?"

229

"Isn't it obvious what I'm doing, Pepper?" She questions in her husky voice. "I'm waiting for him to come back. It should be a fun surprise for him." She taps her manicured fingernail against her chin. "I'm even thinking I'll ride the bus with y'all to

Atlanta."

I move my head incredulously. She's got to be screwing with me. When her expression doesn't change, letting me know she's one hundred percent serious, I pull my eyebrows together. "Why would you put yourself through that?"

So Sinjin can talk shit to you and reiterate how he wishes your band had never come on this tour? So Lucas can ignore you like he's been doing for weeks?

Though I don't say those words directly, I know she must be thinking the same thing, because she releases a little laugh that doesn't reflect in her eyes or in the stiff way she drags her fingers through her hair.

"Trust me, he doesn't hold a grudge for very long," she promises.

"I'm glad you're so sure of yourself." I offer her a harsh smile. "And that you have so much faith in the man you've treated like crap."

Cilla throws back her head and laughs. "You stupid bitch, are you kidding me? Don't think that just because you've been around him for a few weeks you know anything about him because you don't." She stumbles to her bare feet and leans in close to me. Her hair and halter-top reek of vodka and vomit, causing me to clamp my hand over my mouth. "You don't know a thing about any of them. Especially Lucas."

230

I draw away from her, narrowing my eyes. "I know that Sin's been over you for a while now. I know that he's not some last resort and that he's not going to let you make him that. I know that you—"

She sneers. "Oh honey, you don't know a thing about me either."

Undeterred, I continue, "I know that you have issues. That's just about all I need to know about you, Priscilla."

"And all this is coming from Lucas' doormat? Nice. Tell me, Pepper, how does it feel knowing that he's told you to fuck off twice now? It has to hurt."

This isn't the first time she's said something like this to me—and if I'm going to have to be around her for the sake of Lucas' music, it sure as hell won't be the last. Still, that doesn't make it any better. It doesn't stop me from wanting to punch her.

I've never been the one for violence, but between Cilla and Sam, I'm at the end of my incredibly frayed rope.

"Funny," I say while backing out of the narrow space. Cilla follows behind me into the main lounge, her smile completely predatory. I cross my arms over my chest. "That this is coming from the one who still won't take no for an answer. How does that feel?"

Cilla's flinch echoes through her body. She turns away from me slightly and places her palms down flat on the lounge table to keep upright. Her shoulders begin to shake, and as I stand still, waiting for her to make her next move, I can't tell whether she's laughing or crying. When she finally straightens her back and faces me head on, I realize that she's doing both.

"Do you think I want to care about him?" She wipes at the corners of her eyes with the backs of her hands. Grabbing her strappy pumps from the leather couch, she slides past me in the direction of the exit. "Trust me, I don't. And as of this morning, I lost all hope that he'll just come around and get rid of you."

This morning? Whirling around, I grab her upper arm before she can stumble off of the bus. "What the hell are you talking about?" I whisper.

She looks surprised for a moment, but then her eyes narrow and a satisfied smirk lifts the corners of her lips. She's pleased she's caught me off guard, and I'm cursing myself for letting her see that.

"Well, damn, maybe he has come around and realized what a disaster you'll be for him." She jerks out of my grip, massaging her other hand over the spot my fingers held. "Goodnight, Pepper."

Instead of heading back over to the other bus like I initially planned, I stay here. By the time Lucas wanders over to look for me, wearing that self-absorbed grin that always comes from hearing how amazing he is, I'm furious. I've had too much time to think about Cilla's words since she skulked away, and now I can barely see straight.

That's the thing about jealousy, uncertainty—it grabs us by the neck and squeezes until we can't think clearly. No wonder Sinjin pulled me aside to warn me the first night.

Lucas pauses at the entrance of the back compartment and stares me down.

"Everything alright, Si?" he asks gently at the sight of my flushed face.

"Were you with Cilla this morning?" I question, looking up at him from my spot on the edge of the bed.

His shoulders bunch up with tension. "Did she tell you that?" he demands angrily.

My teeth clench. "Were you with her?" I grind out.

Leaning against the doorway, he nods. "I was. But not the way you're thinking. I met up with Tyler after David and I finished what we were doing earlier. Cilla was with him. We shared very few words with each other, none of which were pleasant." Resting my forearms on my thighs, I drop my head forward. My hair sweeps across the floor but right now, I don't care. I feel like an idiot for immediately jumping on him without first asking what had happened, and I'm mortified to meet his gaze. "She made it seem like—" My words catch, and he comes forward, taking my face between his hands.

"You're doing that thing again," he growls. "What the hell did she say to you?"

"It was nothing. I was just flustered. And she was drunk, waiting for Sinjin to come in here."

Lucas lets out a harsh laugh, but his touch stays gentle as he feathers his calloused thumbs over my cheeks. "Then it's good you came before he did. He's not over that shit she pulled with Zoe on his birthday."

"Didn't think he was."

He slides down beside me on the edge of the full-size bed, his body warming mine. "They fixed the bus, so we should be on the road soon," he tells me.

"To your hometown." And Samantha's. Because as pissed as I want to be at

233

Cilla, Sam is the real elephant in the room.

His grin falters. "You need to talk to me," he says. "So let me in, Red. I can't help you—can't do anything for you—unless you do that."

These words are so ironic coming from him that I release a shuddering sigh. Still, there is no use tiptoeing around the subject—I'm just going to have to let it all spill out.

"Lucas ... Sam's been in touch with me."

At least a dozen emotions pass over his features—everything from confusion, to shock, to rage. "Today? She contacted you today?" His voice is cold and flat, and when

I shake my head, he growls, "When?"

"She's been doing it ever since we started this tour."

He sucks in a harsh breath. "Jesus, Sienna. And what did she have to say?" The fear in his voice is undeniable, and it makes me feel just as afraid.

"Nothing that makes any sense. All I know is that ever since she's gotten in touch with me, I'm the Yoko of fucking Your Toxic Sequel. One of my clients has given me the boot, and my mother has called me flipping out about a letter she received that I never wrote. And Sam's contacted my grandmother." The last word is shouted. I get off of the bed, dragging my hands through my hair. "I can take anything she has to throw at me, but to send a letter to Gram?"

Lucas stops my pacing, grabbing my wrist. "You never told me any of this." His tone is soft and dangerous, but I shake my head.

"Why would I?" I shout. "I ask you over and over again what she has on you, and you shoot me down because she's bad for your music. So why the hell would I just tell you?"

Letting go of me, Lucas scrubs his hands roughly over his face. When he stops, he's breathing in short, forceful bursts. "I'm going to see her tomorrow. I'm going to put an end to all of this."

"And then what? Will that end be you deciding to leave me again because she snaps her fingers and holds something over your head?"

He's on his feet, hovering above me before I have time to react. "No. Never again." He shakes his head hard. "I can't let you go, don't you understand that? I used to laugh when I would hear that bullshit about someone being like air, but fuck, that's what you are to me. You are everything I've ever needed." Letting out a low, animalistic noise he throws his head back. "God, I was going to ask you to—"

I feel the room start to spin as I wait for him to finish. "Ask me to what?" I whisper hesitantly.

He pulls something out of his pocket, and I squeeze my eyes closed, shaking my head as he presses it into my hand. Easing back down on the end of the bed, I grip the tiny box until the square corners are jabbing into my skin. He's asking me to marry him.

Of all the moments, he's asking me to marry him right now.

"After Sam," he begins, sinking down on one knee in front of me, "I told myself never again. I never wanted to do that to myself, but with you it's all I can think about. I want you to marry me, Sienna. I want you in my life, in my bed, having my kids someday, being my fucking inspiration."

My chest tightens, like someone is pulling a drawstring taut and refusing to release it, and I cross my arms over myself. "Lucas, tell me what she has on you." I open my eyes, staring down at him. "Please. Just. Tell. Me."

He's trembling as he shakes his head. "There's no way I'm going to have you looking at me like I'm a monster."

Raking in a breath that sets my lungs on fire, I stare down at my lap as the flood begins. The tears are warm and feel bitter against my dry skin. They land on the square ring box, darkening the blue cardboard, drowning what could have been. I ask him once more, and once again he shoots me down.

When I speak again, I can barely breathe, let alone form words but I manage to whisper, "Then I can't, Lucas. I can't marry you."

CHAPTER NINETEEN

I'm by myself in the bed Lucas and I have been sharing when I open my eyes first thing the next morning. I roll over onto my back, staring up at the dim, recessed lighting in the bus ceiling and wonder if the night before was nothing more than a dream. No, correction: I pray that it was all a dream.

But then my gaze lands on my Gibson guitar, which is standing upright beside the nightstand. And sitting on top of that stand rests the little blue box Lucas had tried to give to me last night.

He had asked me to marry him.

And I had said no.

I refused the man I love.

A low moan escapes me as I curl up on my side, bringing my knees to my chest. I close my eyes to hold in the moisture threatening to spill out and press the heel of my palm against my chest. It doesn't help the tight, painful churning going on deep inside of my ribcage, or the way I can't seem to breathe just right.

I said no.

I stay like this—with hundreds of thoughts spiraling through my brain—until I feel the bus lurch to a stop, and I know that we've finally arrived in Atlanta. There are voices filtering from the front of the bus—Lucas and Sinjin and what sounds like Wyatt's deep voice—and I know that, eventually, I'll have to get up and face them all. Today is the day that I fly back home. After I'm done with the job that I've been fortunate enough to secure in Nashville, I have no idea what will happen next.

Because I told him no.

Finally, I climb out of bed and force myself to get dressed. My hands and legs are trembling violently as I smooth down the flouncy, vintage-looking halter dress I bought because, at the time, wearing it had made me feel happy and vibrant. Today, none of those feelings hit me. Now, there's an empty coldness circling around the pit of my stomach.

Instead of making me come to him, Lucas comes to the back of the bus as I finish packing my belongings. He stands in the doorway, looking beautiful in jeans and one of his signature black t-shirts. He gives me a nod, his dark hair falling into his eyes. I let the magnetism between us draw me to him, and when I push his hair back with the side of my hand, I feel like I'm dying a little inside.

The hazel eyes staring down at me are tortured. Haunted. Tortured and haunted and so full of regret.

"I'm going to make sure she leaves you alone," he promise in a low voice. "I swear to it."

I step backward. Bending my head, I stare down at a chip in my pale pink nail polish. "I just want her to stay away from my family." Clenching my teeth, I pull in a rough inhale before looking up at him. "And from you. I'm worried about what she's going to do to you."

"She hasn't done anything so far, Red."

But that's not true. She's terrorized his life. She's demanded his money and his time. She's made it nearly impossible for him to move on, reminding him of … *whatever* it is that he did to her. "I love you. You know that, right?" I ask.

The bus floor creaks as he slowly walks across it. His hands are gentle as they run down the center of my back. "I know you do. And I know why you said no. But I know you'll be back."

I swallow down the tightness building up in my throat. "I can't exactly do that if you don't want me around."

He bends his head to mind and whispers against my temple, "You're it for me, Sienna. I've never needed or wanted anything as much as you. Feelings like these—like what I feel for you—won't stop because of what happened last night. I'm not going to let go of you because of *this*."

I lift my face slightly, the tip of my nose skimming across his straight nose until our eyes meet. I'm lost in his for a moment, lost in him, until I finally say, "I just don't want there to be secrets."

"And if the secret turned me into a monster?" It's the same word he used to describe himself last night. *Monster.* It makes every bone, every muscle in my body scream in absolute fear. What has he done to make him think this? "What the fuck happens then?"

I'm at a loss for words for a moment as I study his pensive expression. What will happen then? "You're not a monster. You could never be that to me."

His smile is sad, and it makes my heart ache more than the look in his eyes. "Never?" he asks, and I shake my head. He crushes me to him, kissing the top of my head. "We better get you to the airport before you miss your flight."

239

Just like the last time I flew from Atlanta to Nashville, this flight is depressing. This time though, I left Lucas of my own volition. That weak part of me that I'm still trying to overcome wants nothing more than to go directly back to him as soon as I arrive in Nashville, but I know it won't solve any of our problems. I dealt with lies and bullshit for years when it came to my mother, and look how my relationship with her has disintegrated.

By the time I step off the plane, I feel sick to my stomach. The nausea only gets worse as I check my text messages while Gram drives home. There's one from Tori and two from Ashley. Tori's message is upbeat, letting me know that she can't wait for me to come to Los Angeles soon, but when I read what Ashley wrote, my heart freezes mid-beat.

9:52AM: *Please tell me the band isn't really breaking up?*

9:54AM: *Because if they are, I still love you but that SUCKS!*

"Is everything okay, sweetheart?" my grandmother asks quietly when I gasp.

I must look like a madwoman as I bob my head up and down. "Everything is fine." Gram offers me a smile that screams she doesn't buy into my answer before she turns her bright blue eyes to the road.

"It's been quiet around the house without you," she muses, trying to make small talk. "It will be nice to have you around for a little while."

When I respond and tell her I'm happy to be back, my words sound like they're coming out in slow motion. The only thing my brain will focus on is Ashley's message.

I'm shaking as I Google Your Toxic Sequel, and it takes me several tries to type coherently enough for the search to yield something worthwhile. Once it does, I scan the newest gossip articles. *Sleaze Cop, Buzz Online*, and *Alternative Entertainment*— they all say the same thing: Your Toxic Sequel is calling it quits. And it's all because of one of the member's relationship with a certain redhead from Music City.

Stunned, I tilt my head back until it touches the headrest.

This can't be happening.

As soon as Gram and I get home, I quietly turn down her offer of eating lunch in the kitchen and race upstairs to my bedroom. Ignoring the stifling heat up here, I sit down on the edge of my bed and call the first person I can think of to confirm the news.

Just before the call goes to her voicemail, Kylie answers happily, speaking theatrically into her phone, "Hello beautiful! I'm so pissed that I missed you this morning, and—"

"Is the band breaking up?" I blurt out.

She's quiet for a few seconds but then she releases a confused laugh. "Um, *no*.

Not unless they're hiding it from me. Why the hell would you think that?"

"I—" I grip the edge of mattress, squeezing it roughly like a stress ball. I clear my throat. "It was on a gossip website, and one of my friends asked me about it."

Kylie releases a heavy sigh. "Babe," she says in the most serious voice I've ever heard her use, "I thought I warned you about this kind of thing a long, *long* time ago.

Never, ever read the shit they write online. It's the devil. It's almost always wrong, and you'll drive yourself up the wall worrying over it. Trust me when I say this because I've been there before." She gives me a moment to process her advice before adding, "But to answer your question, no, the band is absolutely *not* breaking up."

"Thank God," I say in a rushed breath, coming to my feet.

I hear Wyatt whispering something to her in the background, but after she tells him to give her a few minutes alone, she comes back on the line. "Alright, babe. Tell me what's going on. You sound like you're a few seconds away from being pushed over the edge."

Once I start talking, it's almost impossible for me to stop. I walk back and forth across the hardwood floor of my bedroom, telling Kylie everything from the issues with Sam to the YTS fan forums. The only thing that I leave out is Lucas' proposal. It seems wrong to bring that up when the wounds from last night are still so fresh.

"I'm so sorry, babe," Kylie murmurs once I'm done talking. "God, why didn't you say anything to me?"

A painful cry rips from the back of my throat, startling me, and I realize that tears are racing down my cheeks. "I—I didn't want to screw with Lucas' music."

Kylie makes a disgusted noise. "Screw my brother's music. You, Sienna—you're what's important. Music will never be more important than you."

Even after Kylie has to go five minutes later, those words are what stick with me.

After I send Ashley several messages to reassure her that Your Toxic Sequel is definitely not on the verge of ending up on *Where Are They Now: Rockstar Edition*, I spend the rest of the day doing laundry and cleaning the cabin for Gram in hopes that it will keep my mind on anything other than Lucas. It doesn't, and because my grandma is so observant, I make an extra effort to put on a cheerful face so she won't notice how torn I am. But following dinner—which Seth comes over to help eat just to leave in favor of a frat party immediately afterward—she tells me in the politest way possible to go out.

"I mean it, Sienna. There's no point in you sitting here all night with me," she says sternly.

I cast a sideways glance to where she's sitting in her recliner, her feet propped up as she watches an episode of one of her favorite reality shows—the one with roses and ridiculously gorgeous people "looking for true love."

"Are you trying to get rid of me, Gram?" I tease.

Turning the corners of her mouth up, she motions her head back and forth. "No, I'm saying that I'm an eighty-year-old woman. You look like you could use a little company."

Kicking off my pink flip-flops, I lie down on my side and grin over at her. "Actually, you're seventy-nine, Gram. And I'm just fine staying right here."

"You're not going to hurt my feelings," she promises.

"I know, but I'd rather be here with you." I turn my head back to the TV just in time to see a contestant get the boot, but I don't miss the soft smile playing on my grandmother's lips.

Keeping to her schedule, Gram goes to bed a couple of hours later. Alone, I watch old episodes of *Six Feet Under* until my head begins to hurt from staring at the TV screen. As I climb the steps to go upstairs, I reconsider my grandmother's suggestion to go out. Pulling out my phone, I send Ashley a message asking her what's going on at her parents' bar tonight. Twenty minutes later, when I'm settling into bed and about to turn the lamp off, she replies to tell me about a Five Finger Death Punch cover band. A few minutes after that, she sends another text.

10:39PM: *I hope the silence means you're getting dressed? I'm not working tonight, so I'm all yours.*

After I drag on a pair of jeans and a white t-shirt with black leather shoulders, I drive downtown. I loop the nearby area twice before I resign myself to parking in a paid lot several blocks away from The Beacon. I pay for my parking ticket at the automated machine, slide it onto my dashboard, and grab my bag from the front seat.

I don't hear someone coming up behind me, so I jump when I turn around to find a tall, lanky guy standing next to the front of my car. His face is worked into a pinched, angry scowl, and instinctively, I take a step back.

His nostrils flare. "You've. Fucked up. Everything."

Backing up a few more steps, I shake my head quickly, darting my gaze around the empty parking lot in panic. "I think you've got me mistaken for—"

"Sienna? The bitch who's going to ruin Lucas' life? No, I don't have you mistaken." Seething, he moves closer toward me, shoving his hand into his pocket to look for something.

244

My chest constricts, and I struggle to find my voice. When I do, it's small, barely audible. "No, I think you have me mixed up with someone else, I—"

"I followed you from your house, you lying bitch," he yells. And this—this is when the true fear sets in. It's the first time in my entire life I've ever felt it.

I try to take off in the other direction, but the man tackles me to the ground, knocking me onto my back. My head hits the asphalt with a sickening thud, and the air whooshes out of my lungs, leaving me breathless.

As the man sits on top of me, I struggle to breath. To think. To fight.

"Get off of me," I wheeze.

When I open my mouth to scream, his fist slams into my stomach—once, twice. The only thing that stops the third hit is that I guard my belly with my hands, and then, the blow catches my wrist. Burning pain sears through my arm. I try to cry out for help again, but this time, his hands close around my throat.

He wants to hurt me.

No. This guy could kill me.

This guy might kill me, and he knows where I live. Where my grandmother is sleeping at this very moment.

My hands fly up to his arms, pushing and scratching as hard as I can. I dig my fingernails into his skin, dragging roughly as my head starts to spin and my vision clouds. He lets out a howl, moving his hands from my throat to the sides of my face where he squeezes hard.

It's the worst physical pain I've ever felt.

But it's not cutting off my ability to make a noise.

This time, when I scream, it comes out. Hoarse. Broken. Dripping with fear.

His palm crashes into my face, making me dry heave.

Reaching out, I drag my fingers over the ground as I try to find something, anything that will help me fight this man off. When my fingertips tangle into my key chain, I grasp it and jab it up at the man's face.

My car key makes contact with his cheek, and he falls off of me with blood rushing down his face. I stumble to my feet, trying to gather my bearings just long enough to run. In the distance, I can hear someone yelling, but I'm not sure from where.

"Come here, bitch," the man growls, lunging toward me.

I don't think.

I act.

My thumb closes down on the pepper spray Sinjin had given me, and I hold down the trigger until the man crumbles to the ground, screaming and grasping at his face.

I don't move my hands until two men come racing into the parking lot.

Because when I do let go, I lose consciousness altogether.

CHAPTER TWENTY

Lucas

"You're drinking, Luke." Arching her eyebrows, Kylie stirs the tip of her finger around her own drink—cranberry juice and Sprite. "A lot. You should stop. And you should grow the hell up and give Sienna a call. She doesn't bite, I promise."

I down the rest of my beer, my seventh or eighth since coming backstage. "Jesus, I haven't missed your nagging," I grumble. Kylie's mouth drops open, but I stare straight ahead to where Cal's grinning for pictures with Brady and a petite brunette. "Five minutes ago you were saying how amazing you thought the show was and now you're playing psychiatrist."

Setting her drink on the floor, my sister rests her elbows on her knees and cocks her head, her dark hair falling to one side. "It *was* amazing. But now you're getting drunk, and I'm getting worried. I'm not exactly in the mood to worry tonight, Lucas."

She's been saying how worried she is since she met up with us in Atlanta this morning. She was worried after talking to Sienna this afternoon and after we had lunch with our mom and dad, calling me brooding and rude and the biggest asshole she's ever known afterward. After I missed the sound check late this afternoon, my sister was worried yet again.

Nobody had asked where I was, but my sister gave me a disappointed, angry smile when I ran into her backstage right before going on to perform. She probably knew I went to Sam. I didn't see a need to tell her that my ex was nowhere to be found or how I discovered that she really has moved—there are new occupants in that fancy ass apartment I used to pay for and Sam didn't leave a forwarding address with the leasing office. And I sure as fuck wouldn't tell Kylie that the reason I went to see Sam had nothing to do with money.

After all this time, my sister wouldn't have bought it anyway.

"I'm ready for this shit to be over." I drop my head back against the couch.

"The tour?"

The tour. This lie I let myself crawl deeper inside. "Yeah." I release a bitter laugh.

"The tour."

"Ugh. There are so many things I want to say to you—"

"Have I heard them before?"

Kylie is quiet, and I lift my head to challenge her eyes. She shrugs her shoulders and then drops them. "Some of it, yes."

"Then I'm not fucking interested. I get it. I know where I fucked up. I'm going to fix it. Happy?"

"Lucas—" she starts in a defeated voice, but I nod at Wyatt who's talking to two female reporters and ignore the way the jerky movement gives me a headache.

"You flew here to see your husband, not to babysit me."

248

Her cheeks are sucked in as she slides off of the couch, and her brown eyes are hard as she stares me down. "Trust me, babysitting a stubborn dickwad is the last thing that's on my schedule for tonight, so do me a favor and go shove your guitar pick up your ass." She stalks off, and when she reaches Wyatt, he glances over her head at me, his expression grim. He places his mouth against the top of her hair for a few moments, and when he looks back up again, he mouths something. A threat.

So I do the only thing that makes sense.

I grab myself another drink.

For the first time during this tour, I'm not up at seven fucking AM. I stay in my compartment, in my bed, letting what's left of Sienna's sweet scent torture my dreams.

She's everywhere and nowhere, and I know how much I've messed up.

I should have just told her what I did and let her decide for herself.

It would have made everything a hell of a lot easier, and maybe—maybe I'd be able to move on.

My phone vibrating from beneath the pillow is what finally drags my ass out of bed. I swing my legs over the side of the mattress and study the unfamiliar Nashville number on the screen for a few seconds before answering. I've heard the voice on the other line before—Sienna's younger brother—and it's not something I want to wake up to, even if it is after ten. I've gotten into it with this little shit before, and I'm prepared to do it again, but then I stop and listen to what he's saying.

That Sienna has been hurt. Badly.

Attacked.

Beaten in a parking lot.

And by one of my fans.

When the call ends, I'm numb. The feeling comes back a little at a time, and once it's all there, I finally realize that the broken noise resonating through the bus belongs to me.

It takes twenty minutes to charter a helicopter, which Kylie steps in to handle because I've started to lash out at everyone. When she hands me my phone back, she gives me a determined look. "I'm coming with you to Nashville."

I don't refuse her. I can't. My mind is in one place, and one place only, and until I get to Sienna, I won't be able to think clearly.

But in the end, I'm grateful for my sister. It's Kylie who thinks ahead and makes sure there's a rental car waiting for us when we get to Nashville three hours later, and it's my sister who drives us to the hospital, ignoring me by turning up the radio to blast an Aranda song when I tell her to hurry the fuck up.

As we go inside of the hospital, I look up the room number that Sienna's brother had texted to me earlier. There's an agonizing dullness in the center of my chest while Kylie and I take the elevator up to the third floor. When the doors spread, I follow my sister slowly as she rushes down the hallway. I was in such a hurry to get to Nashville, and now, standing here with the scent of bleach and medicine hitting me in the face, all I feel is dread.

So I wait outside of Sienna's door, pulling my shit together, while Kylie goes inside. I hear my sister gasp and a moment later, she murmurs, "Oh god, babe." Dragging in a rough breath, I shove the door open and step through the doorway. Even though Sienna makes an attempt to shield her face, I see everything. I go through a mix of emotions: fear, anger, rage, and guilt. For the time being, I settle on guilt.

Guilt and rage.

I walk over to the hospital bed, each step making the ringing in my ears grow louder. When I get to her, she opens her mouth to say something. At first, I convince myself that she's talking, and I can't hear anything because of the deafening blare in my ears, but then I realize that she's speechless.

And that she's sobbing. Shoulder-wracking, chest-heaving sobs. From the corner of the room, my sister's crying, too.

I feel like the worst fucking thing that's ever lived.

And I want to kill the motherfucker who did this to her.

I'm scared to touch her—terrified out of my goddamn mind that I might hurt her— but she reaches out to me. I slide her fingers through mine.

As soon as she's calm enough to speak, she drags in a long breath. "My brother is friends with a girl who works for the police department." Her gaze falls down to her lap, and she tightens her grip on my hand. "That guy has been in and out of jail. Aggravated assault. Robbery. He told the cops he got my address from somebody he met on a Your Toxic Sequel message board. Followed me from my house to my friend's bar."

I release a harsh sound, but she continues. "Your ex-wife sent me a message this morning. Wanted to know how I was feeling."

Before I can say anything, my sister storms across the room, her hair flying wildly behind her. "This is all you," she hisses, jabbing me hard in the chest with her fingertips.

"This is all *you*, Lucas. Fix it."

I start to release Sienna's hand, but she holds on to it like it's impossible for her to let go as I sink down in the chair closest to the bed. "God, Red, I don't know what to—"

"Tell me," she implores. She grasps bunches of the starched white sheet in her other hand, twisting the fabric around anxiously. "God, Lucas, please tell me what all of this has been about." The last word is a broken whisper, a plea. A silent warning. *Tell me or I'm gone. Tell me what you did, or we're through for good.*

If we were any other place, anywhere but in this goddamn hospital with her fucked up because of me, I'd steer this somewhere else. But I *knew* this conversation was coming, and I feel like I've already been shoved into a pit and buried alive—the worst part of it all is that this is a grave I dug for myself.

Breathing in and out until my chest burns, I glance at my sister, at the blatant disappointment on her face, and then back to Sienna. Despite the pain she's got to be in, she's managed to sit upright. Even through the bruises and cuts, the dark circles beneath her wide blue eyes and the scowl on her face—even through it all, she's still the most beautiful thing I've ever seen.

The best thing I've ever possessed.

And even if it means losing her—and maybe that's what I deserve for what I did years ago—I owe her so much more than she's been given so far.

"After everything went to shit between Sam and me, we didn't stop seeing each other," I begin. Sienna nods her head carefully, her curtain of red hair falling over her bruised face. "Hell, I saw her more after we separated than before." Admitting that still makes me feel like the biggest fucking idiot.

"I fucked up," I whisper harshly. "I did something fucked up and then I told

Samantha about it."

Sienna lets out a breath. "Okay. What is it?"

The room feels like it's shrinking in on me, so before it can finish doing the job, I mutter, "I killed a man. I ended someone's life."

After I came home from Louisville, I had no intention of seeing Samantha. I didn't want to be around her—or anyone else, for that matter—until I pulled myself together.

Figured out what the fuck I needed to do to fix the mess I was in.

Instead, Sam came to me.

I'd stumbled into my house drunk and falling over the couch. So wrecked I wouldn't have noticed that someone else was there, if not for a hand running down my shoulder and over my chest from behind me. I grabbed the arm hard, and a teasing, familiar voice whispered into my ear, "Careful, Lucas, you might hurt me."

Letting Samantha go, I shoved myself to my feet. "What the fuck are you doing here?" I growled. "Get the fuck out of my house, Sam."

She flung her shoulder-length blond hair over her shoulder and skimmed her tongue over her lips. It was supposed to look enticing, but it just made me sick to my stomach. "I missed you. Figured you would want to see me after staying away for so long."

"Believe me, I don't." I swept past her and climbed the steps, but she was right behind me, talking about her flight from Atlanta and how tired she was. She followed me into my bedroom, and as I started to get undressed, she threw herself down on the bed and yawned.

"Get out, Sam."

Stretching her arms out behind her and pressing her palms against the mattress for support, she made a pouting noise. "If you're going to kick me out, you could at least sound convincing." She lolled her head back, and when she looked at me again, she winked one of her gray eyes. "Trust me, you give me what I want, and I'll be on my way."

"It's not happening tonight."

"But you're drunk, and we both know how you get when you drink too much." When I gave her a warning glare that told her I wasn't fucking her tonight, she widened her eyes. "What the hell did you do to my Lucas?"

"I don't want to touch you." I sat down on the edge of my bed, and she tried to climb into my lap. I pushed her away, clenching my teeth. "I can't touch you."

The only thing I wanted to do was go to bed. To forget what I had done.

"You're just drunk, baby," she reminded me. "But I love you, so I'll forgive you." "I fucked up."

Sam suddenly looked irritated as she pressed her lips into a hard line. "I know about that cunt Cilla. You're a free man, Lucas, so you can do whatever it is that you—"

Maybe it was the alcohol, or the words she had said right then, or both, but the next thing that came out of my mouth condemned me. "I killed a man in Louisville."

My ex-wife sat perfectly still for nearly a minute and then she moved her head to the side. "Don't play games, Lucas."

I pulled her close to me so that our noses touched, and repeated my words between gritted teeth. "I. Killed. Someone."

Then I told her what had happened. About Cilla being stalked for months. About the man attacking her in the parking lot of the little shit venue we were playing at. About me going after him, blind with rage, hitting him over and over again until he was unconscious.

"I took Cilla back inside." I dragged my hands through my hair. "And when I went back out, he was gone. He was dead. There wasn't shit I could do. If I'd known ... I wouldn't have just let him fucking die, you've got to understand that."

Sam leaned forward, her face calm in spite of the bomb I just dropped. Maybe she really did think it was all a game.

"You didn't call the cops?" she asked.

"I fucking panicked," I shouted. "I fucking panicked and left him there. They're treating it as a mugging, Sam. What the fuck do I do?"

She thought on my question for a moment, nibbling carefully on her bottom lip. Finally, she slid on top of me, taking my face between her hands. "Nothing. You do nothing because you've done nothing so far. Turning yourself in now would be the end for you. You know that, don't you?"

"Yeah, I do."

She made a sound of approval that reminded me of someone offering encouragement to a small child. It tore me up inside because of all the people to get advice from on something so serious, I was turning to Samantha. The woman who'd been the source of ninety-five percent of my aggravation over the last several years— the same woman I wasn't even able to trust enough to stay married to.

"Does Cilla know what happened?" she asked

I shook my head. "She was so goddamn drunk she couldn't even say her own name without falling over. Once the cops started to show, I got her out of there, took her back to our hotel room." I shook my head once more. "No, she doesn't know. If I told her it would kill her."

When I looked into Sam's gray eyes, I noticed how hard they'd gotten. Dropping her gaze from mine, she wrapped her arms around my shoulders and buried her face in the crook of my neck. "Good," she whispered. "It's good she doesn't remember."

I was stupid enough to believe that my secret—what I had done and who I was— was safe with Samantha. That after that night, we'd never speak of it again, and the only thing I'd have to live with was my own guilt and misery.

But three months later, my ex-wife sent me her first demand for money.

When I'm finished, both my sister and Sienna sit in a dazed silence. Sienna's no longer gripping my hand, and I glare down at a scuffmark on the hospital floor. "That's what Sam has on me," I spit out bitterly. "His name was Bryce Roberts. And I killed him."

"Bryce Roberts," my sister repeats, and I close my eyes and nod. "God, Lucas.

What the fuck?"

I look over at Sienna to find her staring blankly at the wall.

She asked, and I gave her what she wanted to know. And now, I've ruined things with her.

"I sent his family money. An anonymous donation," I add, like it will help the situation. It won't, and nothing I did then or could do now will help. "But god, it was an accident. I swear I didn't mean to kill him." My voice is pleading, and Sienna moves her head up and down.

"No, I understand."

Out of the corner of my eye, I see Kylie leave the room quietly with her face lowered to the floor. As soon as she's gone I get up and move to Sienna's bedside. She doesn't recoil, but she doesn't look at me either.

Fuck.

"I love you," I tell her roughly. "More than anything I've ever loved. And it rips my goddamn soul out that this has happened to you."

At last she turns her face to me, giving me a full view of the damage that was done to her. This was caused because of her being with me. I should have been smarter. Should have hired someone to protect her.

I should have been there to protect her.

"I know you do. And I love you too—it's impossible for me to stop." Sienna closes her eyes tightly, and tears squeeze out the corners. "I just need time to myself to think for a few days. I-I just want to figure things out."

She's terrified of me. After all she's been through in the last twenty-four hours, how can she not be?

"I'll wait to hear from you," I manage, choking on the words, fisting my hands to keep from touching her one final time.

"Sure, Lucas," she whispers.

But after all the lies and the bullshit, the regrets, I still feel like the world has been ripped from beneath my feet when she turns away from me again.

Because everything I've thought about myself since I killed Bryce Roberts has now been confirmed and I can sum it up with just a single word.

Monster.

CHAPTER TWENTY ONE

Sienna

After Lucas and Kylie leave my cold hospital room, I finally ask for some of those pain meds the medical staff has been trying to force down my throat since I was admitted here last night. Hot tears are running down my cheeks, scalding me as I take the tiny plastic cup from my nurse, and by the time I've downed the swig of water she's given me, my shoulders are trembling.

The nurse stands at the foot of my bed, her face wrinkled into a tight mask of concern. Holding her chart close to her chest, she pushes her pen behind her ear and asks me in a gentle voice, "Do you need me to call someone for you, Ms. Jensen?"

I know she's just being kind, but who would I have her call? Gram, who is already worried sick over all of this? Seth, who has spent every moment possible during the last twenty-four hours blasting Lucas for failing to protect me.

Or Lucas himself?

Lucas, the beautiful, tattooed man who makes my chest seize up every time I picture him, every time he steps into a room. The beautiful man whose ex-wife probably orchestrated my attack. The man who, not even half an hour ago, admitted to me that he had murdered a man protecting another woman four years ago.

I feel sorry for Cilla, and for myself, but I also feel my heart break for Lucas.

My throat suddenly feels dry, and I swallow hard, wanting to get rid of some of the bitterness before I answer the nurse. "No—" I squint at her nametag. "Thanks, Nora.

But I'm just tired. I just need to rest. That's all I need."

She puckers her lips sympathetically and pats the bottom of my blanket right next to where my toes are curled into the sheets. "You've been through a lot. Get some rest,

Ms. Jensen, you deserve it. Press the call button if you need anything."

Once she's gone, I flip on the television. Ironically, the newest episode of *Echo Falls*, the paranormal TV show I used to work on the set of, is on, and I let the sounds of unrequited love and sexual frustration serenade me until the tears are gone, and my eyes feel so heavy they ache.

I sleep like shit.

Even though I turn my phone off to avoid calls from Tori and, to my surprise, Sinjin, I filter in and out of consciousness all night—my hazy, waking thoughts focusing on everything from my mother to my own insecurities.

But mostly, it's Lucas who I think about.

And by the time I'm able to force myself into a decent and consistent sleep, there are fresh tears drying on the outside corners of my eyes.

The banging noise of my room's door closing wakes me up the next morning, and I shoot up straight, gasping for air and holding my hands up defensively in front of me. My chest is heaving as my gaze dashes anxiously around the room until it lands on my younger brother.

Clutching my hand over my chest, I scowl at Seth. "You scared the shit out of me."

His mouth sets in a hard line as he walks further into my room and sinks down in the armchair beside my bed. Placing his forearms on thighs, Seth leans forward, pressing his lips to his balled up fists. After a few moments of silence, he looks me over, starting at the top of my head and ending at my hands, which are folded up in my lap.

"I've never seen you look like that."

Self-consciously, I run my hand through my hair, grimacing at how tangled the red locks are. "Of course, you'd state the obvious about my looks and—"

He shakes his head. "Not the bruises, Sienna, or the messed up hair. The look of fear when I woke you up. It's not … natural."

"The key phrase there is that you woke me up," I point out, trying my best to keep my tone dry. Still, my excuse sounds lame even to my own ears.

"You've never woken up like that before."

"How the hell do you know that? Have you been watching me when I sleep, baby brother? Isn't that a tad creepy, even for you?"

Giving me the closest that he's come to a smile since I was checked into the hospital, he pushes himself back into an upright sitting position. "I heard Wolfe was here last night." Probably from the nurse who's the mom of one of his former girlfriends. My brother seems to know everyone in Nashville.

"You called him, didn't you?" I cross my arms over my chest. "Did you not expect him to come? Give the man a little credit, Seth."

Seth gives a noncommittal grunt before shrugging. "Are you going back on tour with him?" he asks quietly, and I stare down at my hands. There's a purplish bruise on the inside of my left wrist where I had blocked one of my attacker's punches, and I massage my right thumb over it in slow, soothing motions.

"I've got a lot of work to do here. As much as I hate—" It's sad, that I don't know what to say next. That I hate myself for pushing once again to find out what it was Lucas was keeping from me? That right now, I hate that knowing everything there is to know about Lucas and realizing just how much I love him, I'm still conflicted? "I have to work," I say again, my voice breaking.

Seth seems to consider this for a long time before he nods once. He looks down at the watch I had given him for his birthday a couple of years ago. Groaning, he stands up and comes over to the bed. He sits down on the side of it. "That girl I was telling you about a few weeks ago? I'm thinking about bringing her to Gram's once you get out of this shithole. You know, so you can meet her and give her shit."

What I do know is exactly what my kid brother is trying to do right now. And coming from Seth, I appreciate the distraction because he only knows half of what's actually going on. All he knows for certain is that I'm hurting. I give him a nod and an appreciative smile that makes my cheeks ache.

"Thank you, Seth. Really. I can't wait to meet her."

He gives me an awkward shrug. "Whatever." When he yawns, I can tell it's fake and a way to pull me away from getting emotional. "I think I'm going back to my room to go to bed—"

"Don't skip. It's too damn early in the year for you to beg off, so save your days for the ones where you … do whatever the hell it is you do when you refuse to go to class." When his mouth flares into a smile, and he parts his lips to say something, I press my hand flat against his chest and turn my face to the side, cringing. "Ugh, I wasn't asking for you to give me an explanation of your extracurricular activities. Go the hell to class."

His bottom lip moves slightly as he bites the inside of it. Finally, he slides off of my bed. "Fine." Bending down, he kisses me on my cheek, his scruffy chin scratching my face. "But you better call me if anything happens."

When he pulls away, both of my eyebrows are raised. "Are you telling me that you—Seth Jensen—will actually answer my phone call?"

He rolls his brown eyes as he walks to the door. "You don't give me enough credit, big sister."

True to his word, even though Lucas turns my hospital room into a florist thanks to all the flowers he has delivered to me, he doesn't return to the hospital to seek me out again. I have all morning to begin the process of sorting out my tangled up thoughts. After one of the physicians comes around a little after noon, and a nurse issues my discharge paperwork shortly thereafter, I'm stunned to find that the person who arrives to pick me up is none other than Kylie McCrae.

Dressed in a green and white Peter Pan-collared dress and white flats, she's smiling when she comes into my room, but her lips are pale. And when she hugs me, taking the utmost care to be gentle, I can feel how violently her shoulders are shaking.

"Are you alright, Kylie?"

She draws away from me, rubbing her hands over her face. "I'm picking you up from the hospital and you're asking me if I'm alright? Yes, I promise I am." When she pushes her oversized sunglasses off her face on top of her head, my chest contracts at the sight of her bloodshot brown eyes and puffy eyelids. "I called your grandmother and asked if you'd mind if I came to get you. She said you wouldn't, and I hope that's true."

"No, I don't mind," I say gently. "Thank you for coming."

Although I'm perfectly capable of carrying it myself, Kylie insists on toting the small overnight bag that Gram dropped off for me yesterday. Kylie leads me to a rental car, an Expedition that she has to practically do acrobatics to get into since she's so tiny.

"Yesterday they had a two hundred thousand dollar bond on that shithead who hurt you, but as of an hour ago there's no longer a bond," she says, breaking the silence a few minutes after she pulls out of the hospital parking lot. "So there's no way in hell that he's going anywhere."

"Lucas' doing?"

Her eyes falter, but then she gazes straight ahead at the Mini Cooper in front of us. "I'm not sure. My brother has a lot of friends. A lot of attorneys. A lot of …"

In my head, I finish the last sentence for her.

A lot of secrets.

"Are you going back to the band tonight?" I ask, but the underlying question is obvious: Has Lucas left already?

"Not if you don't want me to. I'll stay here as long as you need me."

Choosing not to respond to that, I focus my attention on adjusting the A/C vent, playing with the dial until the cold air is blowing into my face. "You've always been amazing to me, Kylie, but I'm guessing that you coming to pick me up wasn't just to tell me that the guy who attacked me won't be getting out of jail anytime soon."

She laughs nervously. "You perceptive bitch, you."

It was funny, I vividly recall her brother saying nearly the same thing to me backstage after the show in Dallas when Cilla had debuted her song "Second Best." It was only a couple of weeks ago, so why the hell does it seem like a lifetime has passed since that night?

"What are you going to do about my brother?" Kylie questions me in a soft voice that's on the verge of breaking.

I twist my head to the right and look out the window. "What he did doesn't change how I feel about him." A strand of my hair blows out of place thanks to the air conditioner, and I tuck it back behind my ear, flinching in pain when my knuckles brush against a bruise along my jawline. "I believe him when he says it was an accident, but why couldn't he have just—"

When my voice cuts off, Kylie whips her head toward me, her short brown tendrils flying around her face. "What? Told you? God, me too. But ... Sienna, I have been riding his ass for years about this, and nothing could have prepared me for what he said in that hospital room yesterday. And I don't think for one second that you wanted to hear that any more than me."

"So you never expected it to be that?"

She returns her gaze to the road. "God, no. Maybe I should have, huh? I mean, now that I really stop to think about it, the signs were all there. Cilla stopped complaining about having a stalker a few weeks after Louisville and then there was the whole thing with Lucas avoiding the damn place. But honestly, I just thought that was because he didn't want the stigma of Cilla's rant being attached to the band." She turns onto the interstate sharply, muttering a curse when some guy honks his horn at her.

"I couldn't sleep last night, so I Googled Bryce. The authorities thought it was a mugging gone wrong—he had drugs on him, and he was high as a kite when he died.

And then he had a history of hurting women and whoever the hell else got in his way."

She bites her bottom lip. "If I had suspected that..."

But she can't bring herself to finish that sentence.

"If you think that I plan on telling anyone what I know, I'm not," I promise, and she gives me a sad smile.

"If I thought that, you wouldn't be in this truck with me. What I want to know is what you plan on doing about ... your personal situation? My brother loves you, and if Sam is going to pull some crazy shit—and use your head, babe, we both know she is, it's just a matter of when she'll choose to do it—I want to know where you stand."

"I...."

Where the hell do I stand? I know exactly where my heart lies, and that's with

Lucas, but my head?

Kylie sniffs hard. "Because I don't want my brother to go away. I don't want his niece or nephew not to know him, and—"

The air feels like it's been punched out of my lungs. "Wait. Kylie, you're not talking about Lucas' niece or nephew that might come five years from now, are you?

You're pregnant?"

"Surprise," she says in a flat voice. "Six weeks, and believe it or not, nobody knows except for you and Lucas. Not even Wyatt." She gives me a rueful smile. "If he knew then he'd be in here with us right now."

"Are you okay? This has to be bad for the baby."

Kylie shakes her head. "I promise, I'm fine." She veers the Expedition onto the exit for Gram's house. When she reaches the stop sign, she presses her forehead to the steering wheel for a moment. "You're sitting there with your face all bruised up, and once again, the only thing you can think of is how I'm feeling. You're pretty unbelievable, you know." She snorts incredulously. "No wonder my brother is madly in love with you."

She's quiet for the rest of the ride, but when I sneak a glance in her direction every minute or so, I see the tears rolling unchecked down her cheeks. When she drives the SUV into my grandmother's driveway, she pulls up as close as she can to the front door. Turning off the ignition, she rests her shoulder blades back against the leather seat and fingers the collar of her green and white dress.

"What the hell are we going to do about all this, Sienna?" Kylie breathes, sounding like she's on the verge of tears. Shutting her eyes, she swipes the pads of her thumbs across her eyelids. "The fact that you've been hurt because of it makes me sick to my stomach."

Realization dawns on me that Kylie's puffy eyes and pale face isn't something solely caused by her brother's confession. She's also been just as worried about me. A sharp pang of guilt pierces my chest.

"Look," I murmur at last, and Kylie's brown eyes snap open to stare at me carefully. "I don't like to leave the people who I love, and who love me." In an effort to avoid her gaze so my chest will stop aching, I look straight ahead at the front door of the house until the rectangular shape of the wood is blurry. "That's why I came back here to Nashville. Because no matter what's happened to me or what I did, I always, *always* knew I could count on Gram and my brother."

"You're a good one. I knew that when I met you a couple years ago."

"I don't know how I'll look at Lucas from now on, but I do know this: I love him. That may make me stupid or weak or even naïve. I don't care. But no matter if we're going to be together or not, I don't want that bitch Sam to do this to him."

"She's going to ask for more money." Kylie frowns. "I know it's coming—the question is when and how much?"

"How do you know that?"

Her shoulders slump forward in defeat. "It's the only thing that makes sense. And he'll keep giving it to her just to bury what he did. What scares me the most is what happens when there's nothing left? When she's taken everything from him, and there's nothing else coming from him that will appease her?"

I watch as the door to the cabin opens up, and my grandmother comes out with a warm smile on her face. But that look melts away quickly when she sees Kylie and me inside of the SUV. Slowly, she reverses back into the house, and the door closes behind her.

I squeeze my eyes together. "It doesn't matter if I stay away or not does it?"

"Lucas loving you puts a fire under her ass, but no, you leaving him doesn't change anything. She's going to keep coming at him no matter what you decide to do."

Sam will keep coming at Lucas until there's nothing left to give.

And how long will that take?

A year?

Another four years?

For the rest of Lucas' life?

Reaching behind her seat, I grab my overnight bag and draw it up to the front of the car, flinching from the pain the movement caused. Kylie gives me a disapproving frown. "Thank you for coming to get me," I whisper.

"Like it or not, you're stuck with me."

"I know I am, but luckily, I like it."

As I climb out of the Expedition, I give Kylie a worried once-over, my eyes stopping when they drop to her flat stomach. She looks down, too. "Take care of yourself, Kylie. And tell Wyatt about the baby, will you? You'll make his year."

For the first time since she picked me up a half an hour ago, she offers me the cheery smile that first drew me to her. "Don't worry, I will. *You* take care of yourself, Sienna. Get some sleep and try to heal. Try not to think about anything other than fixing yourself."

That's easier said than done, but I nod and slam the door. "I'll call you soon."

As I walk slowly up the front steps, I hear the automatic window slide down.

"What should I tell Lucas?" she calls out, and my shoulders go taut.

"That he would be an idiot if he thought I would ever stop loving him."

CHAPTER TWENTY TWO

Over the next day and a half, I force myself to get the much-needed rest that Kylie had suggested—with the way I'm feeling, I really have no other choice. The only thing that screws with my plan is the nightmares. And the two messages from Samantha that pop up in my inbox—one to, once again, ask me how I'm feeling, and the other wanting to know if I had met the real Lucas yet. The Lucas she knows so well.

Seeing her name on my screen—fully comprehending just how much power she has over him—causes my stomach to coil into painful knots that I know won't untangle anytime soon. If ever. Not when Sam is holding so much over Lucas' head.

I don't answer either email, nor do I erase them, though I have no idea what I'm keeping the damn things for. All I know is that they make me absolutely blind with fury and scare the hell out of me.

Because of the crappy dreams and Sam's messages, I leave my house very little—only once to go to the pharmacy to pick up my pain medication. But by Tuesday afternoon not only am I feeling better, but also I'm restless. When Ashley begs me to meet her for lunch, I put aside my apprehension and jump at the chance to get out.

This is when I realize that someone is following me.

As I park my car, I notice that the same black car that was parked on the street near the edge of my driveway when I left the other day to go to Walgreens is sitting in front of a meter across the street from The Beacon.

Maybe I'm overreacting, but panic seeps through my body as I lock my car and rush inside the bar. I'm breathless, wheezing heavily, and glancing behind me. When I crash into a rock hard wall of flesh, sending ripples of pain through my already sore body, I let out a deafening shriek.

"I got you, girl." Nick, the giant redheaded doorman, grasps my shoulders, balancing me. His concerned eyes lock on mine as he continues in a soothing voice,

"Calm down, I got you. Jesus … you're shaking like a leaf."

My breath is coming in and out in short, broken bursts, but I manage to slow it down enough to get a rush of frightened words out. "I think whoever's in that car is following me."

Nick studies my face carefully, and I feel large splotches of embarrassment heating up my skin. I start to question my sanity, question whether or not I should have left my house to begin with, but then I close my eyes and count to ten. When I open them, the thick muscles in Nick's neck are tight.

"Which car is it?" he asks, all business.

He follows me over to the glass door, and I point at the black Nissan with lightly tinted windows. "That's the one," I mutter, rubbing my palm over my chest. My skin feels like it's on fire. I race my tongue over my lips and then pull in a deep breath. "It was parked near my house yesterday, but I didn't pay it any attention then. But now...."

"Can you go check it out, Nicky?" Ashley asks softly from behind us. I spin around, giving her an appreciative look that more than likely borders on the edge of desperation.

Although they butt heads more often than not, Nick doesn't give Ashley any crap about her most recent request. Instead, he nods swiftly, a dangerous gleam leaping into his eyes. "You got it."

While Nick dashes out of the bar, Ashley grabs my wrist and leads me over to a back table. "You don't need to watch anything like that," she soothes. "It's broad daylight, and Nicky deals with the bar shitheads all night long. He can handle whoever that asshole is."

Resting my elbows on the table, I bury my face in my hands, inhaling the scent of vanilla bean sanitizer, before running them back through my hair. I gather my red locks into a tight ponytail and then release my hands. "I'm a fucking mess."

Ashley's back stiffens but then she leans forward, so far that her pink and turquoise hair skims the table. "Dude, you got beat up by some psycho in a parking lot less than four days ago. You're not a mess. You're normal. This is how anybody would react given those circumstances."

The front bell clangs, and both of our heads fly up to see Nick stomping toward us with a familiar body and face in tow. David, Your Toxic Sequel's bodyguard. My hand flies to my chest in relief, and I let my shoulders sag as they both stop short in front of me.

"Tell this motherfucker that I'm not harassing you," David snarls, his brown eyes brimming with fury. "He says he's calling the cops, Sienna."

Coming up out of my seat, I nod my head quickly at Nick. "No, he's fine, I promise! This is one of Your Toxic Sequel's security guards. He's … I guess he's with me." Noticing the pleading look that I'm shooting between Nick and David, Ashley takes this as her cue to intervene and leave. She wiggles her butt off the chair she's sitting on, and motions her head to the back of the bar.

"If she says he's fine, he is. Let's give them a little bit of room, Nicky," she suggests, and Nick begrudgingly follows her toward the bar counter where Ashley pretends to be checking inventory while keeping a cautious eye on what's happening out here between David and me.

We sit down together at the table Ashley and I were sharing, and it takes me a long time to ask, "Lucas? Did Lucas send you to watch over me?"

David confirms with a grunt and a bob of his head. "He said you needed some time. Asked me to come off the tour and keep an eye on you for him."

And he's probably paying you both arms and legs, but of course, I won't say that to David. I feel a deep comfort in knowing that while I've been freaking out and worried the last few days, Lucas took it upon himself to make sure someone was protecting me. "Thank you." I place my hand on his thick forearm, giving it a little squeeze that he probably doesn't even feel. I release a tremulous sigh. "It means a lot to me that you've been making sure I stayed safe."

David's dark brown eyes are apologetic, and he bows his head in shame. "I should've let you know it was me."

"Yeah, probably. I would've been a lot less terrified when I realized that someone was following me."

The awkward conversation between the two of us continues for another few minutes before he excuses himself from the bar, shooting a dark look at Nick as he ducks his head to walk out of the front door.

Ashley comes back out onto the bar floor, slinging a dishtowel over her shoulder. She stares out at the front of the room, at the people passing by the front door outside the bar. "Lucas-Fucking-Wolfe and the shit he'll do for his woman," she sighs, sending a shiver rolling down my spine.

"Yeah," I whisper. "No kidding."

Once again, the black Nissan rental is parked at the top of my driveway this evening, but this time I don't worry about it as I sit on the front porch with my legs stretched out on the swing. When I told Gram about Lucas sending Your Toxic Sequel's bodyguard, I could see the relief on her face. The attack on me shook her badly, and knowing that someone like David is around is enough to give her a little peace.

The sound of my phone buzzing from where I left it on the outdoor table, right next to a new can of pepper spray, interrupts the quietness. I flip it over, and when I peer over at the screen, my heartbeat speeds up. It's Lucas.

This is the first time that he's called me since visiting me in the hospital on Saturday. I grab the phone, weighing it in my palm like I'm considering my options before I suck it up and hit the Accept button. I hear him let out a breath of what sounds like relief as soon as I place the phone to my ear and say hello.

"I'm sorry, Red," he whispers. "There I go again fucking up, huh? I should've warned you about David. I just needed some peace of mind. I couldn't let you go around alone after what the motherfucker did to you."

I wrap my arm around myself, holding my body tightly as I shake my head. "No,

I'm glad that you—"

When I don't continue, he makes a harsh, anguished sound in the back of his throat. "That I'm not there myself, waiting around to kill the next person who tries to touch you?" I can vividly imagine him sitting in the bus galley, with his forehead resting against his palm and every muscle in his body tight from anger. I hate picturing him like that.

"No, Lucas. Don't even—"

"Don't what? Don't admit that that's what I wanted to do to that motherfucker who hurt you? That this time, it wouldn't have been an accident?"

"Where are you?" Fear slices through my heart thinking of whom he could be saying all of this in front of. "You shouldn't talk like that, okay?"

"I'm on the bus. Alone," he growls. "On my way to Nashville."

He was coming here. Lucas was coming back here. For me. Then I close my eyes—of course, he's coming here. He's got a show to play twenty-four hours from now.

"Where's Sinjin?"

"With Zoe. He's meeting us there."

"Ah," I whisper, feeling a wave of happiness wash over me at the thought of Sinjin resolving his issues with Zoe. Sin deserved for something to go his way, especially in the romance department. And Lucas—despite his mistakes and screw-ups—he deserved it too.

Maybe, just maybe, I'm selfish for thinking that.

"I've been doing the shows we didn't have to cancel, but all I can think about is you," he tells me. "The way you taste and smell. The way you laugh. I don't care if I sound like a pussy for admitting this, but I'm messed up without you, and I don't know if anything can fix it this time."

"I just needed time to catch my breath." I tighten my grip around my still-sore body, and the memory of being punched in the stomach comes back to me full force. "I should have told you about Sam's threats earlier."

He releases a rough, grating laugh. "Hell yeah, you should have told me earlier, Red. I told you I'd protect you, and I damn well mean to do it. No more secrets between us—we don't hide shit from each other. I'll never drag you blindfolded into a situation like that again. You're mine now, and I protect what's mine."

"*I* followed you." I stand up and begin to pace the length of the porch, biting on the tip of my thumb as I walk. "I followed you because I love you, and I still love you. Now I just know a little more than I did when I walked in. But … I'm glad to know you'll protect me."

Much, much better.

"So where does this leave us?" he asks.

I hesitate. Where *does* that leave us? "I don't know, but I think we have to figure that out."

"I need to see you." He swallows hard and then I hear him inhale and exhale. "We'll be pulling through in about six or seven hours." Then he gives me the venue, which I immediately know of. When he's finished, he asks me in a low voice, "Be there,

Sienna. Just … I need you."

"You know that I'll always be there for you." This man has come and gone from my life more than once over the last couple years, and to give up now without even trying would be more heartache than never knowing what could have been.

I'm not ready to deal with that type of pain.

I don't think I will ever be.

Sunlight is peeking across the sky when I pull my car into the venue's parking lot a few minutes after six the next morning. Just as Lucas said, the buses have recently pulled in, and the early morning bustle has already started. I take the keys out of my old Mercury sedan, shove them as far as they'll go into my pocket, and walk over to the bus we shared without anyone from security trying to stop me.

One of the drivers is still inside, filling out a log, and when he opens the door for me and takes a close look at my face, he gives me a sympathetic smile. "Welcome back."

I don't have the heart to tell him that I'm not continuing on the tour, so I give him a grateful nod. "Is Lucas back there?"

"Probably sleeping but that doesn't matter. He'll want to be woken up if you're around."

Letting the driver's words roll through my mind, I walk down the bus aisle and past Sinjin's empty section until I reach the back compartment. I find Lucas face down on the full-size bed that we slept in together, his long, muscular legs poking off the edge, and his fingers clenched into the sheets on the side of the mattress that I slept on.

I sit down beside him.

"Lucas," I whisper. He doesn't budge, so I touch his back, running my fingers over the array of tattoos covering his skin. More than six months ago, I had stood over him, watching him sleep and studying his dozens of tattoos. I'd decided that his stopwatch and queen of hearts tattoo found near the bottom of his back was my favorite, but now I can't look at it without my stomach pitching.

It stands for Sam, for her disgusting hold over him, and I hate that he's had to go through her shit alone for so many years.

"Lucas," I try again, shaking his shoulder. He rolls his head to the side, opening his hazel eyes to stare up at me. Wanting to put a little distance between us, at least until we've managed to talk, I slide off the bed and stand beside it.

"Didn't think you'd come." His voice is rough with sleep, and I can't help the involuntary shiver of awareness it sends down my spine. "But I'm so goddamn glad you did, Red."

I wring my hands together, rubbing each finger vigorously. "You must not know me very well to think that I wouldn't keep my word."

He presses his palms to his eyes, scrubbing them inward to wake himself up, and lets out a giant breath. "Come here."

I'm hesitant at first, but then he touches my waist on both sides and urges me to him, his strong hands gliding down the curves of my body gently. I climb on the bed, one knee at a time, sliding my body against his as I rest the side of my face on the pillow beside him. He feathers his knuckles across the bruise on my jaw that I've hidden beneath makeup, and his nostrils flare. "I'm so fucking sorry, Si."

"I know you are."

"No matter what happens to me, I'm going to make sure that nobody ever touches you again," he promises, his eyes hard. "You're mine."

I move my head from side to side. "You make it seem like she's tried to turn you in." When he doesn't say anything, I sit up abruptly and glare down at him. "Lucas? Has she? Is she?"

He doesn't look like he wants to directly address Sam, but he shakes his head. "She's moved, but I've got someone trying to track her down." He offers me a smile that isn't enough to put my mind at ease. "So, at this point, I don't know. But do you think I give a fuck anymore? I looked out for me and only me for years, and then you came along. You made me feel everything—emotions I never expected to feel. You don't know what that's like, because you've always loved. You are love. After I came back here from seeing you beat up and broken because of me, I laid here and I realized that I stopped caring what happens to me a long time ago."

As beautiful and romantic as his words are, hearing him say things like that causes my stomach to harden. Because it makes me feel like this is the beginning of the end.

"Well, I care," I fling back at him, my voice high-pitched and nervous. "I wouldn't have come here if I didn't."

"I killed a man," he admits. "And then, I threw money at his family like it would fix things. It didn't fix a goddamn thing."

"He was stalking someone you cared about." I think of Cilla. No matter what kind of conflict there is between us, I would never want anyone to have to go through what Lucas said Bryce was about to do to her. "If Sam goes to the cops, your story has to count for something."

He pushes himself up into a sitting position, and I roll my head onto his lap. He massages his fingers across the soft red strands at my hairline, and I lift my hand to his face, rubbing the tip of my thumb over his straight nose and then to his lips. "My story is four years too late, Red. I'll go to the cops before Sam does."

"Then we'll figure this out together."

His expression softens. "You're sticking around?"

"On this tour? No," I laugh, shaking my head hard, and he gives me a grim look. "But with you? Always. Didn't Kylie give you my message?"

The look on his face says it all. It's full of love and bewilderment, of appreciation and doubt.

When he answers me, his voice is heavy with emotion. "Yes, but I was convinced it was your pain pills talking."

CHAPTER TWENTY THREE

I spend most of the morning locked in Lucas' tattooed arms.

There's very little talking between us, and no lovemaking, but it's the most intimate we've ever been since our relationship began more than two and a half years ago. After he falls asleep because he's still worn out from last night's show in Memphis, I untangle myself from his body and go out into the bus lounge so that I can call Gram and let her know that I'm okay. By now she's probably wide-awake, and given the events of the last several days, she must be freaking out.

As I dial the number to our house, another call comes through that I accidentally accept. I cringe. I'm not in the mood to talk to anyone other than Gram right now— especially since this person has an unrecognizable out-of-state area code—and I look down at the screen, wanting to just hang up and ignore the caller if they try again. But then again, they might not stop trying to get in touch with me until they actually succeed.

I put the phone up to my ear and try to hide the irritation from seeping into my voice. "Hello?"

"Is this Sienna?" The voice is soft, female with a slight Southern accent. "Hello?"

I clear my throat. "Yes?"

The woman on the other end of the call makes a soft sound, like whispering. Then, in a louder, firmer voice, she hisses, "This is Samantha. The woman whose husband you've been fucking."

Like she needed that introduction. I know her well, and I grind my teeth together. I'm sure that if there were a mirror in front of me, I would see that I'm pale and shaking. But right now, I can't feel anything other than the cold numbness spreading through my body.

"And big surprise, you're silent," Sam taunts.

Clawing my phone to keep from dropping it, I whisper harshly, "He's not your husband. Why the hell are you calling me? Haven't you done enough? And how did you get my phone number?"

She takes a moment to process all of my questions before she speaks. "You're easy to find. And you haven't answered me back. I wanted to hear your voice before—" She stops herself. The little laugh that follows manages to evoke every fear, every bit of desperation, inside me.

"Before what?"

She answers me after a long pause, and each word is emphasized. "Before I put an end to all of this." I try to picture her. Try to close my eyes and remember what she looked like the one time I met her more than six months ago, but the only thing that comes to mind is her icy gray eyes.

Sliding down, my butt hits the floor hard, but I don't even feel it as I hold my elbows close to my chest. "What are you planning to do, Sam?" I demand.

"What I should have done a long time ago."

I tuck in my upper lip and shake my head. "You can't do this to him. Not after he's given you so much of his money." My voice sounds strange to my ears, foreign. Nothing like anything I've ever heard before. "Not after you've put him through so much shit."

"You still support him?" Sam laughs again, this one more forced. Colder. "I can do whatever it is I want, sweetheart. The ball is in my court. All I have to do is go to the cops, and—"

"You *can't* do this," I repeat viciously.

"I'm sorry, but I can't do it anymore. I won't."

So why is she calling to tell me all of this? And why is she apologizing to me?

Leaning my face against my knees, I close my eyes. This woman is dangerous. Dangerous and crazy, and I am scared half to death of how far she's willing to go to tear Lucas' life to shreds.

"Why?" I ask, my voice hoarse. "Why did you put me through so much shit, just so you could do this? Why bring me into it? Why didn't you just turn him in instead of jerking him around for years?" She had dangled his freedom right over his nose, and for what?

When Sam starts to speak again, her words are broken, and I think she's crying. Samantha, who is calling me to wreak havoc and ruin lives, is crying. "Because you love him. Don't you understand that? Because I wanted you to know the real Lucas before I tore everything down. And now that you do?"

"That doesn't change how I feel about him," I hiss. "It doesn't change the fact that I love him. What he did happened because he was trying to protect someone who mattered to him."

"And he's a coward," she snaps. "You forgot about that."

"No." I rake my palm across my chest, over my heart. "You wanted me to see Lucas for who he really was, but I saw you, too. If

285

you wanted the truth to come out about him so badly, you would have turned him in a long time ago. You're the coward."

She's still crying, and she sobs loudly into the phone for several seconds before drawing in an unsteady breath. "This ends now."

"Sam? Samantha?" But she's already gone. And even though I know I shouldn't, I try to call her back. She doesn't answer. I'm sent directly to her voicemail after the first couple of rings. I want to think that there's no reason why she's ignoring them, that this call is just another one of her games, and she has no plans to do anything.

But I can't force myself to believe that. This feels different than before, and panic swells through me.

Because I've made a vow to myself that I wouldn't keep things from Lucas any longer, I immediately wake him up. While I sit on the floor of the lounge, talking to him in hushed tones, he strides back and forth down the aisle, his chest moving slightly as he takes it all in. And he takes it better than I ever imagined. His face is a stone mask when

I'm done speaking.

"She'll do what she wants to do." He stops moving. "But I'm not going to keep chasing after her just to keep myself in the clear. I won't do it anymore."

Those were Sam's exact words from earlier, and they're even more terrifying when they fall from his lips. I grip my hands in my hair, shaking my head wildly.

"There has to be something." I gasp for air, shaking my head. "You don't deserve this."

Kneeling down in front of me, he tilts my chin up with the tip of his index finger. "Maybe I don't, but I messed up. I've been living with what I did for four years now, and these past few days of you and Kylie knowing have been the most liberating fucking time I've had since then." Massaging my cheek with the back of his thumb, he presses his forehead against mine. "Let Sam come after me. She has to already know that I'm going to take her down, too. After all the shit she's put you through—let her come."

After this, he refuses to say or hear anything else about Samantha. We spend the rest of the day up until sound check with a stressed silence lingering between us, and when I tell him that I have to go home, he follows me out to my car.

"You'll come tonight?" he asks, his eyes vulnerable, and I just stare at him. I want to scream. Or hit him. Ask him why he's letting Sam win.

But finally, I close my eyes and urge my lips to twitch into a smile. There's an awful feeling drilling its way through the center of my chest because I feel like he might be telling me goodbye. "I wouldn't miss it."

He drags me to him, kissing me until a sob builds in my chest, and I have to push away from him. I won't look into his hazel eyes, so I turn away, my shoulders limp.

"I love you," he says simply.

I count to ten under my breath slowly, hoping that it will help calm me down before I even attempt to look at him again. As soon as I'm done, I twist around.

He's already left me.

At first, I have no plans to be part of the backstage scene tonight.

I'm nervous and an emotional wreck from everything that's happened over the course of the last week, and I feel like my being around will only make the tension worse. But after Kylie pleads with me to come—and then begs some more—I go ahead and get dressed early in jeans, a slouchy black-and-white long-sleeved pullover from Alternative Apparel that will hide the bruises on my arms, and ballet flats. I consider putting my hair up, but when I examine myself in my dresser mirror, noticing how some of the purplish splotches outlining my face are still visible through my makeup, I release my red locks around my shoulders.

I leave the hairband on my dresser next to a box of tissues.

And, as much as I hate to admit it, I leave some of my hopes for the future at home, too.

An hour later, David escorts me to Your Toxic Sequel's dressing room where I'm met with an awkward silence from Cal and Wyatt— the only band members back there at the moment. They murmur hellos and offer me sympathetic, unsure looks before Kylie comes out of the restroom and scowls at them.

"You told me you weren't coming!" Practically sprinting over to where I'm standing by the door, she grabs my hand, lacing her small fingers through mine, and pulls me over to the loveseat.

"You begged," I retort, sitting back. "It was literally impossible for me to say no and mean it when you did that."

"See," she states in a triumphant voice to Wyatt, "I told you it's impossible to say no to me. You're just … strange." I know that her cheerfulness is all a show. That much is evident in her dark brown eyes and the way her hands tremble when she pushes locks of her short brown hair behind her ears.

"Next time I'll be sure to tell you no," I say dryly.

She chooses to ignore that statement, and instead asks in a high-pitched voice,

"After the show we were thinking about going to that bar you're always talking about."

"The Beacon?"

"I think we all just need to get some stress off our chests." She reaches for her bottle of water on the coffee table, but knocks her hand into Cal's Monster energy drink instead. It falls over, sending the strong-smelling liquid pouring over the edges of the table and onto the thin carpet on the floor. "Shit." When she tries to clean it up, I shake my head.

"I've got it."

After I grab a wad of paper towels from inside of the bathroom, I kneel down on my hands and knees, wiping up the spill. "You know," I start, and Cal leans in close to me. "You should be doing this instead of me."

He smirks and tells me no thanks before his expression turns the most serious

I've ever seen it. "So ... how are you doing?"

I think of the attack. Talking to Sam earlier today. I think of my absolute uncertainty about what's going to happen next, and I swallow back a strangled noise.

"I'm better. Still a little shook up, but I'll be fine," I lie.

He releases a rough sigh. "We were worried about you. All of us, so don't let Sin try to tell you something different."

"Thank you," I whisper.

Giving my shoulder a careful squeeze, Cal rises to his feet. "And speaking of Sinjin, I'm going to go track him down. I haven't seen that asshole since sound check, so who knows what the hell he's gotten himself into."

As soon as Cal leaves, Wyatt volunteers to go too, using his pre-concert chain-smoking as an excuse to escape the dressing room for the time being. "You need me, you call, beautiful," he warns Kylie sternly, and her eyes narrow.

"I text let you know the moment your progeny makes me have to go pee," she answers him, a sardonic smile playing at the corners of her mouth. "And if I decide to walk down the hall, I'll leave you a voicemail first." Making a face at her, he shuts the door behind him, and Kylie slumps forward, sinking her face into her hands. "Okay, I'm a wreck right now," she admits in a muffled voice.

"God, I'm right there with you." Ever since I left the venue earlier this afternoon, I've been trying to reach the number Sam had called me from. I had hoped that if I got her back on the line, I would be able to reason with her, but I hadn't had any such luck. I swallow over a lump in my throat. "Do you know where he is right now?"

Hugging her arms over her stomach, Kylie shakes her head. "Said he had to take care of something with Tyler, but who knows. He's been so annoyingly calm today that I couldn't take being around him anymore."

Had he told her about Sam's call this morning?

I make a fist around the messy stack of dry paper towels beside me on the floor and stand up. Once I take them back to the bathroom, I return and sit on the edge of the loveseat, wringing my hands together. "I'm scared," I confess. "Samantha scares the hell out of me because I don't know what her state of mind is."

"Unbalanced. She's always been like that, even when they were younger," Kylie decides immediately. She rolls her tongue over her lips in preparation to say something else, but then there's a thunderous knock on the dressing room door. Creasing her brow, she yells out, "Come in."

David pops his head into the narrow opening he's made in the door, and looks between Kylie and me with cautious brown eyes. "Have you seen Lucas?"

Kylie shrugs one of her shoulders. "Your guess is as good as mine." She tips her water back and then swipes the back of her hand over her mouth. "Why, what's up?"

Shaking his head from side to side in confusion, the edges of David's lips twist down. "There's a couple of men out here looking for him. Says it's urgent they find him."

Pushing myself up off the floor, I stare at David, waiting for an answer. Knowing that as soon as he speaks, everything will change.

I quickly learn that my intuition is right a moment later when David runs his giant hand over his face. "They're cops, Kylie."

I was right. It all changes here with three words. Three words and my world shudders to a painful stop.

It's all over.

CHAPTER TWENTY FOUR

Lucas

Two weeks later

My plan for my future was simple. After the tour ended, I would turn myself in. I would face the fucking music. I would handle whatever hand I was dealt. I deserved that, and it was a long time coming after what I did.

That all changed when two officers showed up right before the Nashville show for me. It changed even more when I was told why they were there. It wasn't to arrest me, accelerating the plan I had for myself. Samantha—my ex-wife, the woman who gave me so much shit—was dead. She'd listed me as her next of kin, and I was the easiest man in the world to find.

The biggest goddamn shock about Sam's death was delivered to me in an email that I found waiting in my inbox when I got back to my hotel room after finding out that she was gone. It was a video that she'd sent that morning. The message accompanying it was short, a quote from a book. The moment I read the quote, I knew that whatever the fuck she sent me in that file was going to shake my world.

In a time of universal deceit, telling the truth is a revolutionary act.

293

I was right. The video took everything I thought I knew and turned it upside down.

Although Tyler bitched and moaned, the band made a swift and unanimous decision to cancel nearly all the remaining dates on the tour. After all that happened, it seemed like the right thing to do. My head was not where it needed to be, and for the first week and a half after shit jumped headfirst into the fan, I didn't make things any better for myself because I was drawn to re-watching the video Sam had made for me.

Her revolutionary act, delivered four years too late.

The Samantha on the screen doesn't look anything like the woman I saw earlier this summer, or even the woman from a year ago. The Samantha in the video is still a beautiful woman, still blond with a mocking smile and gray eyes that haunted me. When Kylie does a little digging into the history of the file, she discovers that Sam made the video over two years ago. Judging from the somewhat healthy way Sam looks, it sounds about right.

I'm pulled to the twelve-minute film, not because I still love Sam—all those feelings had soured long before she made this recording—but because I think that maybe watching it will help me discover answers and find peace.

It does neither, even as I watch it this one last time tonight.

My ex-wife sits in the middle of that pristine white sofa that used to be in the living room of her apartment in Atlanta. Her short legs are crossed at the ankles, and she arches her thin body forward. On camera, the track marks on the insides of her elbows aren't visible, but she still tries to hide them anyway by pretending to warm herself up with her hands.

Even though she mostly avoids making direct eye contact with the camera, there are rare moments where she does look up. Each time, the look in her gray eyes is intense.

Right now, tonight, it makes me feel like she's staring at me, telling me just a few of her secrets in person.

In a way, she is.

"Lucas," she begins. "I can't do this to your face, so this is the only way I could ever get what I wanted to say out there in the open." Taking a deep breath, she moves her hands in front of her chest as she attempts to work out what she was going to say next. "It's my fault Bryce Roberts died. I did it, and I'm so sorry."

It's always taken a lot to surprise me, but the first time I watched this video in my hotel room in Nashville, I could only stare at the computer screen with my mouth hanging wide open. A few days later, I would hear a similar story from the police, but that night, everything was a numbing shock.

"I killed him," Sam explains, pinching the end of her slightly crooked nose to try to hold back her tears. She doesn't succeed, and they fall freely down her face, rolling down to her skinny chest. "I met him through one of my friends. But he just … he wasn't you. I wanted you. Bryce was nothing to me, because I thought I could get you back. And then I found out you were seeing Priscilla, and I lost it. I lost it, and I asked him to mess with her. Shake her up some. I guess you could say I didn't really give a fuck what happened to her. I still don't. That bitch could die today, and I would be happy."

I was so used to seeing her fake tears that it took me a few days to process how goddamn genuine the video is. It makes watching it that much more insane.

Sam gets up from her seat then, and when she returns, she is lighting a cigarette. Her hand quivers as she brings the filter up to her mouth, but after she takes in a long inhale, she looks a little calmer. A little less like she is only a few words away from having a breakdown and hurling the webcam across the room.

She waits until nothing is left of her cigarette but a crushed brown filter before she drags her hand through her blond hair. "I was with him the night you fought in that fucking parking lot." She stares straight into the camera, her gray eyes hard. "We'd been following a few of your shitty shows, going from town to town. You know, it's kind of ironic. I wanted Bryce to mess with Cilla and that idiot genuinely fell all over himself for her." She chuckles angrily. "Once again I lost a man to that cunt."

"That night, we were fucked up on something—I can't remember what it was, though." Sam focuses her eyes on something behind the camera. "What I do remember is this: After you went back inside that bar to take care of that bitch, I went to help him.

He looked at me, you know, and the first thing he said was Cilla. He called me Cilla. So

I hit him with a tire iron I found in the back of his car."

"You knocked him out. I made sure he wouldn't get back up," my ex-wife coldly confesses.

The first time I saw the video, I had covered my face with my hands and scraped my fingernails back until I was grasping my hair. It was the confession to end all confessions—at least where my life was concerned—and yet, I hadn't felt a goddamn thing but emptiness.

Afterward, what fucks with me the most is that Sam never explains why she let me believe that I was the one who had ended

Bryce's life, other than her hatred for Cilla. Sam only says that she's sorry. That she screwed up. And that she would fix things.

Then she'd broken down sobbing and told me just how much she hated me, swearing that she'd be just as happy with my death as she would be with Cilla's.

Come to think of it, maybe that was the real reason behind all the years of manipulation and lies.

Hatred.

Still, in the end, Sam had fixed things just like she promised in that video she recorded two years ago. She had turned herself in to the police. She'd given her statement. She'd given the cops Bryce Roberts' wallet, which she apparently took from his pocket the night of his murder, probably to use as more blackmail against me when the time was right for her. And then she'd waived her right to an attorney.

And by the time I found out about all of this right before the Nashville show, she was already gone, had already killed herself. She had taken such a toxic cocktail of drugs just before turning herself in, it was a shock her heart hadn't given out mid-confession.

I hate to think of her dying like that.

Even after all the shit we went through, I never wanted that for her.

I was left piecing together the truths between all the lies she had led me to believe. Her video confession was the only help she'd given me.

In life, Sam had been a brief part of the band's history—the woman who was married to Lucas-Fucking-Wolfe—before we hit it big. But in death, somehow she overshadowed every woman I'd ever been with, including Sienna.

At least that's what all the gossip bullshit said.

All I want to do is move on with my life. With my music. With Sienna.

So this time, once Sam's video is done playing, and I know without a doubt I'm not going to get any of the answers I want from it, I delete it for good.

EPILOGUE

Lucas

November

What the fuck do you do when you find out that the secrets that you buried, the lies that you paid to cover up, were just that? Nothing but lies that tore you apart.

Do you linger in the past; holding on to those fucked-up regrets, wishing you could change things?

Or do you move forward?

I decide to do both.

It's not Samantha who has to live with what she did to Bryce— it's me having to face that I lived for four goddamn years thinking that I was a monster and pushing away the woman who wanted to bring me out of all the shadows that I had hidden myself in. The fact that she's here with me tonight is a miracle.

"You look like sin," I tell her, looking up at her reflection as she comes up behind me. She's wearing a tiny black one-shouldered dress that I think should be on my dressing room floor instead of her body, and strappy shoes that make her amazing legs go on for days.

"The best kind." Her hair falls around me as she drapes her bare arms over my shoulders and wraps me up tightly, like she doesn't want to let go. "Last show and then you're all mine." Her clear blue eyes find mine in the mirror, and she takes a long, deep breath. "Are you ready, Mr. Wolfe?"

Reaching back, I ravel her hair tightly through my fingers before I turn my head and find her mouth. I devour her. And she consumes me. It's the only way we will work.

I'm just now figuring that out but better late than never.

When I pull her away, watching in amazement at the way she's looking at me, I offer her a grin. "Sinjin will break my fingers with his drumsticks if I'm not ready." Zoe is supposed to show tonight, and he's bent on impressing her after what had happened the last time he brought her around. There's no Cilla or Wicked Lambs here tonight.

Sinjin, of all the goddamn people, had talked her into going to rehab a month ago.

"Then you should probably let go of my hair," Sienna suggests, and when I do, she flips it back over one of her shoulders, an intentionally sexy move that makes my cock harden. Goddamn, she's beautiful. She stands up straight and holds her arms out.

"Do I look presentable?"

"You look like you should be naked on that couch over there." I jab my finger at the narrow piece of furniture across the room, but then shake my head. "But yes, you're the best thing I've ever laid eyes on. The best thing for me, period."

"And then you have to say stuff like that." She takes a few steps backwards. "I'll see you after the show." Her gaze remains locked with mine as she backs out of the room, and I don't turn back around until after she's gone.

I stare at myself in the mirror. Lucas-Fucking-Wolfe. I stare at the man I was and am, and the one I want to be with her. Then, I get up and leave the dressing room too.

Cal and Wyatt are milling around the backstage hallway, with Wyatt talking shit about my sister's friend Heidi leaving Cal tied up in some hotel room in Utah a week ago. When Cal sees me, he runs his hand over his face in embarrassment and directs his eyes down to the gray concrete floor.

"You got something to add, motherfucker?" he finally challenges.

"Only that I wish she'd left you in public like that." When he mouths a "fuck you," I grin and shrug it off. "Sin and I've got five hundred bucks on who'll come out of this thing ahead—you or Heidi."

As I take off down the hall to the stage entrance, Cal yells after me, "So which one of us are you betting on? It's me, right? I've got Heidi right where I want her."

"You're full of bullshit. My money's always been on Heidi," I yell back, before ducking through the backstage exit.

What do you do when all your secrets come to light, just to be buried again?

You keep fucking playing.

Even though I already know the rescheduled Los Angeles show is sold out, there's still no denying the stunned satisfaction of knowing that thousands of people have dragged their asses out here tonight to see my band perform. Still, through the screams, and the

301

music blaring around me, and thousands of faces, only one stands out to me in the crowd. Sienna's sitting between my sister and her friend Tori in one of the floor seats closest to the stage, beaming up at me.

As Cal kicks off the show with "All Over You," her lips are moving. I can't read them, but it doesn't stop me from murmuring into the mic, "I love you, too. So fucking much it hurts." Thinking it's meant for them, the crowd goes wild, and I give them a cocky grin before I open my mouth to perform.

Two hours later, when we reach the second song of our encore, and my fans are starting to get up out of their seats, I stop them. "I don't do a lot of acoustic shit," I confess into the mic as two members of the stage crew bring out a stool and my guitar. A hush falls over the crowd, and then there's shuffling as they try to get back to where they were sitting. I put the mic on the stand and lean into it. "And I sure as fuck don't usually do covers. But this is the last stop on a tour that seems like it's gone on for months."

Sitting down on the stool, I start to pick the beginning of a song slowly, waiting until my fans pick up on what I'm playing. Ten seconds in, the applause begins to erupt across the stadium. It's deafening, and it gives me that shove I need to move forward.

"I don't think I need to explain why I'm doing this song. Just that it's for the woman I love. I want to spend my life with her. I want to start and end every tour looking at her face. And I want everyone here tonight to know that. She's it for me, always has been. It just took me awhile to get through all the bullshit and figure that out."

Sienna's blue eyes never leave mine as I sing a Tonic song about doing anything for love and the beautiful blue-eyed woman who loves me to the end. When I'm done, and the audience is screaming, I lean back over the mic again.

"I'm going to be a dick and put you on the spot, Sienna," I growl. "Marry me." This time, when her lips move, I can easily read what it is she's trying to say.

"Yes," Sienna accepts.

What do you do when there are no more secrets and all of those regrets are in the past?

I move on with my life, with *her* in it.

The End

The End

THE PLAYLIST

Music, and I bet you guessed this already, played a major role in the writing process for *Consumed*. And I do mean MAJOR. My playlist for the book had over fifty songs! While I love every song on my playlist, here are some of the ones that really inspired me.

1. "Champagne" by Cavo
2. "Last to Know" by Three Days Grace
3. "It's Been Awhile" by Staind
4. "Beautiful with You" by Halestorm
5. "All Falls Down" by Adelitas Way
6. "Buried Alive" by Avenged Sevenfold
7. "You're So Vain" by Marilyn Manson
8. "Tied My Hands" by Seether
9. "Walk Away" by Five Finger Death Punch
10. "Adrenalize" by In This Moment
11. "Dancing with the Dead" by Ten Years
12. "Through Glass" by Stone Sour
13. "Bitch Came Back" by Theory of a Deadman

14. "Rill Rill" by Sleigh Bells

15. "Satisfied" by Aranda

16. "Famous" by Puddle of Mudd

17. "Fade Into You" by Mazzy Star

18. "Every Lie" by My Darkest Days

19. "The Kill" by Thirty Seconds to Mars

20. "Lonely Day" by System of a Down

21. "We Are Broken" by Paramore

22. "I Will Possess Your Heart" by Death Cab for Cutie

23. "My God Is the Sun" by Queens of the Stone Age

24. "If You Could Only See" by Tonic

ACKNOWLEDGMENTS

Thank you so much to my readers for being so amazing. Your enthusiasm and support for my books amaze me on a daily basis, and I feel so blessed to have you.

Thank you for all the emails, reviews, and Facebook messages. You rock my world!

To Kelli Maine, Michelle Valentine, and Kristen Proby— Thank you ladies for putting up with my randomness and making me laugh. I love you three.

To Holly Malgieri and Jenn Foor: YOU TWO ROCK. Thanks for making me grin all the time!

Christine Bezdenejnih Estevez, you are one amazing chick! Thank you for keeping me organized and for loving my books. BIG HUGS for everything you do (and it's a lot)!

Thanks to Letitia Hasser at RBA Designs for creating such a beautiful book cover. And to Stacy Kestwick for her wonderful beta-reading skills and Jenny Sims with Editing4Indies for her unbelievingly quick proofreading—you two rock!

To Cris Hadarly, Becca Manuel, and Abbie Dauenheimer—Thank you ladies a million times for being so effing creative. I love the trailers and collages, and I smile like an idiot every time I look at them.

To all my amazing author friends—you guys kick ass. I'm so blessed to be a part of such a great, caring community. Lots of love to you all.

To the bloggers in the romance community—THANK YOU! Your support and love for my books mean so much to me. I appreciate you all more than you could ever imagine. Thank you for taking such good care of me and all the other indie authors.

ABOUT THE AUTHOR

Emily Snow is *The New York Times* and *USA Today* bestselling author of the *Devoured* series (October 2012, January 2013) and *Tidal* (December 2012). She loves books, sexy bad boys, and really loud rock music, so naturally, she writes stories about naughty rockers. Visit her blog at emilysnowbooks.blogspot.com or chat with her on Twitter @emilysnowbks for news, teasers, and contests.

CPSIA information can be obtained
at www.ICGtesting.com
Printed in the USA
FSHW022003170319
56451FS